Dean Koontz was born and raised in Pennsylvania. The author of many number one bestsellers, he lives with his wife Gerda and their dog Trixie in southern California.

# THE HUSBAND

Landscape gardener Mitchell Rafferty is working in a suburban neighbourhood when his phone rings. And on a bright summer day he has a phone conversation out of his darkest nightmare. 'We have your wife. You get her back for two million cash.' The caller is dead serious. 'See that guy across the street?' . . . Rifle fire shatters the stillness as the man is shot in the head. An object lesson . . . The caller doesn't care that Mitch has no way of raising such a vast sum. This person is confident that Mitch will find a way. If he loves his wife enough. Mitch has got sixty hours to prove that he does. He'll pay anything. He'll pay a lot more than two million dollars . . .

*Books by Dean Koontz*
*Published by The House of Ulverscroft:*

FEAR NOTHING
SEIZE THE NIGHT
FROM THE CORNER OF HIS EYE
ONE DOOR AWAY FROM HEAVEN
BY THE LIGHT OF THE MOON
ODD THOMAS
THE TAKING
LIFE EXPECTANCY
VELOCITY
DEAN KOONTZ'S FRANKENSTEIN:
CITY OF NIGHT *(with Ed Gorman)*
FOREVER ODD

DEAN KOONTZ

# THE HUSBAND

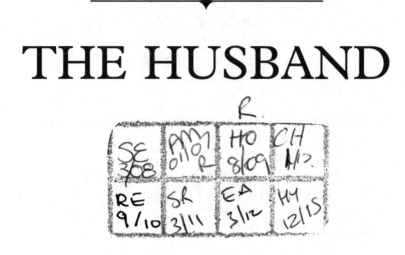

*Complete and Unabridged*

# CHARNWOOD
## Leicester

First published in Great Britain in 2006 by
HarperCollins*Publishers*
London

First Charnwood Edition
published 2007
by arrangement with
HarperCollins*Publishers*
London

British Library CIP Data

Koontz, Dean R. (Dean Ray), *1945 –*
The husband.—Large print ed.—
Charnwood library series
1. Kidnapping—Fiction
2. Suspense fiction
3. Large type books
I. Title
813.5′4 [F]

ISBN 978–1–84617–732–3

Published by
F. A. Thorpe (Publishing)
Anstey, Leicestershire

Set by Words & Graphics Ltd.
Anstey, Leicestershire
Printed and bound in Great Britain by
T. J. International Ltd., Padstow, Cornwall

This novel is dedicated to Andy and Anne Wickstrom, and to Wesley J. Smith and Debra J. Saunders: two good husbands and their good wives, also good friends, who always brighten the corner where they are.

Courage is grace under pressure.

— *Ernest Hemingway*

That Love is all there is,
Is all we know of Love . . .

— *Emily Dickinson*

# Part One

## What Would You Do for Love?

# 1

A man begins dying at the moment of his birth. Most people live in denial of Death's patient courtship until, late in life and deep in sickness, they become aware of him sitting bedside.

Eventually, Mitchell Rafferty would be able to cite the minute that he began to recognize the inevitability of his death: Monday, May 14, 11:43 in the morning — three weeks short of his twenty-eighth birthday.

Until then, he had rarely thought of dying. A born optimist, charmed by nature's beauty and amused by humanity, he had no cause or inclination to wonder when and how his mortality would be proven.

When the call came, he was on his knees.

Thirty flats of red and purple impatiens remained to be planted. The flowers produced no fragrance, but the fertile smell of the soil pleased him.

His clients, these particular homeowners, liked saturated colors: red, purple, deep yellow, hot pink. They would not accept white blooms or pastels.

Mitch understood them. Raised poor, they had built a successful business by working hard and taking risks. To them, life was intense, and saturated colors reflected the truth of nature's vehemence.

This apparently ordinary but in fact momentous morning, the California sun was a buttery ball. The sky had a basted sheen.

Pleasantly warm, not searing, the day nevertheless left a greasy sweat on Ignatius Barnes. His brow glistened. His chin dripped.

At work in the same bed of flowers, ten feet from Mitch, Iggy looked boiled. From May until July, his skin responded to the sun not with melanin but with a fierce blush. For one-sixth of the year, before he finally tanned, he appeared to be perpetually embarrassed.

Iggy did not possess an understanding of symmetry and harmony in landscape design, and he couldn't be trusted to trim roses properly. He was a hard worker, however, and good if not intellectually bracing company.

'You hear what happened to Ralph Gandhi?' Iggy asked.

'Who's Ralph Gandhi?'

'Mickey's brother.'

'Mickey Gandhi? I don't know him, either.'

'Sure you do,' Iggy said. 'Mickey, he hangs out sometimes at Rolling Thunder.'

Rolling Thunder was a surfers' bar.

'I haven't been there in years,' Mitch said.

'Years? Are you serious?'

'Entirely.'

'I thought you still dropped in sometimes.'

'So I've really been missed, huh?'

'I'll admit, nobody's named a bar stool after you. What — did you find someplace better than Rolling Thunder?'

4

'Remember coming to my wedding three years ago?' Mitch asked.

'Sure. You had great seafood tacos, but the band was woofy.'

'They weren't woofy.'

'Man, they had *tambourines*.'

'We were on a budget. At least they didn't have an accordion.'

'Because playing an accordion exceeded their skill level.'

Mitch troweled a cavity in the loose soil. 'They didn't have finger bells, either.'

Wiping his brow with one forearm, Iggy complained: 'I must have Eskimo genes. I break a sweat at fifty degrees.'

Mitch said, 'I don't do bars anymore. I do marriage.'

'Yeah, but can't you do marriage *and* Rolling Thunder?'

'I'd just rather be home than anywhere else.'

'Oh, boss, that's sad,' said Iggy.

'It's not sad. It's the best.'

'If you put a lion in a zoo three years, six years, he never forgets what freedom was like.'

Planting purple impatiens, Mitch said, 'How would you know? You ever asked a lion?'

'I don't have to ask one. I *am* a lion.'

'You're a hopeless boardhead.'

'And proud of it. I'm glad you found Holly. She's a great lady. But *I've* got my freedom.'

'Good for you, Iggy. And what do you do with it?'

'Do with what?'

'Your freedom. What do you do with your freedom?'

'Anything I want.'

'Like, for example?'

'Anything. Like, if I want sausage pizza for dinner, I don't have to ask anyone what *she* wants.'

'Radical.'

'If I want to go to Rolling Thunder for a few beers, there's nobody to bitch at me.'

'Holly doesn't bitch.'

'I can get beer-slammed every night if I want, and nobody's gonna be calling to ask when am I coming home.'

Mitch began to whistle 'Born Free.'

'Some wahine comes on to me,' Iggy said, 'I'm free to rock and roll.'

'They're coming on to you all the time — are they? — those sexy wahines?'

'Women are bold these days, boss. They see what they want, they just take it.'

Mitch said, 'Iggy, the last time you got laid, John Kerry thought he was going to be president.'

'That's not so long ago.'

'So what happened to Ralph?'

'Ralph who?'

'Mickey Gandhi's brother.'

'Oh, yeah. An iguana bit off his nose.'

'Nasty.'

'Some fully macking ten-footers were breaking, so Ralph and some guys went night-riding at the Wedge.'

The Wedge was a famous surfing spot at the

end of the Balboa Peninsula, in Newport Beach.

Iggy said, 'They packed coolers full of submarine sandwiches and beer, and one of them brought Ming.'

'Ming?'

'That's the iguana.'

'So it was a pet?'

'Ming, he'd always been sweet before.'

'I'd expect iguanas to be moody.'

'No, they're affectionate. What happened was some wanker, not even a surfer, just a wannabe tag-along, slipped Ming a quarter-dose of meth in a piece of salami.'

'Reptiles on speed,' Mitch said, 'is a bad idea.'

'Meth Ming was a whole different animal from clean-and-sober Ming,' Iggy confirmed.

Putting down his trowel, sitting back on the heels of his work shoes, Mitch said, 'So now Ralph Gandhi is noseless?'

'Ming didn't eat the nose. He just bit it off and spit it out.'

'Maybe he didn't like Indian food.'

'They had a big cooler full of ice water and beer. They put the nose in the cooler and rushed it to the hospital.'

'Did they take Ralph, too?'

'They had to take Ralph. It was his nose.'

'Well,' Mitch said, 'we *are* talking about boardheads.'

'They said it was kinda blue when they fished it out of the ice water, but a plastic surgeon sewed it back on, and now it's not blue anymore.'

'What happened to Ming?'

7

'He crashed. He was totally amped-out for a day. Now he's his old self.'

'That's good. It's probably hard to find a clinic that'll do iguana rehab.'

Mitch got to his feet and retrieved three dozen empty plastic plant pots. He carried them to his extended-bed pickup.

The truck stood at the curb, in the shade of an Indian laurel. Although the neighborhood had been built-out only five years earlier, the big tree had already lifted the sidewalk. Eventually the insistent roots would block lawn drains and invade the sewer system.

The developer's decision to save one hundred dollars by not installing a root barrier would produce tens of thousands in repair work for plumbers, landscapers, and concrete contractors.

When Mitch planted an Indian laurel, he always used a root barrier. He didn't need to make future work for himself. Green growing Nature would keep him busy.

The street lay silent, without traffic. Not the barest breath of a breeze stirred the trees.

From a block away, on the farther side of the street, a man and a dog approached. The dog, a retriever, spent less time walking than it did sniffing messages left by others of its kind.

The stillness pooled so deep that Mitch almost believed he could hear the panting of the distant canine.

Golden: the sun and the dog, the air and the promise of the day, the beautiful houses behind deep lawns.

Mitch Rafferty could not afford a home in this

neighborhood. He was satisfied just to be able to work here.

You could love great art but have no desire to live in a museum.

He noticed a damaged sprinkler head where lawn met sidewalk. He got his tools from the truck and knelt on the grass, taking a break from the impatiens.

His cell phone rang. He unclipped it from his belt, flipped it open. The time was displayed — 11:43 — but no caller's number showed on the screen. He took the call anyway.

'Big Green,' he said, which was the name he'd given his two-man business nine years ago, though he no longer remembered why.

'Mitch, I love you,' Holly said.

'Hey, sweetie.'

'Whatever happens, I love you.'

She cried out in pain. A clatter and crash suggested a struggle.

Alarmed, Mitch rose to his feet. 'Holly?'

Some guy said something, some guy who now had the phone. Mitch didn't hear the words because he was focused on the background noise.

Holly squealed. He'd never heard such a sound from her, such fear.

'*Sonofabitch*,' she said, and was silenced by a sharp crack, as though she'd been slapped.

The stranger on the phone said, 'You hear me, Rafferty?'

'Holly? Where's Holly?'

Now the guy was talking away from the phone,

not to Mitch: 'Don't be stupid. Stay on the floor.'

Another man spoke in the background, his words unclear.

The one with the phone said, 'She gets up, *punch* her. You want to lose some teeth, honey?'

She was with two men. One of them had hit her. *Hit* her.

Mitch couldn't get his mind around the situation. Reality suddenly seemed as slippery as the narrative of a nightmare.

A meth-crazed iguana was more real than this.

Near the house, Iggy planted impatiens. Sweating, red from the sun, as solid as ever.

'That's better, honey. That's a good girl.'

Mitch couldn't draw breath. A great weight pressed on his lungs. He tried to speak but couldn't find his voice, didn't know what to say. Here in bright sun, he felt casketed, buried alive.

'We have your wife,' said the guy on the phone.

Mitch heard himself ask, 'Why?'

'Why do you think, asshole?'

Mitch didn't know why. He didn't want to know. He didn't want to reason through to an answer because every possible answer would be a horror.

'I'm planting flowers.'

'What's wrong with you, Rafferty?'

'That's what I do. Plant flowers. Repair sprinklers.'

'Are you buzzed or something?'

'I'm just a gardener.'

'So we have your wife. You get her back for two million cash.'

Mitch knew it wasn't a joke. If it were a joke, Holly would have to be in on it, but her sense of humor was not cruel.

'You've made a mistake.'

'You hear what I said? Two million.'

'Man, you aren't listening. I'm a *gardener*.'

'We know.'

'I have like eleven thousand bucks in the bank.'

'We know.'

Brimming with fear and confusion, Mitch had no room for anger. Compelled to clarify, perhaps more for himself than for the caller, he said, 'I just run a little two-man operation.'

'You've got until midnight Wednesday. Sixty hours. We'll be in touch about the details.'

Mitch was sweating. 'This is nuts. Where would I get two million bucks?'

'You'll find a way.'

The stranger's voice was hard, implacable. In a movie, Death might sound like this.

'It isn't possible,' Mitch said.

'You want to hear her scream again?'

'No. Don't.'

'Do you love her?'

'Yes.'

'Really love her?'

'She's everything to me.'

How peculiar, that he should be sweating yet feel so cold.

'If she's everything to you,' said the stranger, 'then you'll find a way.'

11

'There *isn't* a way.'

'If you go to the cops, we'll cut her fingers off one by one, and cauterize them as we go. We'll cut her tongue out. And her eyes. Then we'll leave her alone to die as fast or slow as she wants.'

The stranger spoke without menace, in a matter-of-fact tone, as if he were not making a threat but were instead merely explaining the details of his business model.

Mitchell Rafferty had no experience of such men. He might as well have been talking to a visitor from the far end of the galaxy.

He could not speak because suddenly it seemed that he might so easily, unwittingly say the wrong thing and ensure Holly's death sooner rather than later.

The kidnapper said, 'Just so you'll know we're serious . . .'

After a silence, Mitch asked, 'What?'

'See that guy across the street?'

Mitch turned and saw a single pedestrian, the man walking the slow dog. They had progressed half a block.

The sunny day had a porcelain glaze. Rifle fire shattered the stillness, and the dogwalker went down, shot in the head.

'Midnight Wednesday,' said the man on the phone. 'We're damn serious.'

# 2

The dog stood as if on point: one forepaw raised, tail extended but motionless, nose lifted to seek a scent.

In truth, the golden retriever had not spotted the shooter. It halted in midstep, startled by its master's collapse, frozen by confusion.

Directly across the street from the dog, Mitch likewise stood paralyzed. The kidnapper terminated the call, but Mitch still held the cell phone to his ear.

Superstition promised that as long as the street remained still, as long as neither he nor the dog moved, the violence might be undone and time rewound, the bullet recalled to the barrel.

Reason trumped magical thinking. He crossed the street, first haltingly, then at a run.

If the fallen man was wounded, something might be done to save him.

As Mitch approached, the dog favored him with a single wag of its tail.

A glance at the victim dispelled any hope that first aid might sustain him until paramedics arrived. A significant portion of his skull was gone.

Having no familiarity with real violence, only with the edited-analyzed-excused-and-defanged variety provided by TV news, and with the cartoon violence in movies, Mitch was rendered

13

impotent by this horror. More than fear, shock immobilized him.

More than shock, a sudden awareness of previously unsensed dimensions transfixed him. He was akin to a rat in a sealed maze, for the first time looking up from the familiar passage-ways and seeing a world beyond the glass lid, forms and figures, mysterious movement.

Lying on the sidewalk near its master, the golden retriever trembled, whimpered.

Mitch sensed that he was in the company of someone other than the dog, and felt watched, but more than watched. Studied. Attended. *Pursued*.

His heart was a thundering herd, hooves on stone.

He surveyed the day but saw no gunman. The rifle could have been fired from any house, from any rooftop or window, or from behind a parked car.

Anyway, the presence he sensed was not that of the shooter. He did not feel watched from a distance, but from an intimate vantage point. He felt as if someone *loomed* over him.

Hardly more than half a minute had passed since the dog-walker had been killed.

The crack of the rifle had not brought anyone out of any of the beautiful houses. In this neighborhood, a gunshot would be perceived as a slammed door, dismissed even as it echoed.

Across the street, at the client's house, Iggy Barnes had risen from his knees to his feet. He didn't appear to be alarmed, merely puzzled, as

14

if he, too, had heard a door and didn't understand the meaning of the fallen man, the grieving dog.

Midnight Wednesday. Sixty hours. Time on fire, minutes burning. Mitch couldn't afford to let hours turn to ashes while he was tied up with a police investigation.

On the sidewalk, a column of marching ants changed course, crawling toward the feast within the cratered skull.

In a mostly clear sky, a rare cloud drifted across the sun. The day paled. Shadows faded.

Chilled, Mitch turned from the corpse, stepped off the curb, halted.

He and Iggy couldn't just load the unplanted impatiens into the truck and drive away. They might not be able to do so before someone came along and saw the dead man. Their indifference to the victim and their flight would suggest guilt even to the most unworldly passerby, and certainly to the police.

The cell phone, folded shut, remained in Mitch's hand. He looked upon it with dread.

*If you go to the cops, we'll cut her fingers off one by one . . .*

The kidnappers would expect him to summon the authorities or to wait for someone else to do so. Forbidden, however, was any mention of Holly or of kidnapping, or of the fact that the dogwalker had been murdered as an example to Mitch.

Indeed, his unknown adversaries might have put him in this predicament specifically to test his ability to keep his mouth shut at the moment

15

when he was in the most severe state of shock and most likely to lose his self-control.

He opened the phone. The screen brightened with an image of colorful fish in dark water.

After keying in 9 and 1, Mitch hesitated, but then entered the final digit.

Iggy dropped his trowel, moved toward the street.

Only when the police operator answered on the second ring did Mitch realize that from the moment he'd seen the dead man's shattered head, his breathing had been desperate, ragged, raw. For a moment, words wouldn't come, and then they *blew* out of him in a rough voice he barely recognized.

'*A man's been shot. I'm dead. I mean, he's dead. He's been shot, and he's dead.*'

# 3

Police had cordoned off both ends of the block. Squad cars, CSI vans, and a morgue wagon were scattered along the street with the insouciance of those to whom parking regulations do not apply.

Under the unblinking gaze of the sun, windshields blazed and brightwork gleamed. No cloud remained to be a pirate's patch, and the light was merciless.

The cops wore sunglasses. Behind the dark lenses, perhaps they glanced suspiciously at Mitchell Rafferty, or perhaps they were indifferent to him.

In front of his client's house, Mitch sat on the lawn, his back against the bole of a phoenix palm.

From time to time, he heard rats scrabbling in the top of the tree. They liked to make a high nest in a phoenix palm, between the crown and the skirt.

The feathery shadows of the fronds provided him with no sense of diminished visibility. He felt as if he were on a stage.

Twice in two hours, he had been questioned. Two plainclothes detectives had interviewed him the first time, only one on the second occasion.

He thought he had acquitted himself well. Yet they had not told him that he could go.

Thus far, Iggy had been interviewed only once. He had no wife in jeopardy, nothing to

17

hide. Besides, Iggy had less talent for deception than did the average six-year-old, which would be evident to experienced interrogators.

Maybe the cops' greater interest in Mitch was a bad sign. Or maybe it meant nothing.

More than an hour ago, Iggy had returned to the flower bed. He had nearly completed the installation of the impatiens.

Mitch would have preferred to stay busy with the planting. This inactivity made him keenly aware of the passage of time: Two of his sixty hours were gone.

The detectives had firmly suggested that Iggy and Mitch should remain separated because, in all innocence, if they talked together about the crime, they might unintentionally conform their memories, resulting in the loss of an important detail in one or the other's testimony.

That might be either the truth or malarkey. The reason for keeping them apart might be more sinister, to isolate Mitch and ensure that he remained off balance. Neither of the detectives had worn sunglasses, but Mitch had not been able to read their eyes.

Sitting under the palm tree, he had made three phone calls, the first to his home number. An answering machine had picked up.

After the usual beep, he said, 'Holly, are you there?'

Her abductors would not risk holding her in her own home.

Nevertheless, Mitch said, 'If you're there, please pick up.'

He was in denial because the situation made

18

no sense. Kidnappers don't target the wives of men who have to worry about the price of gasoline and groceries.

*Man, you aren't listening. I'm a gardener.*

*We know.*

*I have like eleven thousand bucks in the bank.*

*We know.*

They must be insane. Delusional. Their scheme was based on some mad fantasy that no rational person could understand.

Or they had a plan that they had not yet revealed to him. Maybe they wanted him to rob a bank for them.

He remembered a news story, a couple years back, about an innocent man who robbed a bank while wearing a collar of explosives. The criminals who necklaced him had tried to use him like a remote-control robot. When police cornered the poor bastard, his controllers detonated the bomb from a distance, decapitating him so he could never testify against them.

One problem. No bank had two million dollars in cash on hand, in tellers' drawers, and probably not even in the vault.

After getting no answer when he phoned home, he had tried Holly's cell phone but hadn't been able to reach her at that number.

He also had called the Realtor's office where she worked as a secretary while she studied for her real-estate license.

Another secretary, Nancy Farasand, had said, 'She called in sick, Mitch. Didn't you know?'

'When I left home this morning, she was a

19

little queasy,' he lied, 'but she thought it would pass.'

'It didn't pass. She said it's like a summer flu. She was so disappointed.'

'I better call her at home,' he said, but of course he had already tried reaching her there.

He had spoken to Nancy more than ninety minutes ago, between conversations with detectives.

Passing minutes unwind a watch spring; but they had wound Mitch tight. He felt as though something inside his head was going to pop.

A fat bumblebee returned to him from time to time, hovering, buzzing close, perhaps attracted by his yellow T-shirt.

Across the street, toward the end of the block, two women and a man were standing on a front lawn, watching the police: neighbors gathered for the drama. They had been there since the sirens had drawn them outside.

Not long ago, one of them had gone into a house and had returned with a tray on which stood glasses of what might have been iced tea. The glasses sparkled in the sunlight.

Earlier, the detectives had walked up the street to question that trio. They had interviewed them only once.

Now the three stood sipping tea, chatting, as if unconcerned that a sniper had cut down someone who had been walking in their community. They appeared to be enjoying this interlude, as though it presented a welcome break from their usual routine, even if it came at the cost of a life.

To Mitch, the neighbors seemed to spend more time staring toward him than at any of the police or CSI technicians. He wondered what, if anything, the detectives had asked them about him.

None of the three used the services of Big Green. From time to time, they would have seen him in the neighborhood, however, because he took care of four properties on this street.

He disliked these tea drinkers. He had never met them, did not know their names, but he viewed them with an almost bitter aversion.

Mitch disliked them not because they seemed perversely to be enjoying themselves, and not because of what they might have said about him to the police. He disliked the three — could have worked up a loathing for them — because their lives were still in order, because they did not live under the threat of imminent violence against someone they loved.

Although irrational, his animosity had a certain value. It distracted him from his fear for Holly, as did his continuous fretful analysis of the detectives' actions.

If he dared to give himself entirely to worry about his wife, he would go to pieces. This was no exaggeration. He was surprised at how fragile he felt, as he never had felt previously.

Each time her face rose in his mind, he had to banish it because his eyes grew hot, his vision blurred. His heart fell into an ominous heavy rhythm.

An emotional display, so out of proportion even to the shock of seeing a man shot, would require an explanation. He dared not reveal the truth, and he didn't trust himself to invent an explanation that would convince the cops.

One of the homicide detectives — Mortonson — wore dress shoes, black slacks, and a pale-blue shirt. He was tall, solid, and all business.

The other — Lieutenant Taggart — wore white sneakers, chinos, and a red-and-tan Hawaiian shirt. He was less physically intimidating than Mortonson, less formal in his style.

Mitch's wariness of Taggart exceeded his concern about the more imposing Mortonson. The lieutenant's precisely trimmed hair, his glass-smooth shave, his perfect veneered teeth, his spotless white sneakers suggested that he adopted casual dress and a relaxed demeanor to mislead and to put at ease the suspects unfortunate enough to come under his scrutiny.

The detectives first interviewed Mitch in tandem. Later, Taggart had returned alone, supposedly to have Mitch 'refine' something he had said earlier. In fact, the lieutenant repeated every question he and Mortonson had asked before, perhaps anticipating contradictions between Mitch's answers and those that he had given previously.

Ostensibly, Mitch was a witness. To a cop, however, when no killer had been identified, every witness also counted as a suspect.

He had no reason to kill a stranger walking a dog. Even if they were crazy enough to think he might have done so, they would have to believe that Iggy was his accomplice; clearly Iggy did not interest them.

More likely, though they knew he'd had no role in the shooting, their instinct told them that he was concealing something.

Now here came Taggart yet again, his sneakers so white that they appeared to be radiant.

As the lieutenant approached, Mitch rose to his feet, wary and sick with worry, but trying to appear merely weary and impatient.

# 4

Detective Taggart sported an island tan to match his Hawaiian shirt. By contrast with his bronze face, his teeth were as white as an arctic landscape.

'I'm sorry for all this inconvenience, Mr. Rafferty. But I have just a couple more questions, and then you're free to go.'

Mitch could have replied with a shrug, a nod. But he thought that silence might seem peculiar, that a man with nothing to hide would be forthcoming.

Following an unfortunate hesitation long enough to suggest calculation, he said, 'I'm not complaining, Lieutenant. It could just as easily have been me who was shot. I'm thankful to be alive.'

The detective strove for a casual demeanor, but he had eyes like those of a predatory bird, hawk-sharp and eagle-bold. 'Why do you say that?'

'Well, if it was a random shooting . . . '

'We don't know that it was,' said Taggart. 'In fact, the evidence points to cold calculation. One shot, perfectly placed.'

'Can't a crazy with a gun be a skilled shooter?'

'Absolutely. But crazies usually want to rack up as big a score as possible. A psychopath with a rifle would have popped you, too. This guy knew exactly who he wanted to shoot.'

24

Irrationally, Mitch felt some responsibility for the death. This murder had been committed to ensure that he would take the kidnapper seriously and would not seek police assistance.

Perhaps the detective had caught the scent of this unearned but persistent guilt.

Glancing toward the cadaver across the street, around which the CSI team still worked, Mitch said, 'Who's the victim?'

'We don't know yet. No ID on him. No wallet. Don't you think that's peculiar?'

'Going out just to walk the dog, you don't need a wallet.'

'It's a habit with the average guy,' Taggart said. 'Even if he's washing the car in the driveway, he has his wallet.'

'How will you identify him?'

'There's no license on the dog's collar. But that's almost a show-quality golden, so she might have a microchip ID implant. As soon as we get a scanner, we'll check.'

Having been moved to this side of the street, tied to a mailbox post, the golden retriever rested in shade, graciously receiving the attention of a steady procession of admirers.

Taggart smiled. 'Goldens are the best. Had one as a kid. Loved that dog.'

His attention returned to Mitch. His smile remained in place, but the quality of it changed. 'Those questions I mentioned. Were you in the military, Mr. Rafferty?'

'Military? No. I was a mower jockey for another company, took some horticulture classes, and set up my own business a year out of high school.'

'I figured you might be ex-military, the way gunfire didn't faze you.'

'Oh, it fazed me,' Mitch assured him.

Taggart's direct gaze was intended to intimidate.

As if Mitch's eyes were clear lenses through which his thoughts were revealed like microbes under a microscope, he felt compelled to avoid the detective's stare, but sensed that he dared not.

'You hear a rifle,' Taggart said, 'see a man shot, yet you hurry across the street, into the line of fire.'

'I didn't know he was dead. Might've been something I could do for him.'

'That's commendable. Most people would scramble for cover.'

'Hey, I'm no hero. My instincts just shoved aside my common sense.'

'Maybe that's what a hero is — someone who instinctively does the right thing.'

Mitch dared to look away from Taggart, hoping that his evasion, in this context, would be interpreted as humility. 'I was stupid, Lieutenant, not brave. I didn't stop to think I might be in danger.'

'What — you thought he'd been shot accidentally?'

'No. Maybe. I don't know. I didn't think anything. I didn't *think*, I just reacted.'

'But you really didn't feel like you were in danger?'

'No.'

'You didn't realize it even when you saw his head wound?'

'Maybe a little. Mostly I was sickened.'

The questions came too fast. Mitch felt off balance. He might unwittingly reveal that he knew why the dogwalker had been killed.

With a buzz of busy wings, the bumblebee returned. It had no interest in Taggart, but hovered near Mitch's face, as if bearing witness to his testimony.

'You saw the head wound,' Taggart continued, 'but you still didn't scramble for cover.'

'No.'

'Why not?'

'I guess I figured if somebody hadn't shot me by then, they weren't going to shoot me.'

'So you still didn't feel in danger.'

'No.'

Flipping open his small spiral-bound notebook, Taggart said, 'You told the 911 operator that you were dead.'

Surprised, Mitch met the detective's eyes again. 'That *I* was dead?'

Taggart quoted from the notebook: ''A man's been shot. I'm dead. I mean, he's dead. He's been shot, and he's dead.''

'Is that what I said?'

'I've heard the recording. You were breathless. You sounded flat-out terrified.'

Mitch had forgotten that 911 calls were recorded. 'I guess I was more scared than I remember.'

'Evidently, you *did* recognize a danger to yourself, but still you didn't take cover.'

27

Whether or not Taggart could read anything of Mitch's thoughts, the pages of the detective's own mind were closed, his eyes a warm but enigmatic blue.

''*I'm dead*,'' the detective quoted again.

'A slip of the tongue. In the confusion, the panic.'

Taggart looked at the dog again, and again he smiled. In a voice softer than it had been previously, he said, 'Is there anything more I should have asked you? Anything you would like to say?'

In memory, Mitch heard Holly's cry of pain.

Kidnappers always threaten to kill their hostage if the cops are brought in. To win, you don't have to play the game by their rules.

The police would contact the Federal Bureau of Investigation. The FBI had extensive experience in kidnapping cases.

Because Mitch had no way to raise two million, the police would at first doubt his story. When the kidnapper called again, however, they would be convinced.

What if the second call didn't come? What if, knowing that Mitch had gone to the police, the kidnapper fulfilled his threat, mutilated Holly, killed her, and never called again?

Then they might think that Mitch had concocted the kidnapping to cover the fact that Holly was already dead, that he himself had killed her. The husband is always the primary suspect.

If he lost her, nothing else would matter. Nothing ever. No power could heal the wound that she would leave in his life.

But to be suspected of harming her — that would be hot shrapnel in the wound, ever burning, forever lacerating.

Closing the notebook and returning it to a hip pocket, shifting his attention from the dog to Mitch, Taggart asked again, 'Anything, Mr. Rafferty?'

At some point during the questioning, the bumblebee had flown away. Only now, Mitch realized that the buzzing had stopped.

If he kept the secret of Holly's abduction, he would stand alone against her kidnappers.

He was no good alone. He had been raised with three sisters and a brother, all born within a seven-year period. They had been one another's confidants, confessors, counsels, and defenders.

A year after high school, he moved out of his parents' house, into a shared apartment. Later, he had gotten his own place, where he felt isolated. He had worked sixty hours a week, and longer, just to avoid being alone in his rooms.

He had felt complete once more, fulfilled, connected, only when Holly had come into his world. *I* was a cold word; *we* had a warmer sound. *Us* rang sweeter on the ear than *me*.

Lieutenant Taggart's eyes seemed less forbidding than they had been heretofore.

Mitch said, 'Well . . . '

The detective licked his lips.

The air was warm, humidity low. Mitch's lips felt dry, too.

Nevertheless, the quick pink passage of Taggart's tongue seemed reptilian, and suggested that he was mentally savoring the taste of pending prey.

Only paranoia allowed the twisted thought that a homicide detective might be allied with Holly's abductors. This private moment between witness and investigator in fact might be the ultimate test of Mitch's willingness to follow the kidnapper's instructions.

All the flags of fear, both rational and irrational, were raised high in his mind. This parade of rampant dreads and dark suspicions did not facilitate clear thinking.

He was half convinced that if he told Taggart the truth, the detective would grimace and say *We'll have to kill her now, Mr. Rafferty. We can't trust you anymore. But we'll let you choose what we cut off first — her fingers or her ears.*

As earlier, when he'd been standing over the dead man, Mitch felt watched, not just by Taggart and the tea-drinking neighbors, but by some presence unseen. Watched, analyzed.

'No, Lieutenant,' he said. 'There's nothing more.'

The detective retrieved a pair of sunglasses from his shirt pocket and put them on.

In the mirrored lenses, Mitch almost didn't recognize the twin reflections of his face. The distorting curve made him look old.

'I gave you my card,' Taggart reminded him.

'Yes, sir. I have it.'

'Call me if you remember anything that seems important.'

The smooth, characterless sheen of the sunglasses was like the gaze of an insect:

emotionless, eager, voracious.

Taggart said, 'You seem nervous, Mr. Rafferty.'

Raising his hands to reveal how they trembled, Mitch said, 'Not nervous, Lieutenant. Shaken. Badly shaken.'

Taggart licked his lips once more.

Mitch said, 'I've never seen a man murdered before.'

'You don't get used to it,' the detective said.

Lowering his hands, Mitch said, 'I guess not.'

'It's worse when it's a woman.'

Mitch did not know what to make of that statement. Perhaps it was a simple truth of a homicide detective's experience — or a threat.

'A woman or a child,' Taggart said.

'I wouldn't want your job.'

'No. You wouldn't.' Turning away, the detective said, 'I'll be seeing you, Mr. Rafferty.'

'Seeing me?'

Glancing back, Taggart said, 'You and I — we'll both be witnesses in a courtroom someday.'

'Seems like a tough case to solve.'

' "Blood crieth unto me from the ground,' Mr. Rafferty,' said the detective, apparently quoting someone. ' "Blood crieth unto me from the ground." '

Mitch watched Taggart walk away.

Then he looked at the grass under his feet.

The progress of the sun had put the palm-frond shadows behind him. He stood in light, but was not warmed by it.

31

# 5

The dashboard clock was digital, as was Mitch's wristwatch, but he could hear time ticking nonetheless, as rapid as the *click-click-click* of the pointer snapping against the marker pegs on a spinning wheel of fortune.

He wanted to race directly home from the crime scene. Logic argued that Holly would have been snatched at the house. They would not have grabbed her on the way to work, not on a public street.

They might unintentionally have left something behind that would suggest their identity. More likely, they would have left a message for him, further instructions.

As usual, Mitch had begun the day by picking up Iggy at his apartment in Santa Ana. Now he had to return him.

Driving north from the fabled and wealthy Orange County coastal neighborhoods where they worked, toward their humbler communities, Mitch switched from the crowded freeway to surface streets, but encountered traffic there, as well.

Iggy wanted to talk about the murder and the police. Mitch had to pretend to be as naively excited by the novelty of the experience as Iggy was, when in fact his mind remained occupied with thoughts of Holly and with worry about what might come next.

Fortunately, as usual, Iggy's conversation soon began to loop and turn and tangle like a ball of yarn unraveled by a kitten.

Appearing to be engaged in this rambling discourse required less of Mitch than when the subject had been the dead dogwalker.

'My cousin Louis had a friend named Booger,' Iggy said. 'The same thing happened to him, shot while walking a dog, except it wasn't a rifle and it wasn't a dog.'

'Booger?' Mitch wondered.

'Booker,' Iggy corrected. 'B-o-o-k-e-r. He had a cat he called Hairball. He was walking Hairball, and he got shot.'

'People walk cats?'

'The way it was — Hairball is cozy in a travel cage, and Booker is carrying him to a vet's office.'

Mitch repeatedly checked the rearview and side mirrors. A black Cadillac SUV had departed the freeway in their wake. Block after block, it remained behind them.

'So Booker wasn't actually *walking* the cat,' Mitch said.

'He was walking *with* the cat, and this like twelve-year-old brat, this faucet-nosed little dismo, shot Booker with a paintball gun.'

'So he wasn't killed.'

'He wasn't quashed, no, and it was a cat instead of a dog, but Booker was totally blue.'

'Blue?'

'Blue hair, blue face. He was fully pissed.'

The Cadillac SUV reliably remained two or three vehicles behind them. Perhaps the driver

33

hoped Mitch wouldn't notice him.

'So Booker's all blue. What happened to the kid?' Mitch asked.

'Booker was gonna break the little dismo's hand off, but the kid shot him in the crotch and ran. Hey, Mitch, did you know there's a town in Pennsylvania named Blue Balls?'

'I didn't know.'

'It's in Amish country. There's another town nearby called Intercourse.'

'How about that.'

'Maybe those Amish aren't as square as Cheez-Its, after all.'

Mitch accelerated to cross an intersection before the traffic light phased to red. Behind him, the black SUV changed lanes, sped up, and made it through on the yellow.

'Did you ever eat an Amish shoofly pie?' Iggy asked.

'No. Never did.'

'It's full-on rich, sweeter than six Gidget movies. Like eating molasses. Treacherous, dude.'

The Cadillac dropped back, returned to Mitch's lane. Three vehicles separated them once more.

Iggy said, 'Earl Potter lost a leg eating shoofly pie.'

'Earl Potter?'

'Tim Potter's dad. He was diabetic, but he didn't know it, and he totally destroyed like a bucket of sweets every day. Did you ever eat a Quakertown pie?'

'What about Earl's leg?' Mitch asked.

34

'Unreal, bro. One day his foot's numb, he can't walk right. Turns out he's got almost no circulation down there 'cause of radical diabetes. They sawed his left leg off above the knee.'

'While he was eating shoofly pie.'

'No. He realized he had to give up sweets.'

'Good for him.'

'So the day before surgery, he had his last dessert, and he chose a whole shoofly pie with like a cow's worth of whipped cream. Did you ever see that stylin' Amish movie with Harrison Ford and the girl with the great knockers?'

By way of Hairball, Blue Balls, Intercourse, shoofly pie, and Harrison Ford, they arrived at Iggy's apartment building.

Mitch stopped at the curb, and the black SUV went past without slowing. The side windows were tinted, so he couldn't see the driver or any passengers.

Opening his door, before getting out of the truck, Iggy said, 'You okay, boss?'

'I'm okay.'

'You look stomped.'

'I saw a guy shot to death,' Mitch reminded him.

'Yeah. Wasn't that radical? I guess I know who's gonna rule the bar at Rolling Thunder tonight. Maybe you should stop in.'

'Don't save a stool for me.'

The Cadillac SUV dwindled westward. The afternoon sun wrapped the suspicious vehicle in glister and glare. It shimmered and seemed to vanish into the solar maw.

Iggy got out of the truck, looked back in at

35

Mitch, and pulled a sad face. 'Ball and chain.'

'Wind beneath my wings.'

'Whoa. That's goob talk.'

'Go waste yourself.'

'I do intend to get mildly polluted,' Iggy assured him. 'Dr. Ig prescribes at least a six-pack of *cerveza* for you. Tell Mrs. Mitch I think she's an uber wahine.'

Iggy slammed the door and walked away, big and loyal and sweet and clueless.

With hands that were suddenly shaky on the wheel, Mitch piloted the truck into the street once more.

Coming north, he had been impatient to be rid of Iggy and to get home. Now his stomach turned when he considered what might wait for him there.

What he most feared was finding blood.

# 6

Mitch drove with the truck windows open, wanting the sounds of the streets, proof of life.

The Cadillac SUV did not reappear. No other vehicle took up the pursuit. Evidently, he had imagined the tail.

His sense of being under surveillance passed. From time to time, his eyes were drawn to the rearview mirror, but no longer with the expectation of seeing anything suspicious.

He felt alone, and worse than alone. Isolated. He almost wished that the black SUV would reappear.

Their house was in an older neighborhood of Orange, one of the oldest cities in the county. When he turned onto their street, except for the vintage of the cars and trucks, a curtain in time might have parted, welcoming him to 1945.

The bungalow — pale-yellow clapboard, white trim, a cedar-shingle roof — stood behind a picket fence on which roses twined. Some larger and some nicer houses occupied the block, but none boasted better landscaping.

He parked in the driveway beside the house, under a massive old California pepper tree, and stepped out into a breathless afternoon.

Sidewalks and yards were deserted. In this neighborhood, most families relied on two incomes; everyone was at work. At 3:04, no latchkey kids were yet home from school.

No maids, no window washers, no gardening services busy with leaf blowers. These homeowners swept their own carpets, mowed their own yards.

The pepper tree braided the sunshine in its cascading tresses, and littered the shadowed pavement with elliptical slivers of light.

Mitch opened a side gate in the picket fence. He crossed the lawn to the front steps.

The porch was deep and cool. White wicker chairs with green cushions stood beside small wicker tables with glass tops.

On Sunday afternoons, he and Holly often sat here, talking, reading the newspaper, watching hummingbirds flit from one crimson bloom to another on the trumpet vines that flourished on the porch posts.

Sometimes they unfolded a card table between the wicker chairs. She crushed him at Scrabble. He dominated the trivia games.

They didn't spend much on entertainment. No skiing vacations, no weekends in Baja. They seldom went out to a movie. Being together on the front porch offered as much pleasure as being together in Paris.

They were saving money for things that mattered. To allow her to risk a career change from secretary to real-estate agent. To enable him to do some advertising, buy a second truck, and expand the business.

Kids, too. They were going to have kids. Two or three. On certain holidays, when they were most sentimental, even four did not seem like too many.

They didn't want the world, and didn't want to change it. They wanted their little corner of the world, and the chance to fill it with family and laughter.

He tried the front door. Unlocked. He pushed it inward and hesitated on the threshold.

He glanced back at the street, half expecting to see the black SUV. It wasn't there.

After he stepped inside, he stood for a moment, letting his eyes adjust. The living room was illuminated only by what tree-filtered sunlight pierced the windows.

Everything appeared to be in order. He could not detect any signs of struggle.

Mitch closed the door behind him. For a moment he needed to lean against it.

If Holly had been at home, there would have been music. She liked big-band stuff. Miller, Goodman, Ellington, Shaw. She said the music of the '40s was suitable to the house. It suited her, too. Classic.

An archway connected the living room to the small dining room. Nothing in this second room was out of place.

On the table lay a large dead moth. It was a night-flyer, gray with black details along its scalloped wings.

The moth must have gotten in the previous evening. They had spent some time on the porch, and the door had been open.

Maybe it was alive, sleeping. If he cupped it in his hands and took it outside, it might fly into a corner of the porch ceiling and wait there for moonrise.

He hesitated, reluctant to touch the moth, for fear that no flutter was left in it. At his touch, it might dissolve into a greasy kind of dust, which moths sometimes did.

Mitch left the night-flyer untouched because he wanted to believe that it was alive.

The connecting door between the dining room and the kitchen stood ajar. Light glowed beyond.

The smell of burnt toast lingered on the air. It grew stronger when he pushed through the door into the kitchen.

Here he found signs of a struggle. One of the dinette chairs had been overturned. Broken dishes littered the floor.

Two slices of blackened bread stood in the toaster. Someone had pulled the plug. The butter had been left out on the counter, and had softened as the day grew warmer.

The intruders must have come in from the front of the house, surprising her as she was making toast.

The cabinets were painted glossy white. Blood spattered a door and two drawer fronts.

For a moment, Mitch closed his eyes. In his mind, he saw the moth flutter and fly up from the table. Something fluttered in his chest, too, and he wanted to believe that it was hope.

On the white refrigerator, a woman's bloody hand print cried havoc as loud as any voice could have shouted. Another full hand print and a smeared partial darkened two upper cabinets.

Blood spotted the terra-cotta tiles on the floor. It seemed to be a lot of blood. It seemed to be an ocean.

The scene so terrified Mitch that he wanted to shut his eyes again. But he had the crazy idea that if he closed his eyes twice to this grim reality, he would go blind forever.

The phone rang.

# 7

He did not have to tread in blood to reach the telephone. He picked up the handset on the third ring, and heard his haunted voice say, 'Yeah?'

'It's me, baby. They're listening.'

'Holly. What've they done to you?'

'I'm all right,' she said, and she sounded strong, but she did not sound all right.

'I'm in the kitchen,' he said.

'I know.'

'The blood — '

'I know. Don't think about that now. Mitch, they said we have one minute to talk, just one minute.'

He grasped her implication: *One minute, and maybe never again.*

His legs would not support him. Turning a chair away from the dinette table, collapsing into it, he said, 'I'm so damn sorry.'

'It's not your fault. Don't beat yourself up.'

'Who are these freaks, are they deranged, what?'

'They're vicious creeps, but they're not crazy. They seem . . . professional. I don't know. But I want you to make me a promise — '

'I'm dyin' here.'

'Listen, baby. I want your promise. If anything happens to me — '

'Nothing's going to happen to you.'

'If anything happens to me,' she insisted, 'promise you'll keep it together.'

'I don't want to think about that.'

'You keep it together, damn it. You keep it together and have a life.'

'You're my life.'

'You keep it together, mower jockey, or I'm going to be way pissed.'

'I'll do what they want. I'll get you back.'

'If you don't keep it together, I'll haunt your ass, Rafferty. It'll be like that *Poltergeist* movie cubed.'

'God, I love you,' he said.

'I know. I love you. I want to hold you.'

'I love you so much.'

She didn't reply.

'Holly?'

The silence electrified him, brought him up from the chair.

'Holly? You hear me?'

'I hear you, mower jockey,' said the kidnapper to whom he had spoken previously.

'You sonofabitch.'

'I understand your anger — '

'You piece of garbage.'

' — but I don't have much patience for it.'

'If you hurt her — '

'I already *have* hurt her. And if you don't pull this off, I'll butcher the bitch like a side of beef.'

An acute awareness of his helplessness brought Mitch crashing down from anger to humility.

'Please. Don't hurt her again. Don't.'

43

'Chill, Rafferty. You just chill while I explain a few things.'

'Okay. All right. I need things explained. I'm lost here.'

Again his legs felt weak. Instead of sitting in the chair, he brushed a broken dish aside with one foot and knelt on the floor. For some reason, he felt more comfortable on his knees than in the chair.

'About the blood,' the kidnapper said. 'I slapped her down when she tried to fight back, but I didn't cut her.'

'All the blood . . . '

'That's what I'm telling you. We put a tourniquet on her arm until a vein popped up, stuck a needle in it, and drew four vials just like your doctor does when you get a physical.'

Mitch leaned his forehead against the oven door. He closed his eyes and tried to concentrate.

'We smeared blood on her hands and made those prints. Spattered some on the counters, cabinets. Dripped it on the floor. It's stage setting, Rafferty. So it looks like she was murdered there.'

Mitch was the turtle, just leaving the START line, and this guy on the phone was the rabbit, already halfway through the marathon. Mitch couldn't get up to speed. 'Staged? Why?'

'If you lose your nerve and go to the cops, they'll never buy the kidnapping story. They'll see that kitchen and think you croaked her.'

'I didn't tell them anything.'

'I know.'

'What you did to the dogwalker — I knew you had nothing to lose. I knew I couldn't mess with you.'

'This is just a little extra insurance,' the kidnapper said. 'We like insurance. There's a butcher knife missing from the rack there in your kitchen.'

Mitch didn't bother to confirm the claim.

'We wrapped it with one of your T-shirts and a pair of your blue jeans. The clothes are stained with Holly's blood.'

They were professional, all right, just like she had said.

'That package is hidden on your property,' the kidnapper continued. 'You couldn't easily find it, but police dogs will.'

'I get the picture.'

'I knew you would. You aren't stupid. That's why we've bought ourselves so much insurance.'

'What now? Make sense of this whole thing for me.'

'Not yet. Right now you're very emotional, Mitch. That's not good. When you're not in control of your emotions, you're likely to make a mistake.'

'I'm solid,' Mitch assured him, although his heart still stormed and his blood thundered in his ears.

'You don't have any room for a mistake, Mitch. Not one. So I want you to chill, like I said. When you've got your head straight, then we'll discuss the situation. I'll call you at six o'clock.'

Though remaining on his knees, Mitch

45

opened his eyes, checked his watch. 'That's over two and a half hours.'

'You're still in your work clothes. You're dirty. Take a nice hot shower. You'll feel better.'

'You've gotta be kidding me.'

'Anyway, you'll need to be more presentable. Shower, change, and then leave the house, go somewhere, anywhere. Just be sure your cell phone is fully charged.'

'I'd rather wait here.'

'That's no good, Mitch. The house is filled with memories of Holly, everywhere you look. Your nerves will be rubbed raw. I need you to be less emotional.'

'Yeah. All right.'

'One more thing. I want you to listen to this . . . '

Mitch thought they were going to twist a scream of pain from Holly again, to emphasize how powerless he was to protect her. He said, 'Don't.'

Instead of Holly, he heard two taped voices, clear against a faint background hiss. The first voice was his own:

'*I've never seen a man murdered before.*'

'*You don't get used to it.*'

'*I guess not.*'

'*It's worse when it's a woman . . . a woman or a child.*'

The second voice belonged to Detective Taggart.

The kidnapper said, 'If you had spilled your guts to him, Mitch, Holly would be dead now.'

In the dark smoky glass of the oven door, he

saw the reflection of a face that seemed to be looking out at him from a window in Hell.

'Taggart's one of you.'

'Maybe he is. Maybe not. You should just assume that everybody is one of us, Mitch. That'll be safer for you, and a lot safer for Holly. Everybody is one of us.'

They had built a box around him. Now they were putting on the lid.

'Mitch, I don't want to leave you on such a dark note. I want to put you at ease about something. I want you to know that we won't touch her.'

'You *hit* her.'

'I'll hit her again if she doesn't do what she's told. But we won't *touch* her. We aren't rapists, Mitch.'

'Why would I believe you?'

'Obviously, I'm handling you, Mitch. Manipulating, finessing. And obviously there is a lot of stuff I won't tell you — '

'You're killers, but not rapists?'

'The point is that everything I *have* told you has been true. You think back over our relationship, and you'll see I've been truthful and I've kept my word.'

Mitch wanted to kill him. Never before had he felt an urge to do serious violence to another human being, but he wanted to *destroy* this man.

He was clutching the phone so fiercely that his hand ached. He was not able to relax his grip.

'I've had a lot of experience working through surrogates, Mitch. You're an instrument to me, a valuable tool, a sensitive machine.'

'Machine.'

'Hang with me a minute, okay? It makes no sense to abuse a valuable and sensitive machine. I wouldn't buy a Ferrari and then never change the oil, never lubricate it.'

'At least I'm a Ferrari.'

'When I'm your handler, Mitch, you won't be pressed beyond your limits. I would expect very high performance from a Ferrari, but I wouldn't expect to be able to drive it through a brick wall.'

'I feel like I've already been through a brick wall.'

'You're tougher than you think. But in the interest of getting the best performance out of you, I want you to know we'll treat Holly with respect. If you do everything we want, then she'll come back to you alive . . . and untouched.'

Holly was not weak. She would not easily be mentally broken by physical abuse. But rape was more than a violation of the body. Rape rended the mind, the heart, the spirit.

Her captor might have raised the issue with the sincere intent of putting some of Mitch's fears to rest. But the sonofabitch had also raised it as a warning.

Mitch said, 'I still don't think you've answered the question. Why should I believe you?'

'Because you have to.'

That was an inescapable truth.

'You have to, Mitch. Otherwise, you might as well consider her dead right now.'

The kidnapper terminated the call.

For a while, Mitch's sense of powerlessness

48

kept him on his knees.

Eventually a recording, a woman with the vaguely patronizing tone of a nursery-school teacher not fully comfortable with children, requested that he hang up the phone. He put the handset on the floor instead, and a continuous beeping urged him to comply with the operator's suggestion.

Remaining on his knees, he rested his forehead against the oven door once more, and closed his eyes.

His mind was in tumult. Images of Holly, tornadoes of memories, tormented him, fragmented and spinning, good memories, sweet, but they tormented because they might be all that he would ever have of her. Fear and anger. Regret and sorrow. He had never known loss. His life had not prepared him for loss.

He strove to clear his mind because he sensed that there was something he could do for Holly right here, now, if only he could quiet his fear and be calm, and *think*. He didn't have to wait for orders from her kidnappers. He could do something important for her now. He could take action on her behalf. He could do something for Holly.

Humbled against the hard terra-cotta tiles, his knees began to ache. This physical discomfort gradually cleared his mind. Thoughts no longer blew through him like shatters of debris, but drifted as fallen leaves drift on a placid river.

He could do something meaningful for Holly, and the awareness of the thing that he could do was right below the surface, floating just beneath his questing reflection. The hard floor was unforgiving, and he began to feel as if he were kneeling on broken glass. He could do something for Holly. The answer eluded him. *Something.* His knees ached. He tried to ignore the pain, but then he got to his feet. The pending insight receded. He returned the telephone handset to its cradle. He would have to wait for the next call. He had never before felt so useless.

# 8

Although still hours away, the approaching night pulled every shadow toward the east, away from the westbound sun. Queen-palm shadows yearned across the deep yard.

To Mitch, standing on the back porch, this place, which had previously been an island of peace, now seemed as fraught with tension as the webwork of cables supporting a suspension bridge.

At the end of the yard, beyond a board fence, lay an alleyway. On the farther side of the alley were other yards and other houses. Perhaps a sentinel at one of those second-floor windows observed him now with high-powered binoculars.

On the phone, he had told Holly that he was in the kitchen, and she had said *I know*. She could have known only because her captors had known.

The black Cadillac SUV had not proved to be in any dark power's employ, imbued with menace only by his imagination. No other vehicle had followed him.

They had expected him to go home, so instead of tailing him, they had staked out his house. They were watching now.

One of the houses on the farther side of the alley might offer a good vantage point if the observer was equipped with high-tech optical gear that provided an intimate view from a distance.

His suspicion settled instead on the detached garage at the rear of this property. That structure could be accessed either from the alley or from the front street via the driveway that ran alongside the house.

The garage, which provided parking for Mitch's truck and Holly's Honda, featured windows on the ground floor and in the storage loft. Some were dark, and some were gilded with reflected sunlight.

No window revealed a ghostly face or a telltale movement. If someone was watching from the garage, he would not be careless. He would be glimpsed only if he wished to be seen for the purpose of intimidation.

From the roses, from the ranunculus, from the corabells, from the impatiens, slanting sunlight struck luminous color like flaring shards in stained-glass windows.

The butcher knife, wrapped in bloody clothes, had probably been buried in a flower bed.

By finding that bundle, retrieving it, and cleaning up the blood in the kitchen, he would regain some control. He'd be able to react with greater flexibility to whatever challenges were thrust upon him in the hours ahead.

If he was being watched, however, the kidnappers would not view his actions with equanimity. They had staged his wife's murder to box him in, and they wouldn't want the box to be deconstructed.

To punish him, they would hurt Holly.

The man on the phone had promised that she would not be *touched*, meaning raped. But he had no compunctions about hitting her.

Given reason, he would hit her again. Punch her. Torture her. Regarding those issues, he had made no promises.

To dress the set of the staged homicide, they had drawn her blood painlessly, with a hypodermic syringe. They had not, however, sworn to spare her forever from a knife.

As instruction in the reality of his helplessness, they might cut her. Any laceration she endured would sever the very tendons of his will to resist.

They dared not kill her. To continue controlling Mitch, they had to let him speak to her from time to time.

But they could cut to disfigure, then instruct her to describe the disfigurement to him on the phone.

Mitch was surprised by his ability to anticipate such hideous developments. Until a few hours ago, he'd had no personal experience of unalloyed evil.

The vividness of his imagination in this area suggested that on a subconscious level, or on a level deeper than the subconscious, he had known that real evil walked the world, abominations that could not be faded to gray by psychological or social analysis. Holly's abduction had raised this willfully repressed awareness out of a hallowed darkness, into view.

The shadows of the queen palms, stretched toward the backyard fence, seemed taut to the snapping point, and the sun-brightened flowers looked as brittle as glass. Yet the tension in the scene increased.

Neither the elongated shadows nor the flowers would snap. Whatever strained toward the breaking point, it would break *within* Mitch. And though anxiety soured his stomach and clenched his teeth, he sensed that this coming change would not be a bad thing.

At the garage, the dark windows and the sun-fired windows mocked him. The porch furniture and the patio furniture, arranged with the expectation of the enjoyment of lazy summer evenings, mocked him.

The lush and sculpted landscaping, on which he had spent so many hours, mocked him as well. All the beauty born from his work seemed now to be superficial, and its superficiality made it ugly.

He returned to the house and closed the back door. He did not bother locking it.

The worst that could have invaded his home had already been here and had gone. What violations followed would be only embellishments on the original horror.

He crossed the kitchen and entered a short hall that served two rooms, the first of which was a den. It contained a sofa, two chairs, and a large-screen television.

These days, they rarely watched any programs. So-called reality TV dominated the airwaves, and legal dramas and police dramas, but all of it bored because none of it resembled reality as he had known it; and now he knew it even better.

At the end of the hallway was the master

54

bedroom. He withdrew clean underwear and socks from a bureau drawer.

For now, as impossible as every mundane task seemed in these circumstances, he could do nothing other than what he had been told to do.

The day had been warm; but a night in the middle of May was likely to be cool. At the closet, he slipped a fresh pair of jeans and a flannel shirt from hangers. He put them on the bed.

He found himself standing at Holly's small vanity, where she daily sat on a tufted stool to brush her hair, apply her makeup, put on her lipstick.

Unconsciously, he had picked up her hand mirror. He looked into it, as if hoping, by some grace that would foretell the future, to see her fine and smiling face. His own countenance did not bear contemplation.

He shaved, showered, and dressed for the ordeal ahead.

He had no idea what they expected of him, how he could possibly raise two million dollars to ransom his wife, but he made no attempt to imagine any possible scenarios. A man on a high ledge is well advised not to spend much time studying the long drop.

As he sat on the edge of the bed, just as he finished tying his shoes, the doorbell rang.

The kidnapper had said he would *call* at six, not come calling. Besides, the bedside clock read 4:15.

Leaving the door unanswered was not an option. He needed to be responsive regardless of how Holly's captors chose to contact him.

If the visitor had nothing to do with her abduction, Mitch was nevertheless obliged to answer the door in order to maintain an air of normalcy.

His truck in the driveway proved that he was home. A neighbor, getting no response to the bell, might circle to the back of the house to knock at the kitchen door.

The six-pane window in that door would provide a clear view of the kitchen floor strewn with broken dishes, the bloody hand prints on the cabinets and the refrigerator.

He should have drawn shut the blinds.

He left the bedroom, followed the hall, and crossed the living room before the visitor had time to ring the bell twice.

The front door had no windows. He opened it and found Detective Taggart on the porch.

# 9

The praying-mantis stare of mirrored lenses skewered Mitch and pinned his voice in his throat.

'I love these old neighborhoods,' Taggart said, surveying the front porch. 'This was how southern California looked in its great years, before they cut down all the orange groves and built a wasteland of stucco tract houses.'

Mitch found a voice that sounded almost like his own, though thinner: 'You live around here, Lieutenant?'

'No. I live in one of the wastelands. It's more convenient. But I happened to be in your neighborhood.'

Taggart was not a man who *just happened* to be anywhere. If he ever went sleepwalking, even then he would have a purpose, a plan, and a destination.

'Something's come up, Mr. Rafferty. And since I was nearby, it seemed as easy to stop in as to call. Can you spare a few minutes?'

If Taggart was not one of the kidnappers, if his conversation with Mitch had been taped without his knowledge, allowing him across the threshold would be reckless. In this small house, the living room, a picture of tranquillity, and the kitchen, smeared with incriminating evidence, were only a few steps apart.

'Sure,' Mitch said. 'But my wife came home

57

with a migraine. She's lying down.'

If the detective was one of *them*, if he knew that Holly was being held elsewhere, he did not betray his knowledge by any change in his expression.

'Why don't we sit here on the porch,' Mitch said.

'You've got it fixed up real nice.'

Mitch pulled the door shut behind him, and they settled into the white wicker chairs.

Taggart had brought a nine-by-twelve white envelope. He put it on his lap, unopened.

'We had a porch like this when I was a kid,' he said. 'We used to watch traffic go by, just watch traffic.'

He removed his sunglasses and tucked them in his shirt pocket. His gaze was as direct as a power drill.

'Does Mrs. Rafferty use ergotamine?'

'Use what?'

'Ergotamine. For the migraines.'

Mitch had no idea whether ergotamine was an actual medication or a word the detective had invented on the spot. 'No. She toughs it out with aspirin.'

'How often does she get one?'

'Two or three times a year,' Mitch lied. Holly had never had a migraine. She rarely suffered headaches of any kind.

A gray-and-black moth was settled on the porch post to the right of the front steps, a night-flyer sleeping in the shade until sunset.

'I have ocular migraines,' Taggart said. 'They're entirely visual. I get the glimmering

58

light and the temporary blind spot for like twenty minutes, but there's no pain.'

'If you've got to have a migraine, that sounds like the kind to have.'

'A doctor probably wouldn't prescribe ergotamine until she was having a migraine a month.'

'It's just twice a year. Three times,' Mitch said.

He wished that he had resorted to a different lie. Taggart having personal knowledge of migraines was rotten luck.

This small talk unnerved Mitch. To his own ear, he sounded wary, tense.

Of course, Taggart had no doubt long ago grown accustomed to people being wary and tense with him, even innocent people, even his mother.

Mitch had been avoiding the detective's stare. With an effort, he made eye contact again.

'We did find an AVID on the dog,' Taggart said.

'A what?'

'An American Veterinary Identification Device. That microchip ID I mentioned earlier.'

'Oh. Right.'

Before Mitch realized that his sense of guilt had sabotaged him again, his gaze had drifted away from Taggart to follow a passing car in the street.

'They inject it into the muscle between the dog's shoulders,' said Taggart. 'It's very tiny. The animal doesn't feel it. We scanned the retriever, got her AVID number. She's from a house one block east, two blocks north of the shooting. Owner's name is Okadan.'

'Bobby Okadan? I do his gardening.'

'Yes, I know.'

'The guy who was killed — that wasn't Mr. Okadan.'

'No.'

'Who was he? A family member, a friend?'

Avoiding the question, Taggart said, 'I'm surprised you didn't recognize the dog.'

'One golden looks like another.'

'Not really. They're distinct individuals.'

'Mishiki,' Mitch remembered.

'That's the dog's name,' Taggart confirmed.

'We do that property on Tuesdays, and the housekeeper makes sure Mishiki stays inside while we're there, out of our way. Mostly I've seen the dog through a patio door.'

'Evidently, Mishiki was stolen from the Okadans' backyard this morning, probably around eleven-thirty. The leash and collar on her don't belong to the Okadans.'

'You mean . . . the dog was stolen by the guy who was shot?'

'So it appears.'

This revelation reversed Mitch's problem with eye contact. Now he couldn't *look away* from the detective.

Taggart hadn't come here just to share a puzzling bit of case news. Apparently this development triggered, in the detective's mind, a question about something Mitch had said earlier — or had failed to say.

From inside the house came the muffled ringing of the telephone.

The kidnappers weren't supposed to call until

six o'clock. But if they called earlier and couldn't reach him, they might be angry.

As Mitch started to rise from his chair, Taggart said, 'I'd rather you didn't answer that. It's probably Mr. Barnes.'

'Iggy?'

'He and I spoke half an hour ago. I asked him not to call here until I had a chance to speak with you. He's probably been wrestling with his conscience ever since, and finally his conscience won. Or lost, depending on your point of view.'

Remaining in his chair, Mitch said, 'What's this about?'

Ignoring the question, returning to his subject, Taggart said, 'How often do you think dogs are stolen, Mr. Rafferty?'

'I never thought about them being stolen at all.'

'It happens. They aren't taken as frequently as cars.' His smile was not infectious. 'You can't break a dog down for parts like you can a Porsche. But they do get snatched now and then.'

'If you say so.'

'Purebred dogs can be worth thousands. As often as not, the thief doesn't intend to sell the animal. He just wants a fancy dog for himself, without paying for it.'

Though Taggart paused, Mitch didn't say anything. He wanted to speed up the conversation. He was anxious to know the point. All this dog talk had a bite in it somewhere.

'Certain breeds are stolen more than others because they're known to be friendly, unlikely to resist the thief. Golden retrievers are one of the most sociable, least aggressive of all the popular breeds.'

The detective lowered his head, lowered his eyes, sat pensively for a moment, as if considering what he wished to say next.

Mitch didn't believe that Taggart needed to gather his thoughts. This man's thoughts were as precisely ordered as the clothes in an obsessive-compulsive's closet.

'Dogs are mostly stolen out of parked cars,' Taggart continued. 'People leave the dog alone, the doors unlocked. When they come back, Fido's gone, and someone's renamed him Duke.'

Realizing that he was gripping the arms of the wicker chair as if strapped in the hot seat and waiting for the executioner to throw the big switch, Mitch made an effort to appear relaxed.

'Or the owner ties the dog to a parking meter outside a shop. The thief slips the knot and walks off with a new best friend.'

Another pause. Mitch endured it.

With his head still bowed, Lieutenant Taggart said, 'It's rare, Mr. Rafferty, for a dog to be stolen out of its owner's backyard on a bright spring morning. Anything rare, anything unusual makes me curious. Any outright *weirdness* really gets under my skin.'

Mitch raised one hand to the back of his neck and massaged the muscles because that seemed like something a relaxed man, a relaxed and unconcerned man, might do.

'It's strange for a thief to enter a neighborhood like that on foot and *walk* away with a stolen pet.

It's strange that he carries no ID. It's more than strange, it's remarkable, that he gets shot to death three blocks later. And it's weird, Mr. Rafferty, that you, the primary witness, knew him.'

'But I didn't know him.'

'At one time,' Taggart insisted, 'you knew him quite well.'

# 10

White ceiling, white railings, white floorboards, white wicker chairs, punctuated by the gray-and-black moth: Everything about the porch was familiar, open and airy, yet it seemed dark now to Mitch, and strange.

His gaze still downcast, Taggart said, 'One of the jakes on the scene eventually got a closer look at the victim and recognized him.'

'Jakes?'

'One of the uniformed officers. Said he arrested the guy on a drug-possession charge after stopping him for a traffic violation about two years ago. The guy never served any time, but his prints were in our system, so we were able to make a quick match. Mr. Barnes says you and he went to high school with the vic.'

Mitch wished that the cop would meet his eyes. As intuitive and perceptive as he was, Taggart would recognize genuine surprise when he saw it.

'His name was Jason Osteen.'

'I didn't just go to school with him,' Mitch said. 'Jason and I were roommates for a year.'

At last reestablishing eye contact, Taggart said, 'I know.'

'Iggy would have told you.'

'Yes.'

Eager to be forthcoming, Mitch said, 'After high school, I lived with my folks for a year,

64

while I took some classes — '

'Horticulture.'

'That's right. Then I got a job with a landscaping company, and I moved out. Wanted an apartment of my own. Couldn't fully afford one, so Jason and I split rent for a year.'

The detective bowed his head again, in that contemplative pose, as if part of his strategy was to force eye contact when it made Mitch uncomfortable and to deny eye contact when Mitch wanted it.

'That wasn't Jason dead on the sidewalk,' Mitch said.

Opening the white envelope that had been on his lap, Taggart said, 'In addition to the identification by an officer and the print match, I have Mr. Barnes's positive ID based on this.'

He withdrew an eight-by-ten color photo from the envelope and handed it to Mitch.

A police photographer had repositioned the cadaver to get better than a three-quarter image of the face. The head was turned to the left only far enough to conceal the worst of the wound.

The features had been subtly deformed by the temple entrance, transit, and post-temple exit of the high-velocity shot. The left eye was shut, the right open wide in a startled cyclopean stare.

'It could be Jason,' Mitch said.

'It is.'

'At the scene, I only saw one side of his face. The right profile, the worst side, with the exit wound.'

'And you probably didn't look too close.'

'No. I didn't. Once I saw he had to be dead, I

didn't want to look too close.'

'And there was blood on the face,' Taggart said. 'We swabbed it off before this photo was taken.'

'The blood, the brains, that's why I didn't look too close.'

Mitch couldn't take his eyes from the photo. He sensed that it was prophetic. One day there would be a photograph like this of his face. They would show it to his parents: *Is this your son, Mr. and Mrs. Rafferty?*

'This is Jason. I haven't seen him in eight years, maybe nine.'

'You roomed with him when you were — what? — eighteen?'

'Eighteen, nineteen. Just for a year.'

'About ten years ago.'

'Not quite ten.'

Jason had always affected a cool demeanor, so mellow he seemed to have surfwaxed his brain, but at the same time he seemed to know the secrets of the universe. Other boardheads called him Breezer, and admired him, even envied him. Nothing had rattled Jason or surprised him.

He appeared to be surprised now. One eye wide, mouth open. He appeared to be shocked.

'You went to school together, you roomed together. Why didn't you stay in touch?'

While Mitch had been riveted by the photo, Taggart had been watching him intently. The detective's stare had the sharp promise of a nail gun.

'We had ... different ideas about things,' Mitch said.

'It wasn't a marriage. You were just room-mates. You didn't have to want the same things.'

'We wanted some of the same things, but we had different ideas about how to get them.'

'Jason wanted to get everything the easy way,' Taggart guessed.

'I thought he was headed for big trouble, and I didn't want any part of it.'

'You're a straight shooter, you walk the line,' Taggart said.

'I'm no better than anyone else, worse than some, but I don't steal.'

'We haven't learned much about him yet, but we know he rented a house in Huntington Harbor for seven thousand a month.'

'A *month?*'

'Nice house, on the water. And so far it looks like he didn't have a job.'

'Jason thought work was strictly for inlanders, smog monsters.' Mitch saw that an explanation was required. 'Surfer lingo for those who don't live for the beach.'

'Was there a time when *you* lived for the beach, Mitch?'

'Toward the end of high school, for a while after. But it wasn't enough.'

'What was it lacking?'

'The satisfaction of work. Stability. Family.'

'You've got all that now. Life is perfect, huh?'

'It's good. Very good. So good it makes me nervous sometimes.'

'But not perfect? What's it lacking now, Mitch?'

Mitch didn't know. He'd thought about that

67

from time to time, but he had no answer. So he said, 'Nothing. We'd like to have kids. Maybe that's all.'

'I have two daughters,' the detective said. 'One's nine and one's twelve. Kids change your life.'

'I'm looking forward to it.'

Mitch realized that he was responding to Taggart less guardedly than he had previously. He reminded himself that he was no match for this guy.

'Aside from the drug-possession charge,' Taggart said, 'Jason stayed clean all these years.'

'He always was lucky.'

Indicating the photo, Taggart said, 'Not always.'

Mitch didn't want to look at it anymore. He returned the photo to the detective.

'Your hands are shaking,' Taggart said.

'I guess they are. Jason was a friend once. We had a lot of laughs. All that comes back to me now.'

'So you haven't seen or spoken to him in ten years.'

'Almost ten.'

Returning the photo to the envelope, Taggart said, 'But you do recognize him now.'

'Without the blood, seeing more of the face.'

'When you saw him walking the dog, before he was killed, you didn't think — *Hey, don't I know that guy?*'

'He was across the street. I only glanced at him, then the shot.'

'And you were on the phone, distracted. Mr.

Barnes says you were on the phone when the shot was fired.'

'That's right. I wasn't focused on the guy with the dog. I just glanced at him.'

'Mr. Barnes strikes me as being incapable of guile. If he lied, I expect his nose might light up.'

Mitch wasn't sure if he was meant to infer, by contrast to Iggy, that he himself was enigmatic and unreliable. He smiled and said, 'Iggy's a good man.'

Looking down at the envelope as he fixed the flap shut with the clasp, Taggart said, 'Who were you on the phone with?'

'Holly. My wife.'

'Calling to let you know she had a migraine?'

'Yeah. To let me know she was going home early with a migraine.'

Glancing at the house behind them, Taggart said, 'I hope she's feeling better.'

'Sometimes they can last all day.'

'So the guy who's shot turns out to be your old roommate. You see why it's weird to me?'

'It is weird,' Mitch agreed. 'It freaks me out a little.'

'You hadn't seen him in nine years. Hadn't spoken on the phone or anything.'

'He was hanging with new friends, a different crowd. I didn't care for any of them, and I didn't run into him anymore at any of the old places.'

'Sometimes coincidences are just coincidences.' Taggart rose from his chair and moved toward the porch steps.

Relieved, blotting his palms on his jeans, Mitch got up from his chair, too.

Pausing beside the steps, head lowered, Taggart said, 'There's not yet been a thorough search of Jason's house. We've only begun. But we found one odd thing already.'

As Earth rolled away from the slowly sinking sun, afternoon light penetrated a gap in the branches of the pepper tree. A dappled orange glare found Mitch and made him squint.

Beyond the sudden light, in shadow, Taggart said, 'In his kitchen there was a catchall drawer where he kept loose change, receipts, an assortment of pens, spare keys . . . We found only one business card in the drawer. It was yours.'

'Mine?'

'"Big Green,"' Taggart quoted. '"Landscape design, installation, and maintenance. Mitchell Rafferty."'

This was what had brought the detective north from the coast. He had gone to Iggy, guileless Iggy, from whom he'd learned that indeed a connection existed between Mitch and Jason.

'You didn't give him the card?' Taggart asked.

'No, not that I remember. What color was the card stock?'

'White.'

'I've only used white for the past four years. Before that, the stock was pale green.'

'And you haven't seen him in like nine years.'

'Maybe nine years.'

'So although you lost track of Jason, it seems like Jason kept track of you. Any idea why?'

'No. None.'

After a silence, Taggart said, 'You've got trouble here.'

'There must be a thousand ways he could've gotten my business card, Lieutenant. It doesn't mean he was keeping track of me.'

Eyes still downcast, the detective pointed to the porch railing. 'I'm talking about this.'

On the white handrail, in the warm stillness, a pair of winged insects squirmed together, as if trysting.

'Termites,' Taggart said.

'They might just be winged ants.'

'Isn't this the time of year when termites swarm? You better have the place inspected. A house can appear to be fine, solid and safe, even while it's being hollowed out right under your feet.'

At last the detective looked up and met Mitch's eyes.

'They're winged ants,' Mitch said.

'Is there anything else you want to tell me, Mitch?'

'Not that I can think of.'

'Take a moment. Be sure.'

Had Taggart been allied with the kidnappers, he would have played this differently. He wouldn't have been so persistent or so thorough. There would have been a sense that it was a game to him, a charade.

*If you had spilled your guts to him, Mitch, Holly would be dead now.*

Their previous conversation could have been recorded from a distance. These days, high-tech directional microphones, what they called shotgun microphones, could pick up voices clearly from hundreds of feet away. He'd seen it

71

in a movie. Little of what he saw in movies was based on any truth, but he thought shotgun microphones were. Taggart might have been as oblivious of the taping as Mitch had been.

Of course, what had been done once could be done twice. A van that Mitch had never seen before stood at the curb across the street. A surveillance specialist might be stationed in the back of it.

Taggart surveyed the street, evidently seeking the object of Mitch's interest.

The houses were suspect, too. Mitch didn't know all of the neighbors. One of the houses was empty and listed for sale.

'I'm not your enemy, Mitch.'

'I never thought you were,' he lied.

'Everyone thinks I am.'

'I'd like to think I don't have any enemies.'

'Everyone has enemies. Even a saint has enemies.'

'Why would a saint have enemies?'

'The wicked hate the good just because they are good.'

'The word *wicked* sounds so . . . '

'Quaint,' Taggart suggested.

'I guess in your work, everything looks black-and-white.'

'Under all the shades of gray, everything *is* black-and-white, Mitch.'

'I wasn't raised to think that way.'

'Oh, even though I see proof every day, I have some trouble staying focused on the truth. Shades of gray, less contrast, less certainty — that's so much more comfortable.'

Taggart took his sunglasses from his shirt pocket and put them on. From the same pocket, he withdrew one of his business cards.

'You already gave me a card,' Mitch said. 'It's in my wallet.'

'That one just has the homicide-division number. I've written my cell phone on the back of this one. I seldom give it out. You can reach me twenty-four/seven.'

Accepting the card, Mitch said, 'I've told you everything I know, Lieutenant. Jason being caught up in this just . . . mystifies me.'

Taggart stared at him from behind twin mirrors that portrayed his face in shades of gray.

Mitch read the cell number. He put the card in his shirt pocket.

Apparently quoting again, the detective said, ''Memory is a net. One finds it full of fish when he takes it from the brook, but a dozen miles of water have run through it without sticking.''

Taggart descended the porch steps. He followed the front walkway toward the street.

Mitch knew that everything he had told Taggart was caught in the detective's net, every word and every inflection, every emphasis and hesitation, every facial expression and twitch of body language, not just what the words said but also what they implied. In that haul of fish, which the cop would read with the vision of a true Gypsy poring over tea leaves, he would find an omen or an indicant that would bring him back with warnings and new questions.

Taggart stepped through the front gate and closed it behind him.

The sun lost its view through the gap in the boughs of the pepper tree, and Mitch was left in shade, but he did not feel a chill because the light had not warmed him in the first place.

# 11

In the den, the big TV was a blind eye. Even if Mitch used the remote to fill the screen with bright idiot visions, this eye could not see him; yet he felt watched by a presence that regarded him with cold amusement.

The answering machine stood on a corner desk. The only message was from Iggy:

'Sorry, bro. I should've called as soon as he left here. But Taggart . . . he's like fully macking triple overhead corduroy to the horizon. He scares you off the board and makes you want to sit quiet on the beach and just watch the monsters break.'

Mitch sat at the desk and opened the drawer in which Holly kept their checkbook and bank statements.

In his conversation with the kidnapper, he had overestimated their checking-account balance, which was $10,346.54.

The most recent monthly statement showed an additional savings-account balance of $27,311.40.

They had bills due. Those were in a different drawer of the same desk. He didn't look at them. He was counting only assets.

Their monthly mortgage payment was automatically deducted from their checking account. The bank statement listed the remaining loan balance as $286,770.

Recently, Holly had estimated that the house

was worth $425,000. That was a crazy amount for a small bungalow in an old neighborhood, but it was accurate. Though old, the neighborhood was desirable, and the greater part of the value lay in the large lot.

Added to their cash on hand, the equity in the house made a total of approximately $175,000. That was far short of two million; and the kidnapper had not sounded like a guy whose intention was to negotiate in good faith.

Anyway, the equity in the house couldn't be converted to cash unless they took a new loan or sold the place. Because the house was jointly owned, he needed Holly's signature in either scenario.

They wouldn't have had the house if Holly hadn't inherited it from her grandmother, Dorothy, who had raised her. The mortgage had been smaller upon Dorothy's death, but to pay inheritance taxes and save the house, they'd had to work out a bigger loan.

So the amount available for ransom was approximately thirty-seven thousand dollars.

Until now, Mitch had not thought of himself as a failure. His self-image had been that of a young man responsibly building a life.

He was twenty-seven. No one could be a failure at twenty-seven.

Yet this fact was indisputable: Although Holly was the center of his life, and priceless, when forced to put a price on her, he could pay only thirty-seven thousand.

A bitterness overcame him for which he had no target except himself. This was not good.

Bitterness could turn to self-pity, and if he surrendered to self-pity, he would *make* a failure of himself. And Holly would die.

Even if the house had been without a mortgage, even if they had half a million in cash and were wildly successful for people their age, he would not have had the funds to ransom her.

That truth brought him to the realization that money would not be what saved Holly. *He* would be what saved her if she could be saved: his perseverance, his wits, his courage, his love.

As he returned the bank statement to the drawer, he saw an envelope bearing his name in Holly's handwriting. It contained a birthday card that she had bought weeks before the day.

On the front of the card was the photograph of an ancient man festooned with wrinkles and wattles. The caption declared *When you're old, I'll still need you, dear.*

Mitch opened the card and read *By then, the only thing I'll have left to enjoy is gardening, and you'll make excellent compost.*

He laughed. He could imagine Holly's laugh in the store when she had opened the card and read that punch line.

Then his laugh became something different from a laugh. In the past five terrible hours, he had more than once come close to tears but had repressed them. The card ruined him.

Below the printed text, she had written *Happy birthday! Love, Holly.* Her writing was graceful but not flamboyant, neat.

In his mind's eye, he saw her hand as she held the pen. Her hands looked delicate, but they were surprisingly strong.

Eventually he recovered his composure by remembering the strength of her fine hands.

He went to the kitchen and found Holly's car keys on the pegboard by the back door. She drove a four-year-old Honda.

After retrieving his cell phone from the charger beside the toaster oven, he went outside and moved his truck to the garage at the back of the property.

The white Honda stood in the second bay, sparkling because Holly had washed it Sunday afternoon. He parked beside the car.

He got out of the truck and shut the driver's door, and stood between the vehicles, sweeping the room with his gaze. If anyone had been here, they would have heard and seen the truck approaching, would have had ample warning and would have fled.

The garage smelled vaguely of motor oil and grease, and strongly of the grass clippings that were bundled in burlap tarps and mounded in the bed of the pickup.

He stared at the low ceiling, which was the floor of the loft that overhung two-thirds of the garage. Windows in the higher space faced the house, providing an excellent vantage point.

Someone had known when Mitch had come home earlier, had known precisely when he had entered the kitchen. The phone had rung, with Holly on the line, moments after he had found the broken dishes and the blood.

Although an observer might have been in the garage, might still be here, Holly would not be with him. He might know where she was being held, but he might *not* know.

If the observer, whose existence remained theoretical, knew where Holly could be found, it would nevertheless be reckless for Mitch to go after him. These people clearly had much experience of violence, and they were ruthless. A gardener would not be a match for any of them.

A board creaked overhead. In a building of this vintage, the creak might have been an ordinary settling noise, old joints paying obeisance to gravity.

Mitch walked around to the driver's door of the Honda, opened it. He hesitated, but got in behind the steering wheel, leaving the door open.

For the purpose of distraction, he started the engine. The garage door stood open, eliminating any danger of carbon-monoxide poisoning.

He got out of the car and slammed the door. Anyone listening would assume he had pulled it shut from inside.

Why he was not at once backing out of the garage might puzzle the listener. One assumption might be that he was making a phone call.

On a side wall were racked the many gardening tools that he used when working on his own property. The various clippers and pruning shears all seemed too unwieldy.

He quickly selected a well-made garden trowel formed from a single piece of machined steel. The handle featured a rubber grip.

The blade was wide and scooped and not as sharp as the blade of a knife. It was sharp enough.

Brief consideration convinced him that, although he might be able to stab a man, he should select a weapon more likely to disable than to kill.

On the wall opposite from the gardening implements, other racks held other tools. He chose a combination lug wrench and pry bar.

# 12

Mitch was aware that a kind of madness, bred of desperation, had come over him. He could bear no more inaction.

With the long-handled lug wrench clutched in his right hand, he moved to the back of the garage where steep open stairs in the north corner led in a single straight flight to the loft.

By continuing to react instead of acting, by waiting docilely for the six-o'clock call — one hour and seven minutes away — he would be performing as the machine that the kidnappers wished him to be. But even Ferraris sometimes ended in junkyards.

Why Jason Osteen had stolen the dog and why he, of all people, had been shot dead as an example to Mitch were mysteries to which no solutions were at hand.

Intuition told him, however, that the kidnappers had known Jason would be linked with him and that this link would make the police suspicious of him. They were weaving a web of circumstantial evidence that, were they to kill Holly, would force Mitch to trial for her murder and would elicit the death penalty from any jury.

Perhaps they were doing this only to make it impossible for him to turn to the authorities for help. Thus isolated, he would be more easily controlled.

Or, once he acquired the two million dollars

by whatever scheme they presented to him, perhaps they had no intention of releasing his wife in return for the ransom. If they could use him to knock over a bank or some other institution by proxy, if they killed Holly after they got the money, and if they were clever enough to leave no traces of themselves, Mitch — and perhaps another fall guy that he had not yet met — might take the rap for every crime.

Alone, grieving, despised, imprisoned, he would never know who his enemies had been. He would be left to wonder why they had chosen him rather than another gardener or a mechanic, or a mason.

Although the desperation that drove him up the loft stairs had stripped away inhibiting fear, it had not robbed him of his reason. He didn't race to the top, but climbed warily, the steel bar held by the pry end, the socket end ready as a club.

The wooden treads must have creaked or even groaned underfoot, but the chug of the Honda's idling engine, echoing off the walls, masked the sounds of his ascent.

Walled on three sides, the loft lay open at the back. A railing extended left from the top of the stairs and across the width of the garage.

In the three walls of the loft, windows admitted afternoon light into that higher space. Visible beyond the balusters — and looming above them — were stacks of cardboard boxes and other items for which the bungalow provided no storage.

The stored goods were arranged in rows, as low as four feet in some places, as high as seven in others. The aisles between were shadowy, and every end offered a blind turn.

At the top of the stairs, Mitch stood at the head of the first aisle. A pair of windows in the north wall directly admitted adequate light to assure him that no one crouched in any shallow niche among the boxes.

The second aisle proved darker than the first, although the intersecting passage at the end was brightened by unseen windows in the west wall, which faced the house. The light at the end would have silhouetted anyone standing boldly in the intervening space.

Because the boxes were not all the same size and were not in every instance stacked neatly, and because gaps existed here and there in the rows, nooks along each aisle offered places large enough for a man to hide.

Mitch had quietly ascended the stairs. The Honda below probably had not been running long enough to raise significant suspicion. Therefore, any sentinel stationed in the loft would be alert and listening, but most likely would not yet have realized the immediate need to be elusive.

The third aisle was brighter for having a window directly at the end of it. He checked out the fourth aisle, then the fifth and final, which lay along the south wall in the light of two dusty windows. He found no one.

The intersecting passage that paralleled the west wall, into which all the east-west aisles terminated, was the only length of the loft that he had not seen in its entirety. Every row of boxes hid a portion of that space.

Raising the lug wrench higher, he eased along the southernmost aisle, toward the front of the loft. He found that the entire length of the last passage was as deserted as the portions he had seen from the farther end of the building.

On the floor, however, against the end of a row of boxes, stood some equipment that should not be here.

More than half the stuff in the loft had belonged to Dorothy, Holly's grandmother. She had collected ornaments and other decorative items for every major holiday.

At Christmas, she'd unpacked fifty or sixty ceramic snowmen of various kinds and sizes. She'd had more than a hundred ceramic Santa Clauses. Ceramic reindeer, Christmas trees, wreaths, ceramic bells and sleighs, groups of ceramic carolers, miniature ceramic houses that could be arranged to form a village.

The bungalow couldn't accommodate Dorothy's full collection for any holiday. She'd unpacked and set out as much as would fit.

Holly hadn't wanted to sell any of the ceramics. She continued the tradition. Someday, she said, they would have a bigger house, and the full glory of each collection could be revealed.

Sleeping in hundreds of cardboard boxes were Valentine's Day lovers, Easter bunnies and lambs and religious figures, July Fourth patriots, Halloween ghosts and black cats, Thanksgiving Pilgrims, and the legions of Christmas.

The gear on the floor in the final aisle was neither ceramic nor ornamental, nor festive. The electronic equipment included a receiver and a recorder, but he couldn't identify the other three items.

They were plugged into a board of expansion receptacles, which was itself plugged into a nearby wall outlet. Indicator lights and LED readouts revealed the equipment to be engaged.

They had been maintaining surveillance of the house. Its rooms and phones were probably bugged.

Confident in his stealth, having seen no one in the loft, Mitch assumed, upon sight of the equipment, that it was not at the moment being monitored, that it must be set to automatic operation. Perhaps they could even access it and download it from a distance.

Simultaneously with that thought, the array of indicator lights changed patterns, and at least one of the LED displays began to keep a running count.

He heard a hissing distinct from the idling Honda in the garage below, and then the voice of Detective Taggart.

'*I love these old neighborhoods. This was how southern California looked in its great years . . .* '

Not just the rooms of the house but the front porch, too, had been bugged.

He knew that he had been outmaneuvered only an instant before he felt the muzzle of the handgun against the back of his neck.

# 13

Although he flinched, Mitch did not attempt to turn toward the gunman or to swing the lug wrench. He would not be able to move fast enough to succeed.

During the past five hours, he had become acutely aware of his limitations, which counted as an achievement, considering that he had been raised to believe he had no limitations.

He might be the architect of his life, but he could no longer believe that he was the master of his fate.

' . . . *before they cut down all the orange groves and built a wasteland of stucco tract houses.*'

Behind him, the gunman said, 'Drop the lug wrench. Don't stoop to put it down. Just drop it.'

The voice was not that of the man on the phone. This one sounded younger than the other, not as cold, but with a disturbing deadpan delivery that flattened every word and gave them all the same weight.

Mitch dropped the club.

' . . . *more convenient. But I happened to be in your neighborhood.*'

Apparently using a remote control, the gunman switched off the recorder.

He said to Mitch, 'You must want her cut to pieces and left to die, the way he promised.'

'No.'

'Maybe we made a mistake, choosing you. Maybe you'd be happy to be rid of her.'

'Don't say that.'

Every word matter-of-fact, all with the same emotional value, which was no value at all: 'A large life-insurance policy. Another woman. You could have reasons.'

'There's nothing like that.'

'Perhaps you'd do a better job for us if, as compensation, we promised to kill her for you.'

'No. I love her. I do.'

'You pull another stunt like this one, she's dead.'

'I understand.'

'Let's go back the way you came.'

Mitch turned, and the gunman also turned, staying behind him.

As he began to retrace his steps along the final aisle, past the first of the southern windows, Mitch heard the lug wrench scrape against the boards as the gunman scooped it off the floor.

He could have pivoted, kicked, and hoped to catch the man as he rose from a quick stoop. He feared the maneuver would be anticipated.

Thus far, he had thought of these nameless men as professional criminals. They probably were that, but they were something else, too. He did not know what else they might be, but something worse.

Criminals, kidnappers, murderers. He could not imagine what might be worse than what he already knew them to be.

Following him along the aisle, the gunman said, 'Get in the Honda. Go for a ride.'

'All right.'

'Wait for the call at six o'clock.'

'All right. I will.'

As they neared the end of the aisle, at the back of the loft, where they needed to turn left and cross the width of the garage to the steps in the northeast corner, something like luck intervened by way of a cord, a knot in the cord, a loop in the knot.

At the moment it happened, Mitch didn't perceive the cause, only the effect. A tower of cardboard boxes collapsed. Some tumbled into the aisle, and one or two fell on the gunman.

According to stenciled legends on the cartons, they contained Halloween ceramics. Packed with more bubble wrap and shredded tissue paper than with decorative objects, the boxes were not heavy, but an avalanche of them almost knocked the gunman off his feet and sent him stumbling.

Mitch dodged one box and raised an arm to deflect another.

The falling first stack destabilized a second.

Mitch almost reached toward the gunman to steady him. But then he realized that any offer of support might be misinterpreted as an attack. To avoid being misunderstood — and shot — he stepped out of his enemy's way.

The old dry wood of the railing at the back of the loft could safely accommodate anyone who leaned casually on it, but it proved too weak to endure the impact of the stumbling gunman. Balusters cracked, nails shrieked loose of their holes, and two butted lengths of the handrail separated at the joint.

The gunman cursed at the storm of boxes. He cried out in alarm as the railing sagged away from him.

He fell to the floor of the garage. The distance was not great, approximately eight feet, yet he landed with a terrible sound, and in a clatter of broken railing, and the gun went off.

# 14

From the toppling of the first box to the concluding punctuation of the gunshot, only a few seconds had passed. Mitch stood in stunned disbelief longer than the event itself had taken to unfold.

Silence shocked him from paralysis. The silence below.

He hurried to the stairs, and under his feet the boards released a great thunder, as though they had stored it up from the storms that long ago had lashed the trees from which they had been milled.

As Mitch crossed the garage on the ground level, past the front of the truck, past the idling Honda, elation contested with despair for control of him. He did not know what he would find and therefore did not know what to feel.

The gunman lay facedown, head and shoulders under an overturned wheelbarrow. He must have slammed into one edge of the wheelbarrow, flipping it over and on top of himself.

An eight-foot fall should not have left him in such a profound stillness.

Breathing hard but not from physical exertion, Mitch righted the wheelbarrow, shoved it aside. Each breath brought him the scent of motor oil, of fresh grass clippings, and as he crouched beside the gunman, he detected the bitter pungency of gunfire, too, and then the sweetness of blood.

He turned the body over and saw the face clearly for the first time. The stranger was in his middle twenties, but he had the clear complexion of a preadolescent boy, jade-green eyes, thick lashes. He did not look like a man who could talk deadpan about mutilating and murdering a woman.

He had landed with his throat across the rolled metal edge of the wheelbarrow tray. The impact appeared to have crushed his larynx and collapsed his trachea.

His right forearm had broken, and his right hand, trapped under him, had reflexively fired the pistol. The index finger remained hooked through the trigger guard.

The bullet had penetrated just below the sternum, angled up and to the left. Minimal bleeding suggested a heart wound, instant death.

If the shot hadn't killed him instantly, the collapsed airway would have killed him quickly.

This was too much luck to be just luck.

Whatever it was — luck or something better, luck or something worse — Mitch didn't at first know whether it was a helpful or an unwelcome development.

The number of his enemies had been reduced by one. A tattered glee, frayed by the rough edge of vengeance, fluttered in him and might have teased out a torn and threadbare laugh if he had not also been at once aware that this death complicated his situation.

When this man did not report back to his

associates, they would call him. When they could not raise him on the phone, they might come looking for him. If they found him dead, they would assume that Mitch had killed him, and soon thereafter Holly's fingers would be taken off one by one, each stump flame-cauterized without benefit of an anesthetic.

Mitch hurried to the Honda and switched off the engine. He used the remote control to shut the garage door.

As shadows closed in, he switched on the lights.

The single shot might not have been heard. If it had been heard, he felt sure that it had not been recognized for what it was.

At this hour, neighbors would not be home from work. Some kids might have returned from school, but they would be listening to CDs or would be deep in an Xbox world, and the muffled shot would be perceived as another bit of music or game percussion.

Mitch returned to the body and stood looking down at it.

For a moment, he was not able to proceed. He knew what needed to be done, but he could not act.

He had lived for almost twenty-eight years without witnessing a death. Now he'd seen two men shot in the same day.

Thoughts of his own death pecked at him, and when he tried to repress them, they could not be caged. The susurration in his ears was only the sound of his rushing blood, driven by the oars of a sculling heart, but his imagination provided dark wings beating at the periphery of his mind's eye.

Although he was squeamish about searching the corpse, necessity brought him to his knees beside it.

From a hand so warm that it seemed death might be a pretense, he removed the pistol. He put it in the nearby wheelbarrow.

If the right leg of the dead man's khakis had not been pulled up in the fall, Mitch wouldn't have seen the second weapon. The gunman carried the snub-nosed revolver in an ankle holster.

After putting the revolver with the pistol, Mitch considered the holster. He undid the Velcro closures, put the holster with the guns.

He dug through the pockets of the sports coat, turned out the pockets of the pants.

He discovered a set of keys — one for a car, three others — which he considered but then returned to the pocket where he'd found them. After a brief hesitation, he retrieved them and added them to the wheelbarrow.

He found nothing more of interest other than a wallet and a cell phone. The former would contain identification, and the latter might be programmed to speed-dial, among other numbers, each of the dead man's collaborators.

If the phone rang, Mitch didn't dare answer it. Even if he spoke in monosyllables and the man at the other end briefly mistook his voice for that of the dead man, he would give himself away by one slip or another.

He switched off the phone. They would be

suspicious when they got voice mail, but they would not act precipitously on mere suspicion.

Restraining his curiosity, Mitch set the wallet and phone aside in the wheelbarrow. Other, more urgent tasks awaited him.

# 15

From the back of the truck, Mitch fetched a canvas tarp that was used for bundling rosebush clippings. The thorns could not easily penetrate it, as they did burlap.

In case one of the other kidnappers came looking for the dead man, Mitch couldn't leave the body here.

The thought of driving around with the corpse in the trunk of his car turned his stomach sour. He would have to buy some antacids.

The tarp had softened with use and was as fissured as the glaze on an antique vase. Although not waterproof, it remained fairly water-resistant.

Because the gunman's heart had stopped instantly, little blood had escaped the wound. Mitch wasn't worried about bloodstains.

He didn't know how long he would have to keep the body in the trunk. A few hours, a day, two days? Sooner or later, fluids other than blood would leak from it.

He spread the tarp on the floor and rolled the cadaver onto it. A wave of revulsion washed through him, inspired by the way the dead man's arms flopped, by the way the head lolled.

Considering Holly's peril, which required him not to recoil from even the most disturbing tasks, he closed his eyes and took several slow, deep breaths. He choked down his revulsion.

The lolling head suggested that the gunman's neck was broken. In that case, he was three ways dead: broken neck, crushed trachea, bullet-torn heart.

This could not be luck. Such layered grisliness could not be a stroke of good fortune. To view it as such would be repellant.

Extraordinary, yes. An extraordinary incident. And strange. But not auspicious.

Besides, he could not yet say that this accident had been to his advantage. It might easily prove to be his undoing.

After rolling the body in the tarp, he did not take time to weave twine through the eyelets and tie the package shut. Worry was a clock ticking, an hourglass draining, and he feared an interruption of one kind or another before this cleanup could be completed.

He dragged the tarp-wrapped corpse to the back of the Honda. As he opened the trunk of the car, a thrill of dread went through him, the absurd thought that he would find another dead man already occupying the space, but of course the trunk was empty.

His imagination had never been a fever swamp, and it had not heretofore been morbid. He wondered if this expectation of a second corpse might be not a flash of fantasy but in fact a presentiment that other dead men lay in his immediate future.

Loading the body into the trunk proved to be an arduous job. The gunman weighed less than Mitch, but he was after all a dead weight.

If Mitch had not been strong and if his

business had not been one that kept him in good physical condition, the corpse might have defeated him. Sweat glazed him by the time he slammed shut the trunk lid and locked it.

A careful inspection revealed no blood on the wheelbarrow. None on the floor, either.

He gathered the broken balusters and the fallen section of the handrail, and he took them out of the garage and concealed them in a half-depleted stack of cordwood that had supplied the living-room fireplace during the previous winter.

Inside once more, he climbed the stairs to the loft and returned to the fateful spot at the end of the southernmost aisle. The cause of the accident soon revealed itself.

Many of the stacked boxes were sealed with tape, but others were tied shut with cord. The neck of the lug wrench was still caught in the loop of a knot.

Carrying the wrench down at his side, somewhat away from his body, the gunman must have snared the dangling loop of cord. He had pulled Halloween down on himself.

Mitch stacked most of the fallen boxes as they had been. He created a new row of short stacks in front of the breach in the railing to conceal the damage.

If the gunman's pals came searching for him, the splintered balusters and the missing section of handrail would suggest to them that a struggle had occurred.

The ragged gap in the railing would still be visible to them from the southeast corner of the lower level. The stairs were at the northeast corner, however, and the gunman's friends might never be in a position to see the damage.

Although Mitch would have liked to vent some anger by smashing the electronic eavesdropping equipment arrayed in the aisle along the west wall, he left it untouched.

When he picked up the long lug wrench, it felt heavier than he remembered.

In the silence, in the stillness, he sensed deception. Felt watched. Felt mocked.

Nearby, web-hung spiders must be patiently dreaming of ripe twitching morsels. A fat spring fly or two must be droning toward silken snares.

More than flies, worse than spiders, something loomed. Mitch turned, but seemed to be alone.

An important truth hid from him, hid not in shadows, hid not behind the boxed holidays, but hid from him in plain sight. He saw but was blind. He heard but was deaf.

This extraordinary perception grew more intense, swelled until it became oppressive, until it had such a physical dimension that his lungs would not expand. Then it rapidly subsided, was gone.

He took the lug wrench downstairs and hung it on the tool rack where it belonged.

From the wheelbarrow, he retrieved the phone, the wallet, the keys, the two guns, and the ankle holster. He put everything on the front passenger's seat of the Honda.

He drove out of the garage, parked beside the house, and went quickly inside to get a jacket. He was wearing a flannel shirt, and though the night ahead would not be cool enough to require a jacket, he needed one.

When he came out of the house, he expected to find Taggart waiting by the Honda for him. The detective didn't show.

In the car once more, he placed the lightweight sports jacket on the passenger's seat, concealing the items that he had taken from the corpse.

The dashboard clock agreed with his wrist-watch — 5:11.

He drove out to the street and turned right, with a thrice-dead man in the trunk of the car and worse horrors loose in his mind.

# 16

Two blocks from his house, Mitch parked at the curb. He left the engine running, kept the windows closed and the doors locked.

He could not recall ever previously locking the doors while he was in the car.

He glanced at the rearview mirror, suddenly certain that the trunk lock had not engaged, that the lid had popped open, presenting the swaddled cadaver for viewing. The trunk remained closed.

In the dead man's wallet were credit cards and a California driver's license in the name of John Knox. For the license photo, the youthful gunman had flashed a smile as winsome as that of a boy-band teen idol.

Knox had been carrying $585, including five one-hundred-dollar bills. Mitch counted the money without taking it out of the currency compartment.

Nothing in the wallet revealed a single fact about the man's profession, personal interests, or associations. No business card, no library card, no health-insurance card. No photos of loved ones. No reminder notes or Social Security card, or receipts.

According to the license, Knox lived in Laguna Beach. Something useful might be learned by a search of his residence.

Mitch needed time to consider the risks of

going to Knox's place. Besides, there was someone else he needed to visit before the scheduled six-o'clock call.

He put the wallet, the dead man's cell phone, and the set of keys in the glove box. He tucked the revolver and the ankle holster under the driver's seat.

The pistol remained on the adjacent seat, under his sports coat.

Through a zigzaggery of low-traffic residential streets, ignoring the speed limits and even a couple of stop signs, Mitch arrived at his parents' place in east Orange at 5:35. He parked in the driveway and locked the Honda.

The handsome house stood on a second tier of hills, with hills above it. The two-lane street, sloping toward flatter land, revealed no suspicious vehicle following in his wake.

A languid breeze had uncoiled from the east. With a thousand times a thousand silvery-green tongues, the tall eucalyptus trees whispered to one another.

He looked up to the single window of the learning room. When he was eight years old, he had spent twenty consecutive days there, with an interior shutter locked across that window.

Sensory deprivation focuses thought, clears the mind. That is the theory behind the dark, silent, empty learning room.

Mitch's father, Daniel, answered the doorbell. At sixty-one, he remained a strikingly good-looking man, still in possession of all his hair, though it had turned white.

Perhaps because his features were so pleasingly bold — perfect features if he had wished to be a stage actor — his teeth seemed too small. They were his natural teeth, every one. He was a stickler for dental hygiene. Laser-whitened, they dazzled, but they looked small, like rows of white-corn kernels in a cob.

Blinking with surprise that was a degree too theatrical, he said, 'Mitch. Katherine never told me you called.'

Katherine was Mitch's mother.

'I didn't,' Mitch admitted. 'I hoped it would be all right if I just stopped by.'

'More often than not, I'd be occupied with one damn obligation or another, and you'd be out of luck. But tonight I'm free.'

'Good.'

'Though I did expect to do a few hours of reading.'

'I can't stay long,' Mitch assured him.

The children of Daniel and Katherine Rafferty, all now adults, understood that, in respect for their parents' privacy, they were to schedule their visits and avoid impromptu drop-ins.

Stepping back from the door, his father said, 'Come in, then.'

In the foyer, with its white-marble floor, Mitch looked left and right at an infinity of Mitches, echo reflections in two large facing mirrors with stainless-steel frames.

He asked, 'Is Kathy here?'

'Girls' night out,' his father said. 'She and Donna Watson and that Robinson woman are off to a show or something.'

'I'd hoped to see her.'

'They'll be late,' his father said, closing the door. 'They're always late. They chatter at each other all evening, and when they pull into the driveway, they're still chattering. Do you know the Robinson woman?'

'No. This is the first I've heard of her.'

'She's annoying,' his father said. 'I don't understand why Katherine enjoys her company. She's a mathematician.'

'I didn't know mathematicians annoyed you.'

'This one does.'

Mitch's parents were both doctors of behavioral psychology, tenured professors at UCI. Those in their social circle were mostly from what academic types recently had begun to call the human sciences, largely to avoid the term *soft sciences*. Among that crowd, a mathematician might annoy like a stone in a shoe.

'I just fixed a Scotch and soda,' his father said. 'Would you like something?'

'No thank you, sir.'

'Did you just *sir* me?'

'I'm sorry, Daniel.'

'Mere biological relationship — '

' — should not confer social status,' Mitch finished.

The five Rafferty children, on their thirteenth birthdays, had been expected to stop calling their parents Mom and Dad, and to begin using first names. Mitch's mother, Katherine, preferred to be called Kathy, but his father would not abide Danny instead of Daniel.

As a young man, Dr. Daniel Rafferty had held strong views about proper child-rearing. Kathy had no firm opinions on the subject, but she had been intrigued by Daniel's unconventional theories and curious to see if they would prove successful.

For a moment, Mitch and Daniel stood in the foyer, and Daniel seemed unsure how to proceed, but then he said, 'Come see what I just bought.'

They crossed a large living room furnished with stainless-steel-and-glass tables, gray leather sofas, and black chairs. The art works were black-and-white, some with a single line or block of color: here a rectangle of blue, here a square of teal, here two chevrons of mustard yellow.

Daniel Rafferty's shoes struck hard sounds from the Santos-mahogany floor. Mitch followed as quietly as a haunting spirit.

In the study, pointing to an object on the desk, Daniel said, 'This is the nicest piece of shit in my collection.'

# 17

The study decor matched the living room, with lighted display shelves that presented a collection of polished stone spheres.

Alone on the desk, cupped in an ornamental bronze stand, the newest sphere had a diameter greater than a baseball. Scarlet veins speckled with yellow swirled through a rich coppery brown.

To the uninformed it might have appeared to be a piece of exotic granite, ground and polished to bring out its beauty. In fact it was dinosaur dung, which time and pressure had petrified into stone.

'Mineral analysis confirms that it came from a carnivore,' said Mitch's father.

'Tyrannosaurus?'

'The size of the entire stool deposit suggests something smaller than a T. rex.'

'Gorgosaurus?'

'If it had been found in Canada, dating to the Upper Cretaceous, then perhaps a gorgosaurus. But the deposit was found in Colorado.'

'Upper Jurassic?' Mitch asked.

'Yes. So it's probably a ceratosaurus dropping.'

As his father picked up a glass of Scotch and soda from the desk, Mitch went to the display shelves.

He said, 'I gave Connie a call a few nights ago.'

Connie was his oldest sister, thirty-one. She lived in Chicago.

'Is she still drudging away in that bakery?' his father asked.

'Yes, but she owns it now.'

'Are you serious? Yes, of course. It's typical. If she puts one foot in a tar pit, she'll never back up, just flail forward.'

'She says she's having a good time.'

'That's what she would say, no matter what.'

Connie had earned a master's degree in political science before she had jumped off the plank into an ocean of entrepreneurship. Some were mystified by this sea change in her, but Mitch understood it.

The collection of polished dinosaur-dung spheres had grown since he had last seen it. 'How many do you have now, Daniel?'

'Seventy-three. I've got leads on four brilliant specimens.'

Some spheres were only two inches in diameter. The largest were as big as bowling balls.

The colors tended toward browns, golds, and coppers, for the obvious reason; however, every hue, even blue, lustered under the display lights. Most exhibited speckled patterns; actual veining was rare.

'I talked to Megan the same evening,' Mitch said.

Megan, twenty-nine, had the highest IQ in a family of high IQs. Each of the Rafferty kids had been tested three times: the week of their ninth, thirteenth, and seventeenth birthdays.

After her sophomore year, Megan had dropped out of college. She lived in Atlanta and operated a thriving dog-grooming business, both a shop and a mobile service.

'She called at Easter, asked how many eggs we dyed,' Mitch's father said. 'I assume she thought that was funny. Katherine and I were just relieved that she didn't announce she was pregnant.'

Megan had married Carmine Maffuci, a mason with hands the size of dinner plates. Daniel and Kathy felt that she had settled for a husband beneath her station, intellectually. They expected that she would realize her error and divorce him — if children didn't arrive first to complicate the situation.

Mitch liked Carmine. The guy had a sweet nature, an infectious laugh, and a tattoo of Tweety Bird on his right biceps.

'This one looks like porphyry,' he said, pointing to a dung specimen with a purple-red groundmass and flecks of something that resembled feldspar.

He had also recently spoken to his youngest sister, Portia, but he did not mention her because he didn't want to start an argument.

Freshening his Scotch and soda at the corner wet bar, Daniel said, 'Anson had us to dinner two nights ago.'

Anson, Mitch's only brother, at thirty-three the oldest of the siblings, was the most dutiful to Daniel and Kathy.

In fairness to Mitch and his sisters, Anson had long been his parents' favorite, and he had never been rebuffed. It was easier to be a dutiful child when your enthusiasms were not analyzed for signs of psychological maladjustment and when your invitations were not met with either gimlet-eyed suspicion or impatience.

In fairness to Anson, he had earned his status by fulfilling his parents' expectations. He had proved, as had none of the others, that Daniel's child-rearing theories could bear fruit.

Top of his class in high school, star quarterback, he declined football scholarships. Instead he accepted those offered only in respect of the excellence of his mind.

The academic world was a chicken yard and Anson a fox. He did not merely absorb learning but devoured it with the appetite of an insatiable carnivore. He earned his bachelor's degree in two years, a master's in one, and had a Ph.D. at the age of twenty-three.

Anson was neither resented by his siblings nor in any slightest way alienated from them. On the contrary, if Mitch and his sisters had taken a secret vote for their favorite in the family, all four of their ballots would have been marked for their older brother.

His good heart and natural grace had allowed Anson to please his parents without becoming like them. This achievement seemed no less impressive than if nineteenth-century scientists, with nothing but steam power and primitive voltaic cells, had sent astronauts to the moon.

'Anson just signed a major consulting contract with China,' Daniel said.

Brontosaurus, diplodocus, brachiosaurus, iguanodon, moschops, stegosaurus, triceratops, and other droppings were labeled by engraving on the bronze stands that held the spheres.

'He'll be working with the minister of trade,' said Daniel.

Mitch didn't know whether petrified stool could be analyzed so precisely as to identify the particular dinosaur species or genus. Perhaps his father had arrived at these labels by the application of theories with little or no hard science supporting them.

In certain areas of intellectual inquiry where absolute answers could not be defended, Daniel embraced them anyway.

'*And* directly with the minister of education,' Daniel said.

Anson's success had long been used to goad Mitch to consider a career more ambitious than his current work, but the jabs never broke the skin of his psyche. He admired Anson but didn't envy him.

As Daniel prodded with another of Anson's achievements, Mitch checked his wristwatch, certain that he would shortly have to leave to take the kidnapper's call in privacy. But the time was only 5:42.

He felt as if he had been in the house at least twenty minutes, but the truth was seven.

'Do you have an engagement?' Daniel asked.

Mitch detected a hopeful note in his father's voice, but he did not resent it. Long ago he had realized that an emotion as bitter and powerful as resentment was inappropriate in this relationship.

Author of thirteen ponderous books, Daniel

believed himself to be a giant of psychology, a man of such iron principles and steely convictions that he was a rock in the river of contemporary American intellectualism, around which lesser minds washed to obscurity.

Mitch knew beyond doubt that his old man was not a rock. Daniel was a fleeting shadow on that river, riding the surface, neither agitating nor smoothing the currents.

If Mitch had nurtured resentment toward such an ephemeral man, he would have made himself crazier than Captain Ahab in perpetual pursuit of the white whale.

Throughout their childhood, Anson had counseled Mitch and his sisters against anger, urging patience, teaching the value of humor as defense against their father's unconscious inhumanity. And now Daniel inspired in Mitch nothing but indifference and impatience.

The day Mitch had left home to share an apartment with Jason Osteen, Anson had told him that having put anger behind himself, he would eventually come to pity their old man. He had not believed it, and thus far he had advanced no further than grudging forbearance.

'Yes,' he said, 'I have an engagement. I should be going.'

Regarding his son with the keen interest that twenty years ago would have intimidated Mitch, Daniel said, 'What was this all about?'

Whatever Holly's kidnappers intended for Mitch, his chances of surviving it might not be high. The thought had crossed his mind that this

110

might be the last chance he had to see his parents.

Unable to reveal his plight, he said, 'I came to see Kathy. Maybe I'll come back tomorrow.'

'Came to see her about what?'

A child can love a mother who has no capacity to love him in return, but in time, he realizes that he is pouring his affection not on fertile ground but on rock, where nothing can be grown. A child might then spend a life defined by settled anger or by self-pity.

If the mother is not a monster, if she is instead emotionally disconnected and self-absorbed, and if she is not an active tormentor but a passive observer in the home, her child has a third option. He can choose to grant her mercy without pardon, and find compassion for her in recognition that her stunted emotional development denies her the fullest enjoyment of life.

For all her academic achievements, Kathy was clueless about the needs of children and the bonds of motherhood. She believed in the cause-and-effect principle of human interaction, the need to reward desired behavior, but the rewards were always materialistic.

She believed in the perfectibility of humanity. She felt that children should be raised according to a system from which one did not deviate and with which one could ensure they would be civilized.

She did not specialize in that area of psychology. Consequently, she might not have become a mother if she hadn't met a man with firm theories of child development and with a system to apply them.

Because Mitch would not have life without his mother and because her cluelessness did not encompass malice, she inspired a tenderness that was not love or even affection. It was instead a sad regard for her congenital incapacity for sentiment. This tenderness had nearly ripened into the pity that he withheld from his father.

'It's nothing important,' Mitch said. 'It'll keep.'

'I can give her a message,' Daniel said, following Mitch across the living room.

'No message. I was nearby, so I just dropped in to say hello.'

Because such a breach of family etiquette had never happened previously, Daniel remained unconvinced. 'Something's on your mind.'

Mitch wanted to say *Maybe a week of sensory deprivation in the learning room will squeeze it out of me.*

Instead he smiled and said, 'I'm fine. Everything's fine.'

Although he had little insight into the human heart, Daniel had a bloodhound's nose for threats of a financial nature. 'If it's money problems, you know our position on that.'

'I didn't come for a loan,' Mitch assured him.

'In every species of animal, the primary obligation of parents is to teach self-sufficiency to their offspring. The prey must learn evasion, and the predator must learn to hunt.'

Opening the door, Mitch said, 'I'm a self-sufficient predator, Daniel.'

'Good. I'm glad to hear that.'

112

He favored Mitch with a smile in which his small super-naturally white teeth appeared to have been sharpened since last he revealed them.

Even to deflect his father's suspicions, Mitch could not summon a smile this time.

'Parasitism,' Daniel said, 'isn't natural to Homo sapiens or to any species of mammal.'

Beaver Cleaver would never have heard that line from *his* dad.

Stepping out of the house, Mitch said, 'Tell Kathy I said hi.'

'She'll be late. They're always late when the Robinson woman joins the pack.'

'Mathematicians,' Mitch said scornfully.

'Especially this one.'

Mitch pulled the door shut. Several steps from the house, he stopped, turned, and studied the place perhaps for the last time.

He had not only lived here but had also been home-schooled here from first grade through twelfth. More hours of his life had been spent in this house than out of it.

As always, his gaze drifted to that certain second-story window, boarded over on the inside. The learning room.

With no children at home any longer, what did they use that high chamber for?

Because the front walk curved away from the house instead of leading straight to the street, when Mitch lowered his attention from the second floor, he faced not the door but the sidelight. Through those French panes, he saw his father.

Daniel stood at one of the big steel-framed

foyer mirrors, apparently considering his appearance. He smoothed his white hair with one hand. He wiped at the corners of his mouth.

Although he felt like a Peeping Tom, Mitch could not look away.

As a child, he had believed there were secrets about his parents that would free him if he were able to learn them. Daniel and Kathy were a guarded pair, however, as discreet as silverfish.

In the foyer now, Daniel pinched his left cheek between thumb and forefinger, and then his right, as if to tweak some color into them.

Mitch suspected that his visit had already more than half faded from his father's mind, now that the threat of a loan request had been lifted.

In the foyer, Daniel turned sideways to the mirror, as though taking pride in the depth of his chest, the slimness of his waist.

How easy to imagine that between the facing mirrors, his father did not cast an infinity of echo reflections, as Mitch had done, and that the single likeness of him possessed so little substance that, to any eye but his own, it would appear as transparent as the image of a spook.

# 18

At 5:50, only fifteen minutes after he had arrived at Daniel and Kathy's house, Mitch drove away. He turned the corner and traveled a quick block and a half.

Perhaps two hours of daylight remained. He could easily have detected a tail if one had pursued him.

He pulled the Honda into the empty parking lot at a church.

A forbidding brick façade, fractured eyes of multicolored glass somber with no current inner light, rose to a steeple that gouged the sky and cast a hard shadow across the blacktop.

His father's fear had been unfounded. Mitch had not intended to ask for money.

His parents had done well financially. They could no doubt contribute a hundred thousand to the cause without being in the least pinched. Even if they would give him twice that sum, and considering his own meager resources, he would still have in hand only a little more than ten percent of the ransom.

Besides, he would not have asked because he knew they would have declined, ostensibly on the basis of their theories of parenting.

Furthermore, he had come to suspect that the kidnappers were seeking more than money. He had no idea what they desired in addition to cash, but snatching the wife of a gardener who

115

earned a five-figure income made no sense unless they wanted something else that only he could provide.

He had been all but certain that they intended to commit a major robbery by proxy, using him as if he were a remote-controlled robot. He could not rule out that scenario, but it no longer convinced him.

From under the driver's seat, he retrieved the snub-nosed revolver and the ankle holster.

He examined the weapon with caution. As far as he could tell, it did not have a safety.

When he broke out the cylinder, he discovered that it held five rounds. This surprised him, as he had expected six.

All he knew about guns was what he had learned from books and movies.

In spite of Daniel's talk about inspiring children to be self-sufficient, he had not prepared Mitch for the likes of John Knox.

*The prey must learn evasion, and the predator must learn to hunt.*

His parents had raised him to be prey. With Holly in the hands of murderers, however, Mitch had nowhere to run. He would rather die than hide and leave her to their mercy.

The Velcro closure on the holster allowed him to strap it far enough above his ankle to avoid exposing it if his pants hiked when he sat down. He didn't favor peg-legged jeans, and this pair accommodated the compact handgun.

He shrugged into the sports coat. Before he got out of the car, he would tuck the pistol under

116

his belt, in the small of his back, where the coat would conceal it.

He examined that weapon. Again he failed to locate a safety.

With some fumbling, he ejected the magazine. It contained eight cartridges. When he pulled the slide back, he saw a ninth gleaming in the breach.

After reinserting the magazine and making sure that it clicked securely into place, he put the pistol on the passenger's seat.

His cell phone rang. The car clock read 5:59.

The kidnapper said, 'Did you enjoy your visit with Mom and Dad?'

He had not been followed to his parents' house or away from it, and yet they knew where he had been.

He said at once, 'I didn't tell them anything.'

'What were you after — milk and cookies?'

'If you're thinking I could get the money from them, you're wrong. They're not that rich.'

'We know, Mitch. We know.'

'Let me talk to Holly.'

'Not this time.'

'Let me talk to her,' he insisted.

'Relax. She's doing fine. I'll put her on the next call. Is that the church you and your parents attended?'

His was the only car in the parking lot, and none were passing at the moment. Across the street from the church, the only vehicles were those in driveways, none at the curb.

'Is that where you went to church?' the kidnapper asked again.

117

'No.'

Although he was closed in the car with the doors locked, he felt as exposed as a mouse in an open field with the vibrato of hawk wings suddenly above.

'Were you an altar boy, Mitch?'

'No.'

'Can that be true?'

'You seem to know everything. You know it's true.'

'For a man who was never an altar boy, Mitch, you are so *like* an altar boy.'

When he didn't at first respond, thinking the statement a non sequitur, and when the kidnapper waited in silence, Mitch at last said, 'I don't know what that means.'

'Well, I don't mean you're pious, that's for sure. And I don't mean you're reliably truthful. With Detective Taggart, you've proved to be a cunning liar.'

In their two previous conversations, the man on the phone had been professional, chillingly so. This petty jeering seemed out of sync with his past performance.

He had, however, called himself a *handler*. He had bluntly said that Mitch was an instrument to be manipulated, finessed.

These taunts must have a purpose, though it eluded Mitch. The kidnapper wanted to get inside his head and mess with him, for some subtle purpose, to achieve a particular result.

'Mitch, no offense, because it's actually kind of sweet — but you're as *naive* as an altar boy.'

'If you say so.'

'I do. I say so.'

This might be an attempt to anger him, anger being an inhibition to clear thinking, or perhaps the purpose was to instill in him such doubt about his competence that he would remain cowed and obedient.

He had already acknowledged to himself the absolute degree of his helplessness in this matter. They could not strop his humility to a sharper edge than now existed.

'Your eyes are wide open, Mitch, but you don't see.'

This statement unnerved him more than anything else that the kidnapper had said. Not an hour ago, in the loft of his garage, that very thought, couched in similar words, had occurred to him.

Having packed John Knox in the trunk of the car, he had returned to the loft to puzzle out how the accident had occurred. Having seen the neck of the lug wrench snared in the loop of the knot, he had settled the mystery.

But just then he had felt deceived, watched, mocked. He had been overcome by an instinctive sense that a greater truth waited in that loft to be discovered, that it hid from him in plain sight.

He had been shaken by the thought that he saw and yet was blind, that he heard and yet was deaf.

Now the mocking man on the telephone: *Your eyes are wide open, Mitch, but you don't see.*

*Uncanny* seemed not to be too strong a word. He felt that the kidnappers could not only watch him and listen to him anywhere, at any time, but

119

also that they could pore through his thoughts.

He reached for the pistol on the passenger's seat. No immediate threat loomed, but he felt safer holding the gun.

'Are you with me, Mitch?'

'I'm listening.'

'I'll call you again at seven-thirty — '

'More waiting? *Why?*' Impatience gnawed at him, and he could not cage it, though he knew the danger of the infection proceeding to a state of foaming recklessness. '*Let's get on with this.*'

'Easy, Mitch. I was about to tell you what to do next when you interrupted.'

'Then, damn it, *tell* me.'

'A good altar boy knows the ritual, the litanies. A good altar boy responds, but he doesn't interrupt. If you interrupt again, I'll make you wait until *eight*-thirty.'

Mitch got a leash on his impatience. He took a deep breath, let it slowly out, and said, 'I understand.'

'Good. So when I hang up, you'll drive to Newport Beach, to your brother's house.'

Surprised, he said, 'To Anson's place?'

'You'll wait with him for the seven-thirty call.'

'Why does my brother have to be involved in this?'

'You can't do alone what has to be done,' said the kidnapper.

'But what has to be done? You haven't told me.'

'We will. Soon.'

'If it takes two men, the other doesn't have to be him. I don't want Anson dragged into this.'

'Think about it, Mitch. Who better than your brother? He loves you, right? He won't want your wife to be cut to pieces like a pig in a slaughterhouse.'

Throughout their beleaguered childhood, Anson had been the reliable rope that kept Mitch tethered to a mooring. Always it was Anson who raised the sails of hope when there seemed to be no wind to fill them.

To his brother, he owed the peace of mind and the happiness that eventually he had found when at last free of his parents, the lightness of spirit that had made it possible for him to win Holly as a wife.

'You've set me up,' Mitch said. 'If whatever you want me to do goes wrong, you've set me up to make it look as if I killed my wife.'

'The noose is even tighter than you realize, Mitch.'

They might be wondering about John Knox, but they didn't know that he was dead in the trunk of the Honda. A dead conspirator was some proof of the story Mitch could tell the authorities.

Or was it? He had not considered all the ways that the police might interpret Knox's death, perhaps most of them more incriminating than exculpatory.

'My point,' Mitch said, 'is that you'll do the same to Anson. You'll wrap him in chains of circumstantial evidence to keep him cooperative. It's how you work.'

'None of that will matter if the two of you do what we want, and you get her back.'

'But it isn't fair,' Mitch protested, and realized that he must in fact sound as ingenuous and credulous as an altar boy.

The kidnapper laughed. 'And by contrast, you feel we've dealt fairly with *you*? Is that it?'

Clenched around the pistol, his hand had grown cold and moist.

'Would you rather we spared your brother and partnered you with Iggy Barnes?'

'Yes,' Mitch said, and was at once embarrassed to have been so quick to sacrifice an innocent friend to save a loved one.

'And that would be fair to Mr. Barnes?'

Mitch's father believed that shame had no social usefulness, that it was a signature of the superstitious mind, and that a person of reason, living a rational life, must be free of it. He believed, as well, that the capacity for shame could be expunged by education.

In Mitch's case, the old man had failed miserably, at least on this score. Although the thug on the phone was the only witness to this willingness to save a brother at the expense of a friend, Mitch felt his face turn warm with shame.

'Mr. Barnes,' the kidnapper said, 'is not the sharpest knife in the drawer. If for no other reason, your friend would not be an acceptable substitute for your brother. Now go to Anson's house and wait for our call.'

Resigned to this development but sick with despair that his brother must be imperiled, Mitch said, 'What should I tell him?'

'Absolutely nothing. I'm *requiring* you to tell

him nothing. I am the experienced handler, not you. When I call, I'll let him hear Holly scream, and then explain the facts.'

Alarmed, he said, 'That's not necessary, making her scream. You promised not to hurt her.'

'I promised not to rape her, Mitch. Nothing you say to your brother will be as convincing as her scream. I know better than you how to do this.'

His cold, sweaty grip on the pistol was problematic. When his hand began to shake, he put the weapon on the passenger's seat once more.

'What if Anson isn't home?'

'He's home. Get moving, Mitch. It's rush hour. You don't want to be late getting to Newport Beach.'

The kidnapper terminated the call.

When Mitch pressed the END button on his phone, the act felt grimly predictive.

He shut his eyes for a moment, trying to gather his unraveled nerves, but then opened them because he felt vulnerable with them closed.

When he started the engine, a flock of crows flew up from the pavement, from the shadow of the steeple to the steeple itself.

# 19

Famous for its yacht harbor, its mansions, and its wonderland of upscale shopping, Newport Beach was not home exclusively to the fabulously wealthy. Anson lived in the Corona del Mar district, in the front half of a two-unit condo.

Shaded by a massive magnolia, approached by a used-brick path, with New England architecture as interpreted by a swooning romantic, the house did not impress, but it charmed.

The door chimes played a few bars of Beethoven's 'Ode to Joy.'

Anson arrived before Mitch pressed the bell push a second time.

Although as fit as an athlete, Anson was a different physical type from Mitch: bearish, barrel-chested, bull-necked. That he had been a star quarterback in high school testified to his quickness and agility, for he looked more like a middle linebacker.

His handsome, broad, open face seemed always to be anticipating a reason to smile. At the sight of Mitch, he grinned.

'*Fratello mio!*' Anson exclaimed, embracing his brother and drawing him into the house. '*Entrino! Entrino!*'

The air was redolent of garlic, onions, bacon.

'Cooking Italian?' Mitch asked.

'*Bravissimo, fratello piccolo!* From a mere

124

aroma and my bad Italian, you make a brilliant deduction. Let me hang up your coat.'

Mitch had not wanted to leave the pistol in the car. The gun was tucked under his belt, in the small of his back.

'No,' he said. 'I'm fine. I'll keep it.'

'Come to the kitchen. I was in a funk at the prospect of another dinner alone.'

'You're immune to funk,' Mitch said.

'There is no such thing as funk antibodies, little brother.'

The house featured a masculine but stylish decor, emphasizing nautical decorative items. Paintings of sailing ships portrayed proud vessels tossed in storms and others making way under radiant skies.

From childhood, Anson had believed that perfect freedom could never be found on land, only at sea, under sail.

He'd been a fan of pirate yarns, stories of naval battles, and tales of adventure on the bounty. He'd read many of them aloud to Mitch, who had sat enthralled for hours.

Daniel and Kathy suffered motion sickness in a rowboat on a pond. Their aversion to the sea had been the first thing to inspire Anson's interest in the nautical life.

In the cozy, fragrant kitchen, he pointed to a pot steaming on the stove. '*Zuppa massaia.*'

'What kind of soup is *massaia*?'

'Classic housewife's soup. Lacking a wife, I have to get in touch with my feminine side when I want to make it.'

Sometimes Mitch found it hard to believe that

a pair as leaden as their parents could have produced a son as buoyant as Anson.

The kitchen clock read 7:24. A traffic backup from an accident had delayed him.

On the table stood a bottle of Chianti Classico and a half-full glass. Anson opened a cabinet, plucked another glass from a shelf.

Mitch almost declined the wine. But one round would not dull his wits and might restore some elasticity to his brittle nerves.

As Anson poured the Chianti, he did a fair imitation of their father's voice. 'Yes, I'm pleased to see you, Mitch, though I didn't notice your name on the visiting-progeny schedule, and I had planned to spend this evening tormenting guinea pigs in an electrified maze.'

Accepting the Chianti, Mitch said, 'I just came from there.'

'That explains your subdued manner and your gray complexion.' Anson raised his glass in a toast. '*La dolce vita*.'

'To your new deal with China,' Mitch said.

'Was I used as a needle again?'

'Always. But he can't push hard enough to puncture me anymore. Sounds like a big opportunity.'

'The China thing? He must've hyped what I told him. They aren't dissolving the Communist Party and giving me the emperor's throne.'

Anson's consulting work was so arcane that Mitch had never been able to understand it. He had earned a doctorate in linguistics, the science of language, but he also had a deep background in computer languages and in digitalization

126

theory, whatever that might be.

'Every time I leave their place,' Mitch said, 'I feel the need to dig in the dirt, work with my hands, *something*.'

'They make you want to flee to something real.'

'That's it exactly. This wine's good.'

'After the soup, we're having *lombo di maiale con castagne*.'

'I can't digest what I can't pronounce.'

'Roast loin of pork with chestnuts,' Anson said.

'Sounds good, but I don't want dinner.'

'There's plenty. The recipe serves six. I don't know how to cut it down, so I always make it for six.'

Mitch glanced at the windows. Good — the blinds were shut.

From the counter near the kitchen phone, he picked up a pen and a notepad. 'Have you gotten any sailing in lately?'

Anson dreamed of one day owning a sailing yacht. It should be large enough not to seem claustrophobic on a long coastal run or perhaps even on a voyage to Hawaii, but small enough to be managed with one mate and an array of sail motors.

He used the word *mate* to mean his fellow sailor but also his companion in bed. Regardless of his bearish appearance and sometimes acerbic sense of humor, Anson was a romantic not just about the sea but also about the opposite sex.

The attraction women felt for him could not be called merely magnetic. He drew them as the gravity of the moon pulls the tides.

Yet he was no Don Juan. With great charm, he turned away most of his pursuers. And each one that he hoped might be his ideal woman always seemed to break his heart, though he would not have put it that melodramatically.

The small boat — an eighteen-foot American Sail — that he currently moored at a buoy in the harbor was by no measure a yacht. But given his luck at love, he might one day own the vessel of his dreams long before he found someone with whom to sail it.

In answer to Mitch's question, he said, 'I haven't had time to do more than bob the harbor like a duck, tacking the channels.'

Sitting at the kitchen table, printing in block letters on the notepad, Mitch said, 'I should have a hobby. You've got sailing, and the old man has dinosaur crap.'

He tore off the top sheet of the pad and pushed it across the table so that Anson, still standing, could read it: YOUR HOUSE IS PROBABLY BUGGED.

His brother's look of astonishment had a quality of wonder that Mitch recognized as similar to the expression that had overtaken him when he had read aloud the pirate yarns and the tales of heroic naval battles that thrilled him as a boy. His initial reaction seemed to be that some strange adventure had begun, and he appeared not to grasp the implied danger.

To cover Anson's stunned silence, Mitch said, 'He just bought a new specimen. He says it's a ceratosaurus dropping. From Colorado, the Upper Jurassic.'

He presented another sheet of paper on which he had printed THEY'RE SERIOUS. I SAW THEM KILL A MAN.

While Anson read, Mitch withdrew his cell phone from an inside coat pocket and placed it on the table. 'Given our family history, it'll be so appropriate — inheriting a collection of polished shit.'

As Anson pulled out a chair and sat at the table, his boyish expression of expectation clouded with worry. He assisted in the pretense of an ordinary conversation: 'How many does he have now?'

'He told me. I don't remember. You could say the den's become a sewer.'

'Some of the spheres *are* pretty things.'

'Very pretty,' Mitch agreed as he printed THEY'LL CALL AT 7:30.

Mystified, Anson mouthed the questions *Who? What?*

Mitch shook his head. He indicated the wall clock — 7:27.

They conducted a self-conscious and inane conversation until the phone rang promptly on the half-hour. The ring came not from Mitch's cell but from the kitchen phone.

Anson looked to him for guidance.

In the event, which seemed likely, that the timing of this call was coincidental and that the expected contact would come on the cell phone, Mitch indicated that his brother should answer it.

Anson caught it on the third ring and brightened when he heard the caller's voice. 'Holly!'

Mitch closed his eyes, bent his head, covered his face with his hands, and from Anson's reaction, knew when Holly screamed.

# 20

Mitch expected to be brought into the call, but the kidnapper spoke only to Anson, and for longer than three minutes.

The substance of the first part of the conversation was obvious, and could be deduced from hearing his brother's half of it. The last couple of minutes proved not easy to follow, in part because Anson's responses grew shorter even as his tone of voice became more grim.

When Anson hung up, Mitch said, 'What do they want us to do?'

Instead of answering, Anson came to the table and picked up the bottle of Chianti. He topped off his glass.

Mitch was surprised to see that his own glass was empty. He could recall having taken only a sip or two. He declined a refill.

Pouring in spite of Mitch's protest, Anson said, 'If your heart's in the same gear as mine, you'll burn off two glasses of this stuff even as you're swallowing it.'

Mitch's hands were trembling, though not from the effect of Chianti, and in fact the wine might steady them.

'And Mickey?' Anson said.

Mickey had been an affectionate nickname that Anson had called his younger brother during a particularly difficult period of their childhood.

When Mitch looked up from his unsteady hands, Anson said, 'Nothing will happen to her. I promise you, Mickey. I swear nothing will happen to Holly. Nothing.'

Through the formative years of Mitch's life, his brother had been a trustworthy pilot, bringing them through storms, or a wingman flying defense as it was needed. He seemed over-reaching now, however, when he promised a safe landing, for surely Holly's kidnappers controlled this flight.

'What do they want us to do?' he asked again. 'Is it even possible, is it something that *can* be done, or is it as crazy as it seemed to me the moment I first heard him demand two million?'

Instead of replying, Anson sat down. Leaning forward, shoulders hunched, beefy arms on the table, the wineglass all but concealed by his large hands, he was an imposing presence.

He still looked bearish but no longer cuddly. The women usually drawn to him as the tides to the moon, upon seeing him in this mood, would take a wide orbit around him.

This particular set to Anson's jaw, the flare of his nostrils, a perceived change in his eyes from a soft seawater green to an emerald hardness heartened Mitch. He knew this look. This was Anson rising to meet injustice, which always brought out in him a stubborn, effective resistance.

Although relieved to have his brother's assistance, Mitch felt guilty, too. 'I'm sorry about this. Man, I never anticipated you'd be dragged into it. I was blindsided by that. I'm sorry.'

'You don't have anything to be sorry about. Nada, zip, zero.'

'If I'd have done something different . . . '

'If you'd done anything different, maybe Holly would be dead now. So what you've done so far is the right thing.'

Mitch nodded. He needed to believe what his brother had said. He felt useless nonetheless. 'What do they want us to do?' he asked again.

'First, Mickey, I want to hear everything that's happened. What the sonofabitch on the phone told me isn't a fraction of it. I need to hear it from the beginning until you rang my bell.'

Surveying the room, Mitch wondered where an eavesdropping device might be hidden.

'Maybe they're listening to us right now, maybe they're not,' Anson said. 'It doesn't matter, Mickey. They already know everything you're going to tell me because *they did it to you.*'

Mitch nodded. He fortified himself with some Chianti. Then he gave Anson an account of this hellish day.

In case they were being monitored, he withheld only the story of his encounter with John Knox in the garage loft.

Anson listened intently and interrupted only a few times to ask clarifying questions. When Mitch finished, his brother sat with eyes closed, ruminating on what he'd been told.

Megan had the highest IQ of the Rafferty children, but Anson had always scored a close second to her. Holly's situation remained as dire now as it had been half an hour ago, but Mitch took comfort in the fact that his brother had joined the fight.

He himself had done nearly as well as Anson on the tests. He felt somewhat cheered not because a higher intelligence had set to work on the problem, but because he was no longer alone.

He had never been any good alone.

Getting up from his chair, Anson said, 'Sit tight, Mickey. I'll be right back,' and left the kitchen.

Mitch stared at the telephone. He wondered if he would recognize a listening device if he took the phone apart.

He glanced at the clock — 7:48. He had been given sixty hours to raise the money, and fifty-two were left.

That didn't seem correct. The events that brought him here had left him feeling wrung out, pressed flat. He felt as if he'd already been through the entire sixty hours.

Because he experienced no effect from what he'd thus far drunk, he finished the wine remaining in his glass.

Anson returned, wearing a sports coat. 'We have places to go. I'll tell you everything in the car. I'd rather you drove.'

'Give me a second to finish this wine,' Mitch said, although his glass was empty.

On the notepad, he printed one more message: THEY CAN TRACK MY CAR.

Although no one had tailed him on his way to his parents' house, the kidnappers had known that he'd gone there. And later, when he had parked in the church lot to take the six-o'clock call, they had known his precise location.

*Is that the church you and your parents attended?*

If they had attached tracking devices to his truck and to the Honda, they had been able to follow him at a distance, out of sight, monitoring his whereabouts electronically.

Although Mitch didn't know the practical details of how such technology worked, he did understand that the use of it meant Holly's abductors were even more sophisticated than he had initially thought. The extent of their resources — that is, their knowledge and their criminal experience — made it increasingly clear that any attempt at resistance would be unlikely to succeed.

On the brighter side, the kidnappers' professionalism argued that any action they directed Mitch and Anson to undertake would have been well thought out and would be likely to succeed, whether robbery by proxy or another crime. With luck, the ransom would be raised.

In response to the warning in the latest note, Anson switched off the flame under the pot of soup, and produced the keys to his SUV. 'Let's take my Expedition. You drive.'

Mitch caught the keys when they were tossed to him, then quickly gathered the notes that he had printed, and threw them in the trash.

He and his brother left by the kitchen door. Anson neither turned off any lights nor engaged the lock, perhaps recognizing that, in this tempest, he could not keep out those whom he wished to bar, only those who had no desire to enter.

Softened by ferns and dwarf nandina, a brick courtyard separated the front and rear condos. The smaller back unit was above a pair of garages.

Anson's two-stall garage contained the Expedition and a 1947 Buick Super Woody Wagon, which he himself had restored.

Mitch got behind the wheel of the SUV. 'What if they have tracking devices on your cars, too?'

As he pulled shut the passenger's door, Anson said, 'Doesn't matter. I'm going to do exactly what they want. If they're able to track us, they'll be reassured.'

Backing out of the garage, into the alley, Mitch said, 'So what do they want, what have we got to do? Hit me with it.'

'They want two million bucks transferred to a numbered account in the Grand Cayman Islands.'

'Yeah, well, I guess that's better than having to give it to them in pennies, two hundred million damn pennies, but whose money do *we* have to rip off?'

The violent light of a red sunset flooded the alleyway.

Anson pressed the remote to close the garage door. He said, 'We don't have to rip off anybody. It's my money, Mickey. They want my money, and for this they can have it.'

# 21

The burning sky made radiant the alley, and a furnace glow filled the Expedition.

Flushed with a fiery reflection of the smoldering sun, Anson's face appeared fierce, and a golden eyeshine gilded his stare, but in his soft voice was the tender truth of him: 'Everything I have is yours, Mickey.'

As if he had crossed a busy city street and, glancing back, saw a primeval forest where a metropolis had just stood, Mitch sat for a moment in bewildered silence, and then said, 'You have two million dollars? Where did you get two million dollars?'

'I'm good at what I do, and I've worked hard.'

'I'm sure you're good at what you do, you're good at everything you do, but you don't live like a rich man.'

'Don't want to. Flash and status don't interest me.'

'I know some people with money keep a low profile, but . . . '

'Ideas interest me,' Anson said, 'and getting real freedom someday, but not having my picture in the society pages.'

Mitch remained lost in the forest of this new reality. 'You mean you have, really have, two million in the bank?'

'I'll have to liquidate investments. It can be done by phone, by computer, once the exchanges open tomorrow. Three hours tops.'

Dry seeds of hope swelled with the irrigation provided by this amazing, this astonishing news.

Mitch said, 'How . . . how much do you have? I mean, altogether.'

'This will almost wipe out my liquidity,' Anson said, 'but I'll still have the equity in the condo.'

'Wipe you out. I can't let that happen.'

'If I earned it once, I can earn it again.'

'Not that much. Not easily.'

'What I do with my money is my business, Mickey. And what I want to do with it is get Holly home safe.'

Through the streaming crimson light, through soft dusky shadows fast hardening toward night, along the alley came a ginger cat.

Caught in cross tides of emotion, Mitch did not trust himself to speak, so he watched the cat and drew slow deep breaths.

Anson said, 'Because I'm not married, don't have kids, these scum came after Holly and you as a way to get at me.'

The revelation of Anson's wealth had so surprised Mitch that he had not at once grasped this obvious explanation of the heretofore inexplicable abduction.

'If there'd been someone closer to me,' Anson continued, 'if I had been more vulnerable that way, then my wife or child would have been snatched, and Holly would've been spared.'

Slinking slowly to a stillness, the ginger cat stopped in front of the Expedition, peered up at Mitch. In a streetscape of reflected fire, only the cat's eyes produced original light, radium-green.

138

'It could've been one of our sisters they grabbed, couldn't it? Megan, Connie, Portia? And this is no different from that.'

Mitch wondered, 'The way you live, so middle-class, how did they know?'

'Someone working in a bank, a stock brokerage, one bent nail where there shouldn't be any.'

'You have any idea who?'

'I haven't had time to think about it, Mickey. Ask me tomorrow.'

Breaking stillness, sneaking forward, the ginger cat passed close by the SUV, vanishing from sight.

In that instant, a bird flew up, a pigeon or a dove that had lingered late over scattered crumbs, thrashing its wings against the driver's-door window as it swooped off toward some safe bower.

Mitch was startled by the sound and by the dreamlike perception that the cat, on vanishing, had become the bird.

Facing his brother again, Mitch said, 'I couldn't see a way to go to the cops. But everything's changed now. You have that option.'

Anson shook his head. 'They shot a guy to death right in front of you to make a point.'

'Yeah.'

'And you got the point.'

'Yeah.'

'Well, so did I. Unless they get what they want, they'll kill without compunction, and they'll pin it on you or on both of us. We get Holly back, and *then* we go to the cops.'

'Two million dollars.'

'It's only money,' Anson said.

Mitch remembered what his brother had said about not caring to have his picture in the society pages, about instead being interested in ideas and in 'getting real freedom someday.'

Now he repeated those four words and said, 'I know what that means. The sailing yacht. A life on the sea.'

'It doesn't matter, Mickey.'

'Sure it matters. With that much money, you're close to having the boat and a life without chains.'

Anson's turn had come to look for the cat or an equivalent distraction in the rouge light, the mordant shadows.

Mitch said, 'I know you're a planner. You always have been. When did you plan to retire, to go for it?'

'It's a child's dream anyway, Mickey. Pirate yarns and naval battles.'

'When?' Mitch insisted.

'In two years. When I turned thirty-five. So it'll be a few years later. And I might make it back quicker than I think. My business is growing fast.'

'The China deal.'

'The China deal and others. I'm *good* at what I do.'

'No way I'd turn you down,' Mitch said. 'I'd die for Holly, so I'm sure as hell willing to let you go broke for her. But I won't let you minimize the sacrifice. It's one mother of a sacrifice.'

Anson reached out, put a hand around the back of Mitch's neck, pulled him close, gently pressed forehead to forehead, so they were not looking at each other but down at the gearshift console between them. 'Tell you something, bro.'

'Tell me.'

'Normally I'd never mention this. But so you don't chew out your own liver with guilt, which is the way you are . . . you should know you aren't the only one who's needed help.'

'What do you mean?'

'How do you think Connie bought her bakery?'

'You?'

'I structured a loan so a portion converts into a tax-free gift each year. I don't want to be repaid. It's fun to do this. And Megan's dog-grooming business.'

Mitch said, 'The restaurant Portia and Frank are opening.'

'That, too.'

Still sitting bowed head to bowed head, Mitch said, 'How did they figure out you had so much?'

'They didn't. I saw what they needed. I've been trying to think what you need, but you've always seemed . . . so damned self-reliant.'

'This is way different from a loan to buy a bakery or open a little restaurant.'

'No shit, Sherlock.'

Mitch laughed shakily.

'Growing up in Daniel's rat maze,' Anson said, 'the only thing any of us had was one another. The only thing that mattered. That's still the way it is, *fratello piccolo*. That's the way it's always going to be.'

'I'll never forget this,' Mitch said.

'Damn right. You owe me forever.'

Mitch laughed again, less shakily. 'Free gardening for life.'

'Hey, bro?'

'Yeah?'

'Are you gonna drip snot on the gearshift?'

'No,' Mitch promised.

'Good. I like a clean car. You ready to drive?'

'Yeah.'

'You sure?'

'Yeah.'

'Then let's roll.'

# 22

Only the thinnest wound of the fallen day bled along the far horizon, and otherwise the sky was dark, and the sea dark; and the moon had not yet risen to silver the deserted beaches.

Anson said he needed to think, and he thought clearly and well aboard a car in motion, because it was akin to a boat under sail. He suggested Mitch drive south.

At that hour, light traffic plied the Pacific Coast Highway, and Mitch stayed in the right-hand lane, in no hurry.

'They'll call the house tomorrow at noon,' Anson said, 'to see what progress I've made with the financials.'

'I don't like this wire transfer to the Cayman Islands.'

'Neither do I. Then they have the money *and* Holly.'

'Better we have a face-to-face,' Mitch said. 'They bring Holly, we bring a couple suitcases of cash.'

'That's also iffy. They take the money, shoot all of us.'

'Not if we make it a condition that we can be armed.'

Anson was dubious. 'That would intimidate them? They're really gonna believe we know guns?'

'Probably not. So we take weapons that don't

143

require us to be great shooters. Like shotguns.'

'Where do we get shotguns?' Anson asked.

'We buy them at a gun shop, at Wal-Mart, wherever.'

'Isn't there a waiting period?'

'I don't think so. Only with handguns.'

'We'd need to practice with them.'

'Not much,' Mitch said, 'just to get comfortable.'

'Maybe we could go out Ortega Highway. Once we had the guns, I mean. There's still some desert they haven't slammed full of houses. We could find a lonely place, fire some rounds.'

Mitch drove in silence, and Anson rode in silence, the eastern hills speckled with the lights of expensive houses, the black sea to the west, and the sky black, with no horizon line visible anymore, sea and sky merging into one great black void.

Then Mitch said, 'It doesn't feel real to me. The shotguns.'

'It feels movie,' Anson agreed.

'I'm a gardener. You're a linguistics expert.'

'Anyway,' Anson said, 'I don't see kidnappers letting us set conditions. Whoever has the power makes the rules.'

They worried southward. The graceful highway curved, rose, and descended into downtown Laguna Beach.

In mid-May the tourist season had begun. People strolled the sidewalks, going to and from dinner, peering in the windows of the closed shops and galleries.

When his brother suggested that they grab

something to eat, Mitch said he wasn't hungry. 'You have to eat,' Anson pressed.

Resisting, Mitch said, 'What're we going to talk about over dinner? Sports? We don't want to be overheard talking about *this*.'

'So we'll eat in the car.'

Mitch parked in front of a Chinese restaurant. Painted on the windows, a dragon rampant tossed its mane of scaly flagella.

While Anson waited in the SUV, Mitch went inside. The girl at the takeout counter promised to have his order in ten minutes.

The animated conversation of the diners at the tables grated on him. He resented their carefree laughter.

Aromas of coconut rice, sweet-chili rice, deep-fried corn balls, cilantro, garlic, sizzling cashews raised an appetite. But soon the fragrant air grew oppressive, oily; his mouth turned dry and sour.

Holly remained in the hands of murderers.

They had hit her.

They had made her scream for him, and for Anson.

Ordering Chinese takeout, eating dinner, attending to *any* tasks of ordinary life seemed like betrayals of Holly, seemed to diminish the desperation of her situation.

If she had heard the threats made to Mitch on the phone — that her fingers would be sawn off, her tongue cut out — then her fear must be unbearable, desolating.

When he imagined her unrelenting fear, thought of her bound in darkness, the humility arising from his helplessness began at last to make way for greater anger, for rage. His face was hot, his eyes stinging, his throat so swollen with fury he could not swallow.

Irrationally, he envied the happy diners with an intensity that made him want to knock them out of their chairs, smash their faces.

The orderly decor offended him. His life had fallen into chaos, and he burned with the desire to spend his misery in a violent spree.

Some secret savage splinter of his nature, long festering, now flamed to full infection, filling him with the urge to tear down the colorful paper lanterns, shred the rice-paper screens, rip from the walls the red-enameled wooden letters of the Chinese language and spin them, as if they were martial-arts throwing stars, to slash and gouge everything in their path, to shatter windows.

Presenting two white bags containing his order, the counter girl sensed the pending storm in him. Her eyes widened, and she tensed.

Only a week ago, a deranged customer in a pizzeria had shot and killed a cashier and two waiters before another customer, an off-duty cop, had brought him down with two shots. This girl probably replayed in her mind the TV reports of that slaughter.

The realization that he might be frightening her was a lifeline that reeled Mitch back from fury to anger, then to a passive misery that dropped his blood pressure and quieted his thundering heart.

Leaving the restaurant, stepping into the mild spring night, he saw that his brother, in the

146

Expedition, was on his cell phone.

As Mitch got behind the steering wheel, Anson concluded the call, and Mitch said, 'Was it them?'

'No. There's this guy I think we should talk to.'

Giving Anson the larger bag of takeout, Mitch said, 'What guy?'

'We're in deep water with sharks. We're no match for them. We need advice from someone who can keep us from being eaten like chum.'

Although earlier he had given his brother the option of going to the authorities, Mitch said, 'They'll kill her if we tell anyone.'

'They said no cops. We aren't going to the police.'

'It still makes me nervous.'

'Mickey, I see the risks. We're playing a trip wire with a violin bow. But if we don't try to make some music, we're screwed anyway.'

Tired of feeling powerless, convinced that docile obedience to the kidnappers would be repaid with contempt and cruelty, Mitch said, 'Okay. But what if they're listening to us right now?'

'They're not. To bug a car and listen in real time, wouldn't they have to plant more than a microphone? Wouldn't they have to package it with a microwave transmitter and a power source?'

'Would they? I don't know. How would I know?'

'I think so. It would be too much equipment, too bulky, too complicated to conceal easily or to set up quickly.'

With chopsticks, which he had requested, Anson ate Szechuan beef from one container, rice with mushrooms from another.

'What about directional microphones?'

'I've seen the same movies you have,' Anson said. 'Directional mikes work best when the air is still. Look at the trees. We have a breeze tonight.'

Mitch ate moo goo gai pan with a plastic fork. He resented the deliciousness of the food, as though he would be more faithful to Holly if he gagged down a flavorless meal.

'Besides,' Anson said, 'directional mikes don't work between one moving vehicle and another.'

'Then let's not talk about it till we're moving.'

'Mickey, there's a very thin line between sensible caution and paranoia.'

'I passed that line hours ago,' Mitch said, 'and for me there's no going back.'

# 23

The moo goo gai pan left an unsavory aftertaste that Mitch tried unsuccessfully to wash away with Diet Pepsi as he drove.

He headed south on Coast Highway. Buildings and trees screened the sea from sight except for glimpses of an abyssal blackness.

Sipping from a tall paper cup of lemon tea, Anson said, 'His name is Campbell. He's ex-FBI.'

Alarmed, Mitch said, 'This is exactly who we *can't* turn to.'

'Emphasis on the ex, Mickey. *Ex*-FBI. He was shot, and shot bad, when he was twenty-eight. Other guys would have lived on disability, but he built his own little business empire.'

'What if they've got a tracking device on the Expedition, and they figure out we're powwow-ing with an ex-FBI agent?'

'They won't know that he was. If they know anything at all about him, they might know I did a large piece of business with him a few years ago. That'll just look like I'm putting together the ransom.'

The tires droned on the blacktop, but Mitch felt as though the highway under them were no more substantial than the skin of surface tension on a pond, across which a mosquito might skate confidently until a feeding fish rose and took it.

'I know what soil bougainvillea needs, what

149

sunlight loropetalum requires,' he said. 'But this stuff is another universe to me.'

'Me too, Mickey. Which is why we need help. No one has more real-world knowledge, more street smarts than Julian Campbell.'

Mitch had begun to feel that every yes-no decision was a switch on a bomb detonator, that one wrong choice would atomize his wife.

If this continued, he would soon worry himself into paralysis. Inaction would not save Holly. Indecision would be the death of her.

'All right,' he relented. 'Where does this Campbell live?'

'Get to the interstate. We're going south to Rancho Santa Fe.'

East-northeast of San Diego, Rancho Santa Fe was a community of four-star resorts, golf courses, and multimillion-dollar estates.

'Jam it,' Anson said, 'and we'll be there in ninety minutes.'

When together, they were comfortable with silences, perhaps because each of them, as a kid, had separately and alone spent much time in the learning room. That chamber was better soundproofed than a radio-station studio. No noise penetrated from the outside world.

During the drive, Mitch's silence and his brother's were different from each other. His was the silence of futile thrashing in a vacuum, of a mute astronaut tumbling in zero gravity.

Anson's was the silence of feverish but ordered thought. His mind raced along chains of deductive and inductive reasoning faster than

150

any computer, without the hum of electronic calculation.

They had been on I-5 for twenty minutes when Anson said, 'Do you sometimes feel we were held for ransom our entire childhood?'

'If not for you,' Mitch said, 'I'd hate them.'

'I *do* hate them sometimes,' Anson said. 'Intensely but briefly. They're too pathetic to hate for more than a moment. It would be like wasting your life hating Santa Claus because he doesn't exist.'

'Remember when I got caught with the copy of *Charlotte's Web*?'

'You were almost nine. You spent twenty days in the learning room.' Anson quoted Daniel: ''Fantasy is a doorway to superstition.''

'Talking animals, a humble pig, a clever spider — '

''A corrupting influence,'' Anson quoted. ''The first step in a life of unreason and irrational beliefs.''

Their father saw no mystery in nature, just a green machine.

Mitch said, 'It would have been better if they hit us.'

'Much better. Bruises, broken bones — that's the kind of thing that gets the attention of Child Protective Services.'

After another silence, Mitch said, 'Connie in Chicago, Megan in Atlanta, Portia in Birmingham. Why are you and I still here?'

'Maybe we like the climate,' Anson said. 'Maybe we don't think distance heals. Maybe we feel we have unfinished business.'

The last explanation resonated with Mitch. He had often thought about what he would say to his parents if the opportunity arose to question the disparity between their intentions and methods, or the cruelty of trying to strip from children their sense of wonder.

When he left the interstate and drove inland on state highways, desert moths swirled as white as snowflakes in the headlights and burst against the windshield.

Julian Campbell lived behind stone walls, behind an imposing iron gate framed by a massive limestone chambranle. The ascendants of the chambranle featured rich carvings of leafy vines that rose to the capping transverse, joining to form a giant wreath at the center.

'This gate,' Mitch said, 'must've cost as much as my house.'

Anson assured him: 'Twice as much.'

# 24

To the left of the main gate, the stacked-stone estate wall incorporated a guardhouse. As the Expedition drifted to a stop, the door opened, and a tall young man in a black suit appeared.

His clear dark eyes read Mitch as instantly as a cashier's scanner reads the bar code on a product. 'Good evening, sir.' He at once looked past Mitch to Anson. 'Pleased to see you, Mr. Rafferty.'

With no sound that Mitch could detect, the ornate iron gates swung inward. Beyond lay a two-lane driveway paved with quartzite cobblestones, flanked by majestic phoenix palms, each tree lighted from the base, the great crowns forming a canopy over the pavement.

He drove onto the estate with the feeling that, all forgiven, Eden had been restored.

The driveway was a quarter of a mile long. Vast, magically illuminated lawns and gardens receded into mystery on both sides.

Anson said, 'Sixteen manicured acres.'

'There must be a dozen on the landscape staff alone.'

'I'm sure there are.'

From red tile roofs, limestone walls, mullioned windows radiant with golden light, columns, balustrades, and terraces, the architect had conjured as much grace as grandeur. So large that it should have been intimidating, the

Italianate house instead looked welcoming.

The driveway ended by encircling a reflecting pond with a center fountain from which crisscrossing jets, like sprays of silver coins, arced and sparkled in the night. Mitch parked beside it.

'Does this guy have a license to print money?'

'He's in entertainment. Movies, casinos, you name it.'

This splendor overawed Mitch but also raised his hopes that Julian Campbell would be able to help them. Having built such wealth after being critically wounded and released from the FBI on permanent disability, having been dealt such a bad hand yet having played it to win, Campbell must be as street-smart as Anson promised.

A silver-haired man, with the demeanor of a butler, greeted them on the terrace, said his name was Winslow, and escorted them inside.

They followed Winslow across an immense white-marble receiving foyer capped by a coffered plaster ceiling with gold-leaf details. After passing through a living room measuring at least sixty by eighty feet, they came finally into a mahogany-paneled library.

In response to Mitch's question, Winslow revealed that the book collection numbered over sixty thousand volumes. 'Mr. Campbell will be with you momentarily,' he said, and departed.

The library, which incorporated more square footage than Mitch's bungalow, offered half a dozen seating areas with sofas and chairs.

They settled into armchairs, facing each other

154

across a coffee table, and Anson sighed. 'This is the right thing.'

'If he's half as impressive as the house — '

'Julian is the best, Mickey. He's the real deal.'

'He must think a lot of you to meet on such short notice, past ten o'clock at night.'

Anson smiled ruefully. 'What would Daniel and Kathy say if I turned away your compliment with a few words of modesty?'

' 'Modesty is related to diffidence,' ' Mitch quoted. ' 'Diffidence is related to shyness. Shyness is a synonym for timidity. Timidity is a characteristic of the meek. The meek do *not* inherit the earth, they serve those who are self-confident and self-assertive.' '

'I love you, little brother. You're amazing.'

'I'm sure you could quote it word for word, too.'

'That's not what I mean. You were raised in that Skinner box, that rat maze, and yet you're maybe the most modest guy I know.'

'I've got issues,' Mitch assured him. 'Plenty of them.'

'See? Your response to being called modest is self-criticism.'

Mitch smiled. 'Guess I didn't learn much in the learning room.'

'For me, the learning room wasn't the worst,' Anson said. 'What I'll never scrape out of my mind is the shame game.'

Memory flushed Mitch's face. ' 'Shame has no social usefulness. It's a signature of the superstitious mind.' '

'When did they first make you play the shame game, Mickey?'

'I think I was maybe five.'

'How often did you have to play it?'

'I guess half a dozen times over the years.'

'They put me through it eleven times that I remember, the last when I was thirteen.'

Mitch grimaced. 'Man, I remember that one. You were given a full week of it.'

'Living naked twenty-four/seven while everyone else in the house remains clothed. Being required to answer in front of everyone the most embarrassing, the most intimate questions about your private thoughts and habits and desires. Being watched by two other family members at every toilet, at least one of them a sister, allowed no smallest private moment . . . Did that cure *you* of shame, Mickey?'

'Look at my face,' Mitch said.

'I could light a candle off that blush.' Anson laughed softly, a warm and bearish laugh. 'Damn if we're getting him anything for Father's Day.'

'Not even cologne?' Mitch asked.

This was a jokey routine from childhood.

'Not even a pot to piss in,' Anson said.

'What about the piss without the pot?'

'How would I wrap it?'

'*With love*,' Mitch said, and they grinned at each other.

'I'm proud of you, Mickey. You beat 'em. It didn't work with you the way it worked with me.'

'The way what worked?'

'They broke me, Mitch. I have no shame, no capacity for guilt.' From under his sports coat, Anson withdrew a pistol.

156

# 25

Mitch held his smile in anticipation of the punch line, as if the pistol would prove to be not a weapon but instead a cigarette lighter or a novelty-store item that shot bubbles.

If the salty sea could freeze and keep its color, it would have been the shade of Anson's eyes. They were as clear as ever, as direct as always, but they were further colored by a quality that Mitch had never seen before, that he could not identify, or would not.

'Two *million*. Truth is,' Anson said almost sadly, without bite or rancor, 'I wouldn't pay two million to ransom *you*, so Holly was dead the moment she was snatched.'

Mitch's face set marble-hard, and his throat seemed to be full of broken stones that weighed down speech.

'Some people I've done consulting work for — sometimes they come across an opportunity that is crumbs to them but meat to me. Not my usual work, but things that are more directly criminal.'

Mitch had to struggle to focus his attention, to hear what was said, for his head was filled with a roar of lifelong perceptions collapsing like a construct of termite-eaten timbers.

'The people who kidnapped Holly are the team I put together for one of those jobs. They made a bundle from it, but they found out my take was bigger than I told them, and now they're greedy.'

So Holly had been kidnapped not solely because Anson had enough money to ransom her, but also because — *primarily* because — Anson had cheated her abductors.

'They're afraid to come directly after me. I'm a valuable resource to some serious people who'd pop anyone who popped me.'

Mitch assumed he would soon meet some of those 'serious people,' but whatever threat they might pose to him, it could not equal the devastation of this betrayal.

'On the phone,' Anson revealed, 'they said if I don't ransom Holly, they'll kill her and then shoot you down in the street one day, like they shot Jason Osteen. The poor dumb babies. They think they know me, but they don't know what I really am. Nobody does.'

Mitch shivered, for his mental landscape had turned wintry, his thoughts a storm of sleet, an icy and unrelenting barrage.

'Jason was one of them, by the way. Sweet brainless Breezer. He thought his pals were going to shoot the dog to make their point with you. By shooting him instead, they made a sharper point *and* improved the split of the remaining partners.'

Of course, Anson had known Jason as long as Mitch had known him. But Anson evidently had remained in touch with Jason long after Mitch had lost track of his former roommate.

'Is there something you want to say to me, Mitch?'

Perhaps another man in his position would have had a thousand angry questions, bitter denunciations, but Mitch sat frozen, having just experienced an emotional and intellectual polar shift, his previous equatorial view of life having flipped arctic in an instant. The landscape of this new reality was unknown to him, and this man who so resembled his brother was not the brother he had known, but a stranger. They were foreigners to each other, with no common language, here on a desolate plain.

Anson seemed to take Mitch's silence as a challenge or even an affront. Leaning forward in his chair, he sought a reaction, though he spoke in the brotherly voice that he had always used before, as if his tongue was so accustomed to the soft tones of deceit that it could not sharpen itself to the occasion.

'Just so you won't feel that you mean less to me than Megan, Connie, and Portia, I should clarify something. I didn't give them money to start businesses. That was bullshit, bro. I handled you.'

Because a response was clearly wanted, Mitch did not give one.

A man with a fever can suffer chills, and Anson's stare remained icy though its intensity revealed a feverishly agitated mind. 'Two million wouldn't wipe me out, bro. The truth is . . . I've got closer to eight.'

From behind the burly bearish charm, a goatish other watched, and Mitch sensed, without fully understanding what he meant, that

159

he and his brother, alone in the room, were in fact not alone.

'I bought the yacht in March,' Anson said. 'Come September, I'll run my consulting service at sea, with a satellite uplink. Freedom. I've earned it, and no one's gonna bleed me for two cents of it.'

The library door closed. Someone had arrived — and wanted privacy for what came next.

Rising from his chair, pistol ready, Anson tried once more to sting a reaction from Mitch. 'You can take some comfort from the fact that this will be over for Holly quicker now than midnight Wednesday.'

Defined by a confidence and grace that suggested miscegenation with a panther somewhere in his heritage, a tall man arrived, his iron-gray eyes bright with curiosity, his nose raised as if seeking an elusive scent.

To Mitch, Anson said, 'When I'm not home to take their call at noon, and when they can't get you on your cell phone, they'll know my buttons can't be pushed. They'll whack her, dump her, and run.'

The confident man wore tasseled loafers, black silk slacks, and a gray silk shirt the shade of his eyes. A gold Rolex brightened his left wrist, and his manicured fingernails were buffed to a shine.

'They won't torture her,' Anson continued. 'That was bluff. They probably won't even screw her before they kill her, though I would if I were them.'

Two solid men stepped from behind Mitch's

chair, flanking him. Both had pistols fitted with silencers, and their eyes were like those you usually saw only from the free side of a cage.

'He's carrying a piece in the small of his back,' Anson told them. To Mitch, he said, 'I felt it when I hugged you, bro.'

In retrospect, Mitch wondered why he hadn't mentioned the pistol to Anson once they were in the Expedition, in motion, and not likely to be monitored. Perhaps in the deepest catacombs of his mind had been interred a distrust of his brother that he had not been able to acknowledge.

One of the gunmen had a bad complexion. Like aphids at a leaf, acne had pitted his face. He told Mitch to stand, and Mitch got up from the chair.

The other gunman lifted the back of his sports coat and took the pistol from him.

When told to sit down, Mitch obeyed.

At last he spoke to Anson, but only to say, 'I pity you,' which was true, though it was a wretched kind of pity, with some compassion but no tenderness, leeched of mercy but transfused with revulsion.

However this pity might be qualified, Anson wanted none of it. He had said that he was proud of Mickey for not being molded in their parents' forge, that he himself felt broken. Those were lies, the lubricating oil of a manipulator.

His pride was reserved for his own cunning and ruthlessness. At Mitch's declaration of pity, disdain narrowed Anson's eyes, and his clear

161

contempt brought a harder edge of brutality to his features.

As if he sensed that Anson was sufficiently offended to do something rash, the man in silk raised one hand, Rolex glittering, to stay a gunshot. 'Not here.'

After a hesitation, Anson returned his pistol to the shoulder holster under his sports coat.

Unsought, into Mitch's mind came the seven words that Detective Taggart had spoken to him eight hours before, and though he did not know their source and did not fully see their appropriateness to the moment, he felt compelled to speak them. ''Blood crieth unto me from the ground.''

For an instant, Anson and his associates were as motionless as figures in a painting, the library hushed, the air still, the night crouched at the French doors, and then Anson walked out of the room, and the two gunmen retreated a few steps, remaining alert, and the man in silk perched on the arm of the chair in which Anson had sat.

'Mitch,' he said, 'you've been quite a disappointment to your brother.'

# 26

Julian Campbell had the golden glow that could have been achieved only with a tanning machine of his own, a sculpted physique that was proof of a home gym and a personal trainer, and a smooth face that, for a man in his fifties, suggested a plastic surgeon on retainer.

The wound that had ended his FBI career was not evident, nor any sign of disability. His triumph over his physical injuries evidently equaled his economic success.

'Mitch, I'm curious.'

'About what?'

Instead of answering, Campbell said, 'I'm a practical man. In my business I do what I need to do, and I don't get acid indigestion over it.'

Mitch translated those words to mean that Campbell did not allow himself to be troubled by guilt.

'I know a lot of men who do what needs done. Practical men.'

In thirteen and a half hours, the kidnappers would call Anson's house. If Mitch wasn't there to take the call, Holly would be killed.

'But this is the first time I've seen a man drop the dime on his own brother just to prove he's the hardest hardcase around.'

'For money,' Mitch corrected.

Campbell shook his head. 'No. Anson could have asked me to teach these pussies a lesson.

They aren't as tough as they think.'

Below this darkest level of the day's descent lay something darker.

'In twelve hours, we could have them begging to *pay* us to take your wife back unharmed.'

Mitch waited. For now there was nothing to do but wait.

'These guys have mothers. We burn down one mom's house, maybe smash another old lady's face, she needs a year of reconstructive surgery.'

Campbell was as matter-of-fact as if he had been explaining the terms of a real-estate deal.

'One of them has a daughter by an ex-wife. She means something to him. We stop the kid on her way home from school, strip her naked, set her clothes on fire. We tell her dad — next time we burn little Suzie *with* her clothes.'

Earlier, in his naivete, Mitch had been willing to have Iggy dragged into this mess to spare Anson.

Now he wondered if he would have been willing for other innocent people to be beaten, burned, and savaged in order to save Holly. Perhaps he should be thankful that the choice had not been offered to him.

'If we tweaked twelve of theirs in twelve hours, those pussies would send your wife home with apologies and a Nordstrom gift certificate for a new wardrobe.'

The two gunmen never took their eyes off Mitch.

'But Anson,' Campbell continued, 'he wants to make a statement so nobody ever underestimates him again. Indirectly, the statement's also for my benefit. And I gotta say . . . I'm impressed.'

Mitch could not let them see the true intensity of his terror. They would assume that extreme fear would make him reckless, and they would watch him even more diligently than they watched him now.

He must appear to be fearful but, more than fearful, despairing. A man in the grip of despair, who has utterly abandoned hope, is not a man with the will to fight.

'I'm curious,' Campbell repeated, coming around at last to where he had started. 'For your brother to be able to do this to you . . . what did *you* do?'

'Loved him,' Mitch said.

Campbell regarded Mitch as a wading heron regards a swimming fish, and then smiled. 'Yes, that would do it. What if one day he found himself reciprocating?'

'He's always wanted to go far, and to get there fast.'

'Sentiment is an encumbrance,' Campbell said.

In a voice weighed low with despair, Mitch said, 'Oh, it's a chain and an anchor.'

From the coffee table where one of the gunmen had put it, Campbell picked up the pistol that had been taken from Mitch. 'Have you ever fired this?'

Mitch almost said that he had not, but then realized that the magazine lacked one bullet, the round with which Knox accidentally shot himself. 'Once. I fired it once. To see what it felt like.'

Amused, Campbell said, 'And did it feel scary?'

'Scary enough.'

'Your brother says you're not a man for guns.'

'He knows me better than I know him.'

'So where did you get this?'

'My wife thought we should keep one in the house.'

'How right she was.'

'It's been in a nightstand drawer since the day we bought it,' Mitch lied.

Campbell rose to his feet. With his right arm extended full length, he pointed the pistol at Mitch's face. 'Stand up.'

# 27

Meeting the blind stare of the pistol, Mitch rose from the armchair.

The two nameless gunmen moved to new positions, as though their intent was to cut down Mitch in triangulated fire.

'Take off your coat and put it on the table,' Campbell said.

Mitch did as he was told, and then followed another instruction to turn out the pockets of his jeans. He put his ring of keys, his wallet, and a couple of wadded Kleenex on the coffee table.

He recalled being a boy in darkness and silence. Instead of concentrating for days on the simple lesson his incarceration was meant to teach him, he had conducted imaginary conversations with a spider named Charlotte, a pig named Wilbur, a rat named Templeton. That had been the closest he had come to defiance — then or since.

He doubted that these men would shoot him while in the house. Even when scrubbed away and no longer visible to the eye, blood left a protein signature that special chemicals and lights could reveal.

One of the gunmen picked up Mitch's coat, searched the pockets, and found only the cell phone.

To his watchful host, Mitch said, 'How did you go from being an FBI hero to this?'

Campbell's puzzlement was brief. 'Is that the yarn Anson spun to get you here? Julian Campbell — FBI hero?'

Although the gunmen had seemed as humorless as carrion-eating beetles, the one with smooth skin laughed, and the other smiled.

'You probably didn't make your money in entertainment, either,' Mitch said.

'Entertainment? That could be true enough,' Campbell said, 'if you have an elastic definition of entertainment.'

The acne-scarred gunman had produced a folded plastic garbage bag from a hip pocket. He shook it open.

Campbell said, 'And Mitch, if Anson told you these two gentlemen are candidates for the priesthood, I should warn you they aren't.'

The carrion beetles were further amused.

The gunman with the plastic bag stuffed it with the sports coat, cell phone, and other items that they had taken off Mitch. Before throwing away the wallet, he stripped out the cash and gave it to Campbell.

Mitch remained on his feet, waiting.

The three men were more relaxed with him than they had first been. They knew him now.

He was Anson's brother but only by blood. He was an evader, not a hunter. He would obey. They knew he would not effectively resist. He would retreat within himself. Eventually he would beg.

They knew him, knew his kind, and after the gunman finished putting items in the garbage bag, he produced a pair of handcuffs.

Before Mitch could be asked to extend his hands, he offered them.

The man with the cuffs hesitated, and Campbell shrugged, and the man with the cuffs snapped them around Mitch's wrists.

'You seem very tired,' Campbell said.

'Funny how tired,' Mitch agreed.

Putting down the gun they had confiscated, Campbell said, 'It's that way sometimes.'

Mitch didn't bother to test the cuffs. They were tight, and the shackle chain between the wrists was short.

As Campbell counted the forty-odd dollars that had been taken from Mitch's wallet, his voice had an almost tender quality: 'You might even fall asleep on the way.'

'Where are we going?'

'I knew a guy who fell asleep one night, on a drive like the one you're taking. It was almost a shame to wake him when we got there.'

'Are you coming?' Mitch asked.

'Oh, I haven't in years. I'll stay here with my books. You don't need me. You'll be all right. Everyone's all right, at the end.'

Mitch looked around at the aisles of books. 'Have you read any?'

'The histories. I'm fascinated by history, how almost no one ever learns from it.'

'Have you learned from it?'

'I *am* history. I'm the thing nobody wants to learn.'

Campbell's hands, as dexterous as those of a magician, folded Mitch's money into his own wallet with an economy of movement that was nevertheless theatrical.

'These gentlemen will be taking you to the car pavilion. Not through the house, but across the gardens.'

Mitch assumed that the household staff — night maids, the butler — either were not aware of the hard side of Campbell's business or collaborated in a pretense of ignorance.

'Good-bye, Mitch. You'll be all right. It's not long now. You might even doze on the way.'

Flanking Mitch, each holding him by one arm, the gunmen walked him across the library to the French doors. The man with the pitted face, on his right, pressed the muzzle of a pistol into his side, not cruelly, only as a reminder.

Just before stepping across the threshold, Mitch glanced back and saw Campbell reviewing the titles on a shelf of books. He stood with the hipshot grace of a loitering ballet dancer.

He appeared to be choosing a book to take to bed. Or maybe not to bed. A spider does not sleep; neither does history.

Terrace to steps, descending to another terrace, the gunmen expertly conveyed Mitch.

The moon lay drowned in the swimming pool, as pale and undulant as an apparition.

Along garden pathways where hidden toads sang, across a broad lawn, through a copse of tall lacy silver sheens shimmering like the scales of schooling fish, by a roundabout route, they came to a large but elegant building encircled by a romantically lighted loggia.

The gunmen's vigilance never wavered during the walk.

Night-blooming jasmine twined the columns of the loggia and festooned the eaves.

Mitch drew slow deep breaths. The heavy fragrance was so sweet as to be almost narcoleptic.

A slow-moving black long-horned beetle crossed the floor of the loggia. The gunmen guided Mitch around the insect.

The pavilion contained exquisitely restored cars from the 1930s and 1940s — Buicks, Lincolns, Packards, Cadillacs, Pontiacs, Fords, Chevrolets, Kaizers, Studebakers, even a Tucker Torpedo. They were displayed like jewels under precisely focused arrays of pin lights.

Estate vehicles in daily use were not kept here. Evidently, by taking him to the main garage, they would have risked encountering members of the household staff.

The gunman with the pitted face fished from his pocket a set of keys and opened the trunk of a midnight-blue Chrysler Windsor from the late 1940s. 'Get in.'

For the same reason they had not shot him in the library, they would not shoot him here. Besides, they wouldn't want to risk doing damage to the car.

The trunk was roomier than those of contemporary cars. Mitch lay on his side, in the fetal position.

'You can't unlock it from the inside,' the scarred man said. 'They had no child-safety awareness in those days.'

His partner said, 'We'll be on back roads where no one will hear you. So if you make a lot of noise, it won't do you any good.'

Mitch said nothing.

The scarred man said, 'It'll just piss us off. Then we'll be harder on you at the other end than we have to be.'

'I don't want that.'

'No. You don't want that.'

Mitch said, 'I wish we didn't have to do this.'

'Well,' said the one with smooth skin, 'that's how it is.'

Backlighted by the pin spots, their faces hung over Mitch like two shadowed moons, one with an expression of bland indifference, the other tight and cratered with contempt.

They slammed the lid, and the darkness was absolute.

# 28

Holly lies in darkness, praying that Mitch will live.

She fears less for herself than for him. Her captors at all times wear ski masks in her presence, and she assumes they would not bother to conceal their faces if they intended to kill her.

They aren't just wearing them as a fashion statement. No one looks good in a ski mask.

If you were hideously disfigured, like the Phantom of the Opera, maybe you would want to wear a ski mask. But it defied reason that all four of these men would be hideously disfigured.

Of course, even if they hoped not to harm her, something could go awry with their plans. In a moment of crisis, she might be shot accidentally. Or events could change the kidnappers' intentions toward her.

Always an optimist, having believed since childhood that every life has meaning and that hers will not pass before she finds its purpose, Holly does not dwell on what might go wrong, but envisions herself released, unharmed.

She believes envisioning the future helps shape it. Not that she could become a famous actress merely by envisioning herself accepting an Academy Award. Hard work, not wishes, builds careers.

Anyway, she doesn't want to be a famous

actress. She would have to spend a lot of time with famous actors, and most of the current crop creep her out.

Free again, she will eat marzipan and chocolate peanut-butter ice cream and potato chips until she either embarrasses herself or makes herself sick. She hasn't thrown up since childhood, but even vomiting is an affirmation of life.

Free, she will celebrate by going to Baby Style, that store in the mall, and buying the huge stuffed bear she saw in their window when she passed by recently. It was fluffy and white and so cute.

Even as a teenage girl, she liked teddy bears. Now she needs one anyway.

Free, she will make love to Mitch. When she is done with him, he'll feel as if he's been hit by a train.

Well, that isn't a particularly satisfying romantic image. It's not the kind of thing that sells millions of Nicholas Sparks novels.

*She made love to him with every fiber of her being, body and soul, and when at last their passion passed, he was splattered all over the room as if he had thrown himself in front of a locomotive.*

Envisioning herself as a best-selling novelist would be a waste of effort. Fortunately, her goal is to be a real-estate agent.

So she prays that her beautiful husband will live through this terror. He *is* physically beautiful, but the most beautiful thing about him is his gentle heart.

Holly loves him for his gentle heart, for his sweetness, but she worries that certain aspects of his gentleness, such as his tendency toward passive acceptance, will get him killed.

He possesses a deep and quiet strength, too, a spine of steel, which is revealed in subtle ways. Without that, he would have been broken by his freak-show parents. Without that, Holly would not have led him on a chase all the way to the altar.

So she prays for him to stay strong, to stay alive.

During her prayers, during her ruminations about kidnappers' fashions and gluttony and vomiting and big fluffy teddy bears, she works steadily at the nail in the floorboard. She has always been an excellent multitasker.

The wood floor is rough. She suspects that the planks are thick enough to have required heavier than usual flooring nails.

The nail that interests her has a large flat head. The size of the head suggests that this nail may be large enough to qualify as a spike.

In a crisis, a spike might serve as a weapon.

The flat head of the nail is not snug to the wood. It is raised maybe a sixteenth of an inch. This gap gives her a little leverage, a grip with which to work the nail back and forth.

Though the nail isn't loose, one of her virtues is perseverance. She will keep working at the nail, and she will *envision* it loose, and eventually she will extract it from the plank.

She wishes she had acrylic fingernails. They look nice; and when she's a real-estate agent, she'll certainly need to have them. Good acrylic fingernails might give her an advantage with the spike.

On the other hand, they might break and split easier than her real fingernails. If she had them, they might prove to be a terrible disadvantage.

Ideally, when she had been kidnapped, she would have had acrylic nails on her left hand and none on her right. And two steel teeth set with a gap in the front of her mouth.

An ankle cuff and a length of chain shackle her right leg to a ringbolt in the floor. This leaves both of her hands free to work on the not-yet-loose nail.

The kidnappers have made some consider-ations for her comfort. They have provided her with an air mattress to lie on, a six-pack of bottled water, and a bedpan. Earlier they had given her half of a cheese-and-pepperoni pizza.

This is not to suggest that they are nice people. They are not nice people.

When they needed her to scream for Mitch, they hit her. When they needed her to scream for Anson, they pulled her hair suddenly, sharply, and so hard that she thought her scalp was coming off.

Although these are not people you would ever meet in church, they are not cruel sheerly for the fun of it. They are evil, but they have a business goal, so to speak, on which they remain focused.

One of them is evil *and* crazy.

He's the one who worries her.

They have not made her privy to their scheme, but Holly vaguely understands that they are

176

imprisoning her in order to use Mitch to manipulate Anson.

She doesn't know why or how they think Anson can tap a fortune to ransom her for Mitch, but she is not surprised that he stands at the center of the whirlwind. She has long felt that Anson is not only what he pretends to be.

Now and then she has caught him staring at her in a way that the loving brother of her husband should never stare. When he realizes he has been caught, the predatory lust in his eyes and the hungry cast of his face vanish under his usual charm so instantaneously that it's easy to believe you must have imagined the glint of savage interest.

Sometimes when he laughs, his mirth sounds manufactured to her. She seems to be alone in this perception. Everyone else finds Anson's laugh infectious.

She has never shared her doubts about Anson. Until she met Mitch, all that he had were his sisters — who had fled to far points of the compass — his brother, and his passion for working in fertile earth, for making green things grow. Her hope has always been to enrich his life, not to subtract anything from it.

She can put her life in Mitch's strong hands and fall at once into a dreamless sleep. In a sense, that is what marriage is about — a good marriage — a total trusting with your heart, your mind, your life.

But with her fate in Anson's hands, as well, she might not sleep at all, and if she sleeps, there will be nightmares.

She worries, worries, worries the nail until her fingers ache. Then she uses two different fingers.

As the dark silent minutes pass, she tries not to brood about how a day that began with such joy could spiral into these desperate circumstances. After Mitch had gone to work and before the masked men had burst into her kitchen, she had used the kit that she'd bought the previous day but that she'd been too nervous to consult until this morning. Her period is nine days overdue, and according to the pregnancy test, she is going to have a baby.

For a year, she and Mitch have been hoping for this. Now here it is, on this of all days.

The kidnappers are unaware that *two* lives are at their mercy, and Mitch is unaware that not only his wife but also his child depend upon his cunning and his courage, but *Holly* knows. This knowledge is at once a joy and an anguish.

She envisions a child of three — sometimes a girl, sometimes a boy — at play in their backyard, and laughing. She envisions it more vividly than she has envisioned anything before, in the hope that she can make it come to pass.

She tells herself that she will be strong, that she will not cry. She does not sob or otherwise disturb the stillness, but sometimes tears come.

To shut off that hot flow, she works more aggressively at the nail, the stubborn damn nail, in the blinding dark.

After a long period of silence, she hears a solid thud with a hollow metallic quality: *ca-chunk*.

Alert, wary, she waits, but the thud does not repeat. No other noise follows it.

The sound is tantalizingly familiar. A mundane noise — and yet her instinct tells her that her fate hangs on that *ca-chunk*.

She is able to replay the sound in her memory, but she is not at first able to connect it to a cause.

After a while, Holly begins to suspect that the sound was imagined rather than real. More accurately, that it occurred in her head, not beyond the walls of this room. This is a peculiar notion, but it persists.

Then she recognizes the source, something she has heard perhaps hundreds of times, and although it has no ominous associations for her, she is chilled. The *ca-chunk* is the sound of a lid slamming shut on a car trunk.

Just the lid slamming shut on a car trunk, whether imagined or actually heard, should not cause crystals of creeping frost to form in the hollows of her bones. She sits very erect, the nail forgotten for the moment, breathing not at all, then shallowly, quietly.

# Part Two

## Would You Die for Love? Would You Kill?

# 29

In the late 1940s, if you owned a car like a Chrysler Windsor, you knew the engine was big because it made a big sound. It had the throb of a bull's heart, low fierce snort and heavy stamp of hooves.

The war was over, you were a survivor, large swaths of Europe lay in ruin, but the homeland was untouched, and you wanted to feel *alive*. You didn't want a sound-proofed engine compartment. You didn't want noise-control technology. You wanted power, balanced weight, and speed.

The car's dark trunk reverberated with engine knock and rumble transferred along the drive shaft, through the body and the frame. The thrum and stutter of road noise rose and fell in direct relation to the tempo of the turning wheels.

Mitch smelled faint traces of exhaust gases, perhaps from a leak in the muffler, but he was in no danger of being overcome by carbon monoxide. Stronger were the rubbery scent of the mat on which he lay and the acidity of his own fear sweat.

Although as dark as the chamber in his parents' house, this mobile learning room otherwise failed to impose sensory deprivation. Yet one of the greatest lessons of his life was being driven home to him mile by mile.

His father says there is no tao, no natural law

we are born to understand. In his materialist view, we should conduct ourselves not according to any code, only according to self-interest.

Rationality is always in a man's self-interest, Daniel says. Therefore, any act that is rational is right and good and admirable.

Evil does not exist in Daniel's philosophy. Stealing, rape, murder of the innocent — these and other crimes are merely *irrational* because they put he who commits them in jeopardy of his freedom.

Daniel does acknowledge that the degree of irrationality depends on the criminal's chances of escaping punishment. Therefore, those irrational acts that succeed and have only positive consequences for the perpetrator may be right and admirable, if not good for society.

Thieves, rapists, murderers, and their ilk might benefit from therapy and rehabilitation, or they might not. In either case, Daniel says, they are not evil; they are recovering — or irredeemable — irrationalists, only that and nothing more.

Mitch had thought that these teachings had not penetrated him, that he'd not been singed by the fire of a Daniel Rafferty education. But fire produced fumes; he'd been smoked in his father's fanaticism so long that some of what steeped into him had stayed.

He could see, but he had been blind. He could hear, but he had been deaf.

This day, this night, Mitch had come face-to-face with evil. It was as real as stone.

Although an irrational man should be met

with compassion and therapy, an evil man was owed nothing more or less than resistance and retribution, the fury of a righteous justice.

In Julian Campbell's library, when the gunman had produced the handcuffs, Mitch had at once held out his hands. He had not waited for instructions.

If he had not appeared worn down, had not seemed meek and resigned to his fate, they might have cuffed his hands behind him. Reaching the revolver in his ankle holster would have been more difficult; using it with accuracy would have been impossible.

Campbell had even commented on Mitch's weariness, by which he had meant primarily the weariness of mind and heart.

They thought they knew the kind of man he was, and maybe they did. But they didn't know the kind of man he could become when the life of his wife was in the balance.

Amused by his lack of familiarity with the pistol that they had confiscated, they had not imagined he would have a second weapon. Not only good men are disadvantaged by their expectations.

Mitch pulled up the leg of his jeans and retrieved the revolver. He unstrapped the holster and discarded it.

Earlier, he had examined the weapon and had not found a safety. In movies, only some pistols had safeties, never revolvers.

If he lived through the next two days and got Holly back alive, he would never again allow himself to be put in a position where he had to rely on Tinseltown's grasp of reality for his or his family's survival.

When he had first swung open the cylinder, he had discovered five rounds in five chambers, where he expected six.

He would have to score two hits out of five rounds. Direct hits, not just wing shots.

Perhaps one of the gunmen would open the trunk. It would be better if the two were there, giving him the advantage of surprise with both.

Both would have their weapons drawn — or only one. If one, Mitch must be quick enough to target his armed adversary first.

A peaceable man, planning violence, was plagued by thoughts that were not helpful: *As a teenager, cursed by the explosions of acne that had left his face a moonscape, the scarred gunman must have suffered much humiliation.*

Sympathy for the devil was a kind of masochism at best, a death wish at worst.

For a while, rocking to the rhythms of road and rubber, and of internal combustion, Mitch tried to imagine all the ways that the violence might go down when the trunk lid went up. Then he tried *not* to imagine.

According to his radiant watch, they traveled more than half an hour and then, slowing, changed from blacktop to an unpaved road. Small stones rattled through the undercarriage, rapped hard against the floor pan.

He smelled dust and licked the alkaline taste of it from his lips, but the air never became foul enough to choke him.

After twelve minutes at an easy speed, on the

dirt road, the car came slowly to a stop. The engine idled for half a minute, and then the driver switched it off.

After forty-five minutes of drone and drum, the silence was like a sudden deafness.

One door opened, then the other.

They were coming.

Facing the back of the car, Mitch splayed his legs, bracing his feet in opposite corners of the space. He could not sit erect until the lid raised, but he waited with his back partly off the floor of the trunk, as if in the middle of doing a series of stomach crunches at the gym.

The cuffs all but required that he hold the revolver in a two-hand grip, which was probably better anyway.

He didn't hear footsteps, just the gallop of his heart, but then he heard the key in the trunk lock.

Through his mind's eye blinked an image of Jason Osteen being shot in the head, blinked and blinked, repeating like a film loop, Jason slammed by the bullet, skull exploding, slammed by the bullet, skull exploding . . .

As the lid lifted, Mitch realized that the trunk did not have a convenience light, and he began to sit up, thrusting the revolver forward.

The full-pitcher moon spilled its milk, backlighting the two gunmen.

Mitch's eyes were adapted to absolute blackness, and theirs were not. He sat in darkness, and they stood in moonlight. They thought he was a meek and broken and helpless man, and he was not.

187

He didn't consciously squeeze off the first shot, but felt the hard recoil and saw the muzzle flash and heard the crash, and then he was aware of squeezing the trigger the second time.

Two point-blank rounds knocked one silhouette down out of the moon-soaked night.

The second silhouette backed away from the car, and Mitch sat all the way up, squeezing off one, two, three more rounds.

The hammer clicked, and there was just the quiet of the moon, and the hammer clicked, and he reminded himself *Only five, only five!*

He had to get out of the trunk. With no ammunition, he was a fish in a barrel. Out. Out of the trunk.

# 30

Rising too fast, Mitch knocked his head against the lid, almost fell back, but maintained forward momentum. He scrambled out of the trunk.

His left foot came down on solid ground, but he planted his right on the twice-shot man. He staggered, stepped on the body again, and it shifted under him, and he fell.

He rolled away from the gunman, to the verge of the road. He was stopped by a wild hedge of mesquite, which he identified by its oily smell.

He had lost the revolver. It didn't matter. No ammunition.

Around him lay a parched moon-silvered landscape: the narrow dirt road, desert scrub, barren soil, boulders.

Sleek, its ample chrome features lustrous with lunar polish, the Chrysler Windsor seemed strangely futuristic in this primitive land, like a ship meant to sail the stars. The driver had switched off the headlights when he killed the engine.

The gunman on whom Mitch had twice stepped, when exiting the trunk, had not cried out. He had not reared up or clutched at Mitch. He was probably dead.

Maybe the second man had been killed, too. Coming out of the trunk, Mitch had lost track of him.

If one of the last three rounds had found its

target, the second man should have been a buffet for vultures on the dirt road behind the car.

The sandy soil of the roadbed was rich in silica. Glass is made from silica, mirrors from glass. The single-lane track offered much higher reflectivity than any surface in the night.

Lying facedown and flat, head cautiously raised, Mitch could see a significant distance along the pale ribbon as it dwindled through the gnarled and bristling scrub, in the direction from which they had come. No second body lay on the road.

If the guy hadn't been at least winged, surely he would have charged, firing, as Mitch clambered out of the Chrysler.

Hit, he might have hobbled or crawled into the scrub or behind a formation of stone. He could be anywhere out there, assessing his wound, reviewing his options.

The gunman would be angry but not scared. He lived for action like this. He was a sociopath. He wouldn't scare easily.

Definitely, unequivocally, Mitch was afraid of the man hiding in the night. He also feared the one who was lying on the road at the back of the Chrysler.

The guy near the car might be dead, but even if he was crowbait, Mitch was afraid of him anyway. He didn't want to go near him.

He had to do what he didn't want to do, because whether the sonofabitch was a carcass or unconscious, he possessed a weapon. Mitch needed a weapon. And quick.

He had discovered that he was capable of

violence, at least in self-defense, but he hadn't been prepared for the rapidity with which events unfolded following the first shot, for the speed with which decisions must be made, for the suddenness with which new challenges could arise.

On the farther side of the road, several blinds of scraggly vegetation offered concealment, as did low batters of weathered rock.

If the light breeze that had been active toward the coast had made its way this far inland, the desert had swallowed it to the last draught. Any movement of the brush would reveal not the hand of Nature but instead his enemy.

As far as he could tell in this murk, all was still.

Acutely aware that his own movement made a mark of him, hampered by the handcuffs, Mitch wriggled on his belly to the man behind the car.

In the gunman's open and unblinking eyes, the mortician moon had laid coins.

Beside the body rested a familiar shape of steel made sterling in this light. Mitch seized it gratefully, almost squirmed away, but realized that he had found the useless revolver.

Wincing at the faint jingle produced by the short chain between his handcuffs, he patted down the corpse — and pressed his fingers in a wetness. Sickened, shuddering, he wiped his hand on the dead man's clothes.

As he was about to conclude that this guy had gotten out of the Chrysler without a weapon, he discovered the checked grip of the pistol protruding from under the corpse. He pulled the gun free.

A shot cracked. The dead man twitched, having taken the round meant for Mitch.

He flung himself toward the Chrysler and heard a second shot and heard the whispery whine of passing death and heard a bullet ricochet off the car. He also heard a closer whisper, although he might have imagined two near misses with one round and might in fact have heard nothing after the insectile shriek of the ricochet.

With the car between himself and the shooter, he felt safer, but then almost at once not safe at all.

The gunman could come around the Chrysler at either the front end or the back. He had the advantage of choosing his approach and initiating the action.

Meanwhile, Mitch would be forced to keep an alert watch in both directions. An impossible task.

Already the other might be on the move.

Mitch thrust up from the ground and away from the car. He ran in a crouch, off the road, through the natural hedge of mesquite, which crackled revealingly and at the same time shushed as if warning him to be quiet.

The land sloped down from the road, which was good. If it had sloped up, he would have been visible, his broad back an easy target, the moment the gunman rounded the Chrysler.

He had lucked into firm but sandy soil, instead of shale or loose stones, so he didn't make a clatter as he ran. The moon mapped his route, and he weaved among clumps of brush instead of thrashing through them, mindful that keeping his balance was more difficult with his hands cuffed in front of him.

At the bottom of the thirty-foot slope, he turned right. Based on the position of the moon, he believed that he was heading almost due west.

Something like a cricket sang. Something stranger clicked and shrilled.

A colony of pampas-grass clumps drew his attention with scores of tall feathery panicles. They glowed white in the moonlight, and reminded him of the plumed tails of proud horses.

From the round clumps sprayed very narrow, sharp-edged, pointed, recurved blades of grass three to five feet in length. They were waist-high on Mitch. When dry, these blades could scratch, prickle like needles, even cut.

Each clump respected the territorial integrity of the other. He was able to pass among them.

In the heart of the colony, he felt safely screened by the white feathery panicles that rose higher than his head. He remained on his feet and, through gaps between the plumes, he peered back the way that he had come.

The ghostly light did not reveal a pursuer.

Mitch shifted his position, gently pushed aside a panicle, and another, surveying the edge of the roadway at the top of the slope. He didn't see anyone up there.

He did not intend to hide in the pampas for long. He had fled his vulnerable position at the car only to gain a couple of minutes to think.

He wasn't concerned that the remaining gunman would drive away in the Chrysler. Julian Campbell wasn't the kind of boss to whom you could report failure with the confidence that you would keep either your job or your head.

Besides, to the guy out there on the hunt, this was sport, and Mitch was the most dangerous game of all. The hunter was motivated by vengeance, by pride, and by the taste for violence that had led him into this kind of work in the first place.

Had he been able to hide until dawn or slip away, Mitch would not have done so. He wasn't boiling over with macho enthusiasm for a confrontation with this second professional killer, but he understood too well the consequences of avoiding it altogether.

If the remaining gunman lived and reported back to Campbell, Anson would know sooner rather than later that his *fratello piccolo*, his little brother, was alive and free. Mitch would lose his ease of movement and the advantage of surprise.

Most likely, Campbell didn't expect a report from his pair of executioners until morning. Perhaps he would not even seek them out until the following afternoon.

Indeed, Campbell might miss the Chrysler Windsor before he missed the men. That depended on which of his machines he most valued.

Mitch needed to be able to catch Anson by surprise, and he needed to be in his brother's house at noon to take the call from the kidnappers. Holly was on a higher and narrower ledge than ever.

He could not hide, and his enemy would not. For predator and prey — whoever might be which — this had to be a fight to the death.

# 31

Surrounded by noble white plumes that suggested an encircling protectorate of helmeted knights, Mitch in the pampas grass recalled the hard crack of the two shots that had almost drilled him as he had been taking the pistol from the dead gunman.

If his adversary's weapon had been equipped with a sound suppressor, as it had been in the library, the reports would not have been so loud. He might not have heard them.

In this desolate place, the gunman had not been concerned about attracting unwanted attention, but he had not removed the silencer just for the satisfaction of a louder bang. He must have had another reason.

Sound suppressors were most likely illegal. They facilitated quiet murder. They were meant for use in close quarters — as in a mansion where the household staff was not reliably corrupt.

Logic led Mitch quickly to conclude that a sound suppressor was useful *only* in discreet situations *because it diminished the accuracy of the weapon.*

When you were standing over your captive in a library or when you forced him to kneel before you on a lonely desert road, a pistol with a sound suppressor might serve you well. But at a distance of twenty feet, or thirty, perhaps it reduced the accuracy to such a degree that you were more certain to hit your target by throwing the pistol than by shooting it.

Small stones rattled like tumbling dice.

The sound seemed to have arisen west of him. He turned in that direction. With caution, he parted the pampas panicles.

Fifty feet away, the gunman crouched like a hunchback troll. He was waiting for any repercussions of the noise that he had made.

Even when still, the man could not be mistaken for a thrust of rock or for desert flora, because he'd drawn attention to himself in the process of crossing a long barren swath of alkaline soil. That patch of ground appeared not merely reflective but luminous.

If Mitch had not paused here, if he had continued west, he would have encountered the killer in the open, perhaps coming face-to-face as in a Western-movie showdown.

He considered lying in wait, letting his stalker draw closer before firing.

Then instinct suggested that the colony of pampas grass and similar features of the landscape were exactly the places that would most interest the gunman. He expected Mitch to hide; and he would regard the pampas with suspicion.

Mitch hesitated, for the advantage still seemed to be his. He could fire from cover, while the troll stood in the open. He had not yet squeezed off a shot with this pistol, while his adversary had expended two.

A spare magazine. Given that mayhem was the

gunman's business, he probably carried a spare magazine, maybe two.

He would approach the pampas colony cautiously. He would not make an easy target of himself.

When Mitch fired and missed because of distance, angle, distorting light, and lack of experience, the gunman would return fire. Vigorously.

The pampas offered visual cover, not protection. A barrage of eight rounds followed at least by another volley of ten would not be survivable.

Still crouching, the trollish figure took two tentative steps forward. He paused again.

Inspiration came to Mitch, a bold idea that for a moment he considered discarding as reckless but then embraced as his best chance.

He let the panicles ease into their natural positions. He slipped out of the colony opposite from the point at which the gunman approached it, hoping to keep it between them as long as possible.

To a choir of crickets and the more sinister clicking-shrilling of the unknown insect musician, Mitch hurried eastward, along the route that he had taken earlier. He passed the point at which he had descended the embankment; that unscreened ascent would leave him too exposed if he failed to reach the top before the gunman rounded the pampas colony.

About sixty feet farther, he arrived at a wide shallow swale in the otherwise uniform face of the slope. Chaparral thrived in this depression and spilled up over the edges of it.

In need of his cuffed hands to climb, Mitch jammed the pistol under his belt. Previously, moonlight had shown him the way, but now moonshadows obscured and deceived. Always conscious that quiet was as important as swift progress, he insinuated himself upward through the chaparral.

He stirred up a musky scent that might have had a plant source but that suggested he was trespassing in one kind of animal habitat or another. Brush snared, poked, scratched.

He thought of snakes, and then he refused to think of them.

When he reached the top without drawing gunfire, he eeled out of the swale, onto the shoulder of the road. He crawled to the center of the dirt lane before standing.

If he attempted to circle behind where he thought the gunman might be headed, he would find that meanwhile the gunman would have done some anticipating of his own, would have changed course in hope of surprising his quarry even as his quarry schemed to surprise him. Stalking and counter-stalking, they could spend a lot of precious time wandering the wilderness, now and then finding each other's spoor, until one of them made a mistake.

If that was the game, the fatal mistake would be Mitch's, for he was the less experienced player. As had been true thus far, his hope lay in not fulfilling his enemy's expectations.

Because Mitch had surprised them with the revolver, the gunman would expect him to have as savage an instinct for self-preservation as any cornered animal. He had proved, after all, not to be paralyzed by fear, self-pity, and self-loathing.

But the gunman might not expect a cornered animal, once having broken free, to return voluntarily to the corner that it had recently escaped.

The vintage Chrysler stood sixty feet west of him, the trunk lid still half raised.

Mitch hurried to the car and paused beside the corpse. Eyes filled with the starry wonder of the heavens, the acne-scarred gunman lay supine.

Those eyes were two collapsed stars, black holes, exerting such gravity that Mitch assumed they would pull him to destruction if he stared at them too long.

In fact, he felt no guilt. In spite of his father, he realized that he believed in meaning and in natural law, but killing in self-defense was no sin by any tao.

Neither was it an occasion for celebration. He felt that he had been robbed of something precious. Call it innocence, but that was only part of what he had lost; with innocence had gone a capacity for a certain kind of tenderness, a heretofore lifelong expectation of an impending, sweet, ineffable joy.

Looking back, Mitch studied the ground for footprints he might have left. In sunshine, the hard-packed dirt might betray him; but he saw no tracks now.

Under the moon's mesmerizing stare, the desert seemed to be asleep and dreaming, rendered in the silver-and-black palette of most dreams, every shadow as hard as iron, every object as insubstantial as smoke.

When he looked into the trunk, where the moon declined to peer, the darkness suggested the open mouth of some creature without mercy. He could not see the floor of the space, as though it were a magical compartment offering storage for an infinite amount of baggage.

He withdrew the pistol from under his belt.

He lifted the lid higher, climbed into the trunk, and pulled the lid partway shut again.

After a little experimentation, he figured out that the sound suppressor was threaded to the barrel of the pistol. He unscrewed it and set it aside.

Sooner rather than later, when he failed to find Mitch hiding in pampas grass or in chaparral, or in a niche of weather-sculpted rock, the gunman would come back to watch the Chrysler. He would expect his prey to return to the car in the hope that the keys might be in the ignition.

This professional killer would not be capable of understanding that a good husband could never drive away from his vows, from his wife, from his best hope of love in a world that offered little of it.

If the gunman established a surveillance point behind the car, he might cross the road in the moonlight. He would be cautious and quick, but a clear target nonetheless.

The possibility existed that he would watch the front of the vehicle. But if time passed and nothing happened, he might undertake another general exploration of the area and, on returning, cross Mitch's sights.

Only seven or eight minutes had passed since the pair had opened the trunk to receive a greeting of gunfire. The surviving man would be patient. But eventually, if his surveillance and his searches were not fruitful, he would consider packing up and getting out of here, regardless of how much he might fear his boss.

At that time, if not before, he would come to the back of the car to deal with the corpse. He would want to load it into the trunk.

Now Mitch half sat, half lay, swaddled in darkness, his head raised just enough to see across the sill of the trunk.

He had killed a man.

He intended to kill another.

The pistol felt heavy in his hand. He smoothed his trembling fingers along its contours, seeking a clickable safety, but he found none.

As he stared at the lonely moon-glazed road crowded by the spectral desert, he understood that what he had lost — innocence, and that fundamentally childlike expectation of impending, ineffable joy — was gradually being replaced by something else, and not by something bad. The hole in him was filling, with what he could not yet say.

From the car trunk he had a limited view of the world, but in that wedge he perceived far more this night than he would have been capable of perceiving previously.

The silvery road receded from him but also

approached, offering him a choice of opposite horizons.

Some stone formations contained chips of mica that sparkled in the moonlight, and where the rock rose in silhouette against the sky, the stars appeared to have salted themselves upon the earth.

Out of the north, southbound, on its feathered sails, a great horned owl, as pale as it was immense, swooped low and silent across the road, then rowed itself higher into the night, much higher and away.

Mitch sensed that what he seemed to be gaining for what he had lost, what so quickly healed the hole in him, was a capacity for awe, a deeper sense of the mystery of all things.

Then he pulled back from the brink of awe, to terror and to grim determination, when the gunman returned with an intention that had not been foreseen.

# 32

So stealthily had the killer returned that Mitch
was unaware of his presence until he heard one
of the car doors click open and swing wide with
the faintest creak.

The man had approached from the front of
the Chrysler. Risking exposure in the brief
glow of the car's interior lights, he got in and
pulled the door shut as softly as it could be
closed.

If he had gotten behind the wheel, he must
intend to leave the scene.

No. He wouldn't drive away with the trunk lid
open. And surely he wouldn't leave the corpse.

Mitch waited in silence.

The gunman was silent, too.

Slowly the silence became a kind of pressure
that Mitch could feel on his skin, on his
eardrums, on his unblinking eyes, as if the car
were descending into a watery abyss, an
ever-increasing weight of ocean bearing down
on it.

The gunman must be sitting in the dark,
surveying the night, waiting to learn whether the
throb of light had drawn attention, whether he
had been seen. If his return inspired no
response, what would he do next?

The desert remained breathless.

In these circumstances, the car would seem as
sensitive to motion as a boat on water. If Mitch

moved, the killer would be alerted to his presence.

A minute passed. Another.

Mitch pictured the smooth-faced gunman sitting up there in the car, in the gloom, at least thirty years old, maybe thirty-five, yet with such a remarkably soft smooth face, as if life had not touched him and never would.

He tried to imagine what the man with the smooth face was doing, planning. The mind behind that mask remained inaccessible to Mitch's imagination. He might have more profitably pondered what a desert lizard believed about God or rain or jimsonweed.

After a long stillness, the gunman shifted positions, and the movement proved to be a revelation. The unnerving intimacy of the sound indicated that the man wasn't behind the wheel of the Chrysler. He was in the backseat.

He must have been sitting forward, watchful, ever since getting into the car. When at last he leaned back, the upholstery made a sound like leather or vinyl does when stressed, and the seat springs quietly complained.

The backseat of the car formed the back wall of the trunk. He and Mitch were within a couple feet of each other.

They were almost as close to each other as they had been on the walk from the library to the car pavilion.

Lying in the trunk, Mitch thought about that walk.

The gunman made a low sound, either a stifled cough or a groan further muffled by the intervening wall of upholstery.

Perhaps he had been wounded, after all. His condition wasn't sufficiently serious to persuade him to pack up and leave, although it might be painful enough to discourage a lot of roaming.

Clearly, he settled in the car because he hoped that eventually, in desperation, his quarry would return to it. He figured Mitch would be circumspect in his approach, thoroughly scoping out the immediate surrounding territory, but would not expect death to be waiting for him in the shadows of the backseat.

In this makeshift learning room, Mitch thought about that walk between the library and the car pavilion: the moon like a lily pad floating in the pool, the muzzle of the pistol pressed into his side, the songs of the toads, the lacy branches of the silver sheens, *the pistol pressed into his side* . . .

A car of this vintage would not feature a fire wall or a crash panel between the trunk and the passenger compartment. The back of the rear seat might have been finished with a quarter-inch fiberboard panel or even just with cloth.

The backrest might contain six inches of padding. A bullet would meet some resistance.

The barrier wasn't bulletproof. No one armored with a mere sofa cushion would expect to walk unscathed through a barrage of ten high-velocity rounds.

Currently Mitch half lay and half sat on his left side, facing the night through the open trunk lid.

He would need to roll onto his right side in

order to bring the pistol to bear on the back wall of the trunk.

He weighed a hundred and seventy pounds. No degree in physics was required to figure out that the car would respond to that much weight shifting position.

Turn fast, open fire — and maybe he would discover that he was wrong about the partition between trunk and passenger compartment. If there was indeed a metal panel, he might not only be nailed by a ricochet but also fail to hit his target.

Then he would be wounded and out of ammunition, and the gunman would know where to find him.

A bead of sweat slipped along the side of his nose to the corner of his mouth.

The night was mild, not hot.

An urge to act pulled his nerves as taut as bowstrings.

# 33

As Mitch lay in indecision, he heard in memory Holly's scream, and the sharp *slap* of her being hit.

A real sound refocused his attention on the present: his enemy, in the passenger compartment, stifling a series of coughs.

The noise had been so effectively muffled that it wouldn't have been heard beyond the car. As before, the coughing lasted only a few seconds.

Maybe the gunman's cough related to a wound. Or he was allergic to desert pollen.

When the guy coughed again, Mitch would seize the opportunity to change positions.

Beyond the open trunk, the desert seemed to darkle, brighten, darkle rhythmically, but in fact the acuity of his vision sharpened briefly with each systolic thrust of his pounding heart.

A sudden illusion of snow, however, had a basis in reality. Moonlight frosted the phosphorescent wings of swarming moths that whirled like flakes of winter across the road.

Mitch's cuffed hands gripped the pistol so fiercely that his knuckles began to ache. His right forefinger hooked the trigger guard, rather than the trigger itself, because he feared that a nervous twitch would cause him to fire before he intended.

His teeth were clenched. He heard himself

inhale, exhale. He opened his mouth to breathe more quietly.

Even though his heart raced, time ceased to be a river running and became a creeping flow of mud.

Instinct had served Mitch well in recent hours. Likewise, a sixth sense might at any moment alert the gunman that he was not alone.

A sludge of seconds filled an empty minute, filled another, and another — and then the man's third bout of stifled coughing gave Mitch cover to roll from his left side to his right. The maneuver complete, he lay with his back to the open end of the trunk, very still.

The gunman's silence seemed to have a quality of heightened vigilance, of suspicion. The world now came to Mitch's five senses through a distorting lens of extreme anxiety.

What angle of fire? What pattern?

*Think.*

The man with the smooth face would not be sitting upright. He would slump to take full advantage of the darkness in the backseat.

In other circumstances, the assassin might have preferred a corner, where he could further ensure his invisibility. But because the raised lid of the trunk obstructed an easy view of him through the rear window of the car, he could safely sit in the center, the better to cover both front doors.

Keeping the cuff chain taut, Mitch quietly put down the pistol. He dared not risk knocking the weapon against something during the exploration he needed to perform.

Blindly reaching forward with both hands, he found the back wall of the trunk. Although firm under his fingertips, the surface had a cloth covering.

The Chrysler might not have been restored with a hundred percent fidelity. Campbell might have chosen some custom upgrades, including more refined materials in the trunk.

A pair of synchronized spiders, his hands crept left to right across the surface, testing. He pressed gently, and then a little harder.

Beneath his questing fingertips, the surface flexed slightly. Quarter-inch fiberboard, covered in cloth, might flex that way. It did not have the feel of metal.

The panel accepted his pressure in silence, but when he relaxed his hands, it returned to form with a subtle buckling noise.

From the passenger compartment came the protest of stressed upholstery, a short twist of sound and nothing more. The gunman had most likely adjusted his position for comfort — though he might have turned to listen more intently.

Mitch felt the floor, seeking the pistol, and rested his hands on it.

Lying on his side, knees drawn up, with no room to extend his arms, he was not in a good shooting position.

If he tried to move toward the open end of the trunk before firing, he would give himself away. A mere second or two of warning might be enough for the experienced gunman to roll off the backseat, onto the floor.

Mitch went through it in his mind one more

time, to be sure that he had not overlooked anything. The smallest miscalculation could be the death of him.

He raised the pistol. He would shoot left to right, then right to left, a double spray, five rounds in each arc.

When he squeezed the trigger, nothing happened. Just a faint but crisp metallic *snick*.

His heart was both hammer and anvil, and he had to hear *through* that roar, but he was pretty sure the gunman had not moved again, had not detected the small sound of the stubborn pistol.

Earlier he had explored the weapon and hadn't found a safety click.

He eased off the trigger, hesitated, squeezed again.

*Snick.*

Before panic could seize him, serendipity fluttered against his cheek and into his open mouth: a moth, not as cold as they had looked when whirling like snowflakes.

Reflexively, he sputtered, spat out the insect, gagging, and pulled the trigger again. A stop was incorporated into the trigger — maybe *that* was the safety — through which you had to pull to fire, a double action, and because he pulled harder than before, the pistol boomed.

The recoil, exacerbated by his position, rocked him, and the crash couldn't have been louder if it had been the door to Hell slamming behind him, and he was surprised by a blow-back of debris, bits of singed cloth and flecks of fiberboard spraying his face, but he squinched his eyes shut and kept firing, left to right, the gun

211

trying to pull up, pull wild, then right to left, *controlling* the weapon, not just shooting it, and though he had thought he would be able to count the rounds as he fired them, he lost track after two, and then the magazine was depleted.

# 34

If the gunman wasn't dead, even if wounded, he could return fire through the backrest. The car trunk was still a potential deathtrap.

Abandoning the useless pistol, Mitch scrambled out, knocking a knee against the sill, an elbow against the bumper, dropped to his hands and knees in the road, then thrust to his feet. He ran in a crouch for ten yards, fifteen, before stopping and looking back.

The gunman hadn't gotten out of the Chrysler. The four doors were closed.

Mitch waited, sweat dripping off the tip of his nose, off his chin.

Gone were the snowflake moths, the great horned owl, the songs of crickets, the click-shrill of the sinister something.

Under the mute moon, in the petrified desert, the Chrysler looked anachronistic, like a time machine in the early Mesozoic, sleek and gleaming two hundred million years before it was built.

When the air, as dry as salt, began to sear his throat, he stopped breathing through his mouth, and when the sweat began to dry on his face, he asked himself how long he should wait before assuming that the man was dead. He looked at his watch. He looked at the moon. He waited.

He needed the car.

He had timed the trip on the dirt track at

twelve minutes. They had been making perhaps twenty-five miles per hour on that last leg of the journey. The math put him five miles from a paved road.

Even when he got that far back toward civilization, he might find himself in lonely territory without much traffic. Besides, in his current condition, dirty and rumpled and no doubt wild-eyed, no one would give him a ride, except maybe an itinerant psychopath cruising for a victim.

Finally he approached the Chrysler.

He circled the vehicle, staying as far from the sides of it as the width of the road would allow, alert for a smooth ghostly face peering from the shadows within. After arriving without incident at the trunk from which he had twice escaped, he paused and listened.

Holly was in a bad place, and if the kidnappers tried to reach Mitch, they wouldn't have any luck because his cell phone was in that white plastic bag back at Campbell's estate. The noon call to Anson's house would be his only chance to reconnect with them before they decided to chop their hostage and move on to another game.

Without further hesitation, he went to the back door on the driver's side and opened it.

Lying on the seat, eyes open, bloody but still alive, was the smooth-faced man, with his pistol aimed at the door. The muzzle looked like an eyeless socket, and the gunman looked triumphant when he said, 'Die.'

He tried to pull the trigger, but the pistol

wobbled in his hand, and then he lost his grip on it. The weapon dropped to the floor of the car, and the gunman's hand dropped into his lap, and now that his one-word threat had turned out to be a prediction of his own fate, he lay there as if making an obscene proposition.

Leaving the door open, Mitch walked to the side of the road and sat on a boulder until he could be certain that, after all, he was not going to vomit.

# 35

Sitting on the boulder, Mitch had much to consider.

When this was finished, *if* it was ever finished, maybe the best thing would be to go to the police, tell his story of desperate self-defense, and present them with the two dead gunmen in the trunk of the Chrysler.

Julian Campbell would deny that he had employed them or at least that he had directed them to kill Mitch. Men like these two were most likely paid in cash; from Campbell's point of view, the fewer records the better, and the gunmen hadn't been the type to care that, if paid in cash with no tax deductions, they would eventually be denied their Social Security.

The possibility existed that no authorities were aware of the dark side to Campbell's empire. To all appearances, he might be one of California's most upstanding citizens.

Mitch, on the other hand, was a humble gardener already set up to take the fall for his wife's murder in the event that he failed to ransom her. And in Corona del Mar, on the street in front of Anson's house, the trunk of his Honda contained the body of John Knox.

Although he believed in the rule of law, Mitch didn't for a minute believe that crime-scene investigation was as meticulous — or CSI technicians as infallible — as portrayed on TV.

The more evidence that suggested his guilt, even if it was planted, the more they would find to support their suspicion, and the easier they would find it to ignore the details that might exonerate him.

Anyway, the most important thing right now was to remain free and mobile until he ransomed Holly. He *would* ransom her. Or die trying.

After he'd met Holly and fallen almost at once in love, he had realized that he'd previously been only half alive, *buried* alive in his childhood. She had opened the emotional casket in which his parents had left him, and he had risen, flourished.

His transformation had amazed him. He had thought himself fully alive, at last, when they married.

This night, however, he realized that part of him had remained asleep. He had awakened to a clarity of vision no less exhilarating than it was terrifying.

He had encountered evil of a purity that a day previously he had not thought existed, that he had been educated to deny existed. With the recognition of evil, however, came a growing awareness of more dimensions in every scene, in nearly every object, than he had seen before, greater beauty, strange promise, and mystery.

He did not know precisely what he meant by that. He only knew that it was the case, that he'd opened his eyes to a higher reality. Behind the layered and gorgeous mysteries of this new world around him, he sensed a truth that veil by veil would reveal itself.

In this state of enlightenment, funny that he should find the most urgent task before him to be the disposal of a pair of dead men.

A laugh rose in him, but he swallowed it. Sitting in the desert, near midnight, with no company but corpses, laughing at the moon did not seem to be the first step on the right path out of here.

From high in the east, a meteor slid westward like the pull-tab of a zipper, opening the black sky to reveal a glimpse of whiteness beyond, but the teeth of the zipper closed as quickly as they opened, keeping the sky clothed, and the meteor became a cinder, a vapor.

Taking the falling star as an omen to get on with his grisly work, Mitch knelt beside the scarred gunman and searched his pockets. He quickly found the two things he wanted: the handcuff key and the keys to the Chrysler Windsor.

Having freed himself of the cuffs, he threw them in the open trunk of the car. He rubbed his chafed wrists.

He dragged the body of the gunman to the south shoulder of the road, through the screening brush, and left it there.

Getting the second one out of the backseat involved unpleasant wrestling, but in two minutes the dead pair were lying side by side, faceup to the wonder of the stars.

At the car once more, Mitch found a flashlight on the front seat. He'd figured there would be one because they must have intended to bury him nearby and would have needed a light to guide them.

The car's weak ceiling lamp had not shown him as much of the backseat as he needed to see. He examined it with the flashlight.

Because the gunman had not died instantly, he'd had time to bleed, and he'd done a thorough job of it.

Mitch counted eight holes in the backrest, rounds that punched through from the trunk. The other two had evidently been deflected or fully stopped by the structure of the seat.

In the back of the front seat were five holes; but only one bullet had drilled all the way through. A pockmark in the glovebox door indicated the end point of its trajectory.

He found the spent slug on the floor in front of the passenger's seat. He threw it away into the night.

Once he got off the dirt track and onto paved roads, though he would be in a hurry, he would have to obey the posted speed limits. If a highway-patrol officer stopped him and got one glimpse of the blood and destruction in the backseat, Mitch would probably be eating at the expense of the state of California for a long time.

The two gunmen had not brought a shovel.

Considering their professionalism, he doubted they would have left his body to rot where hikers or off-road racers might have found it. Familiar with the area, they had known a feature of the landscape that served as a natural tomb unlikely to be discovered casually.

Searching for that burial place at night, with a flashlight, did not appeal to Mitch. Nor did the prospect of the bone collection that he might find there.

He returned to the bodies and relieved them of their wallets to make identification more difficult. He was becoming less squeamish about handling them — and his new attitude disturbed him.

After dragging the dead men farther from the road, he interred them in a tight grove of waist-high manzanita. Shrouds of leathery leaves concealed them from easy discovery.

Although the desert seems hostile to life, many species thrive in it, and a number are carrion eaters. Within an hour, the first of these would be drawn to the double treat in the manzanita.

Some were beetles like the one that the gunmen had taken care not to crush underfoot as they had led him along the car-pavilion loggia.

In the morning, the desert heat would begin to do its work as well, significantly hastening the process of decomposition.

If they were ever found, their names might never be known. And which of them suffered terrible acne scars and which had a smooth face would matter to no one, and count for nothing.

In the car pavilion, as they had been closing him into the trunk of the Chrysler, he had said *I wish we didn't have to do this*.

*Well*, said the one with the smooth skin, *that's how it is*.

Another shooting star drew his attention to the deep clear sky. A brief bright scar, and then the heavens healed.

He returned to the car and closed the trunk lid.

Having gotten the best of two experienced killers, perhaps he should have felt empowered, proud, and fierce. Instead, he had been further humbled.

To spare himself the stench of blood, he rolled down the windows in all four doors of the Chrysler Windsor.

The engine started at once: a full-throated song of power. He switched on the headlights.

He was relieved to see that the fuel gauge indicated the tank was nearly three-quarters full. He didn't want to stop at any public place, not even at a self-service station.

He had turned the car around and driven four miles on the dirt road when, topping a rise, he came upon a sight that caused him to brake to a stop.

To the south, in a shallow bowl of land, lay a lake of mercury with concentric rings of sparkling diamonds floating on it, moving slowly to the currents of a lazy whirlpool, as majestic as a spiral galaxy.

For a moment the scene was so unreal that he thought it must be a hallucination or a vision. Then he understood that it was a field of grass, perhaps squirreltail with its plumelike flower spikes and silky awns.

The moonlight silvered the spikes and struck sparkles from the high sheen of the awns. A wind eddy, the laziest of spiral breezes, pulsed around the bowl of land with such grace and consistent timing that, were there music for this dance of

221

grass, it would be a waltz.

In mere grass was hidden meaning, but the stink of blood brought him back from the mystic to the mundane.

He continued to the end of the dirt road and turned right because he recalled that they had turned left on the way here. The paved roads were well marked, and he returned not to the Campbell estate — which he hoped he would not see again — but to the interstate.

Post-midnight traffic was light. He drove north, never faster than five miles per hour above the speed limit, an excess that the law rarely punished.

The Chrysler Windsor was a beautiful machine. Seldom do dead men return to haunt the living in such style.

# 36

Mitch arrived in the city of Orange at 2:20 A.M., and parked on a street that was a block away from the one on which his house stood.

He rolled up the four windows and locked the Chrysler.

With his shirttail pulled out to conceal it, he carried a pistol under his belt. The weapon had belonged to the smooth-faced gunman who, having said *Die*, failed to find the strength to flex his trigger finger one last time. It contained eight cartridges; Mitch hoped that he would not need any of them.

He was parked under an old jacaranda in full flower, and when he moved into the light from the street lamp, he saw that he walked on a carpet of purple petals.

Warily, he approached his property along the alleyway behind it.

A rattling induced him to switch on his flashlight. From between two trash cans that had been set out for morning collection, a city-adapted possum, like a large pale-faced rat, twitched its pink nose.

Mitch clicked off the light and proceeded to his garage. The gate at the corner of the building was never locked. He passed through it into the backyard.

His house keys, with his wallet and other personal items, had been confiscated in Campbell's library.

He kept a spare key in a small key safe that was padlocked to a ringbolt low on the garage wall, concealed behind a row of azaleas.

Risking the flashlight but hooding it with his fingers, Mitch parted the azaleas. He dialed in the combination, disengaged the lock, plucked the key from the safe, and switched off the light.

Making not a sound, he let himself into the garage, which was keyed to match the house.

The moon had traveled westward; and trees let little of that light through the windows. He stood in the dark, listening.

Either the silence convinced him that he was alone or the darkness reminded him too much of the car trunk that he had twice escaped, and he switched on the garage lights.

His truck was where he had left it. The Honda's space was empty.

He climbed the stairs to the loft. The boxes were still stacked to disguise the gap in the railing.

At the front of the loft, he discovered that the recorder and electronic surveillance gear were gone. One of the kidnappers must have come to collect the equipment.

He wondered what they thought had happened to John Knox. He worried that Knox's disappearance had already had consequences for Holly.

When a fit of tremors shook him, he forced his mind away from that dark speculation.

He was not a machine, and neither was she. Their lives had meaning, they had been brought together by destiny for a purpose, and they would fulfill their purpose.

He had to believe that was true. Without it, he had nothing.

Leaving the garage dark, he entered the house through the back door, confident that the place was no longer watched.

The staged murder scene in the kitchen remained as he had last seen it. The spattered blood, dry now. Hand prints on the cabinetry.

In the adjacent laundry room, he took off his shoes and examined them in the fluorescent light. He was surprised to find no blood.

His socks were not stained, either. He stripped them off anyway and threw them in the washing machine.

He found small smears on his shirt and jeans. In the shirt pocket, he found Detective Taggart's card. He saved the card, tossed the clothes in the machine, added soap, and started the wash cycle.

Standing at the laundry sink, he scrubbed his hands and forearms with soap and a soft-bristle brush. He wasn't washing away evidence. Perhaps certain memories were what he hoped to flush down the drain.

With a wet rag, he wiped his face, his neck.

His weariness was profound. He needed rest, but he had no time for sleep. Anyway, if he tried to sleep, his mind would be ridden by dreads both known and nameless, would be ridden hard in circles, howling, to wide-eyed exhaustion.

In shoes and underwear, carrying the pistol, he returned to the kitchen. From the refrigerator, he got a can of Red Bull, a high-caffeine drink, and chugged it.

Finishing the Red Bull, he saw Holly's purse open on a nearby counter. It had been there earlier in the day.

Earlier, however, he had not taken time to notice the debris scattered on the counter beside the purse. A wadded cellophane wrapper. A small box, the top torn open. A pamphlet of instructions.

Holly had bought a home pregnancy-test kit. She had opened it and evidently had used it, sometime between when he had left for work and when the kidnappers had taken her.

Sometimes as a child in the learning room, when you have spoken to no one for a long time, nor heard a voice other than your muffled own, and when you have been denied food — though never water — for as much as three days, when for a week or two you have seen no light except for the brief daily interruption when your urine bottles and waste bucket are traded for fresh containers, you reach a point where the silence and the darkness seem not like *conditions* any longer but like *objects* with real mass, objects that share the room with you and, growing by the hour, demand more space, until they press on you from all sides, the silence and the darkness, and weigh on you from above, squeezing you into a cubic minim that your body can occupy only if it is condensed like an automobile compressed by a junkyard ram. In the horror of that extreme claustrophobia, you tell yourself that you cannot endure another minute, but you do, you endure another minute, another, another, an hour, a day, you endure, and then the door opens, the banishment ends, and there is light, there is always eventually light.

Holly had not revealed that her period was overdue. False hopes had been raised twice before. She had wanted to be sure this time before telling him.

Mitch had not believed in destiny; now he did. And if a man believes in destiny, after all, he must believe in one that is golden, one that shines. He will not wait to see what he is served, damn if he will. He'll butter his bread thick with fate and eat the whole loaf.

Carrying the pistol, he hurried to the bedroom. The switch by the door turned on one of two bedside lamps.

With single-minded purpose, he went to the closet. The door stood open.

His clothes were disarranged. Two pair of jeans had slipped from their hangers and lay on the closet floor.

He didn't remember having left the closet in this condition, but he snatched a pair of jeans from the floor and pulled them on.

Shrugging into a dark-blue long-sleeved cotton shirt, he turned from the closet and for the first time saw the clothes strewn on the bed. A pair of khakis, a yellow shirt, white athletic socks, white briefs and T-shirt.

They were his clothes. He recognized them.

They were mottled with dark blood.

By now he knew the look of planted evidence.

Some new outrage was to be hung around his neck.

He retrieved the pistol from the closet shelf where he had put it while dressing.

The door stood open to the dark bathroom.

Like a dowser's divining rod, the pistol guided him to that darkness. Crossing the threshold, he flipped the light switch and with bated breath stepped into the bathroom brightness.

He expected to find something grotesque in the shower or a severed something in the sink. But all was normal.

His face in the mirror was clenched with dread, as tight as a fist, but his eyes were as wide as they had ever been and were no longer blind to anything.

Returning to the bedroom, he noticed something out of place on the nightstand with the extinguished lamp. He clicked the switch.

Two colorful polished spheres of dinosaur dung stood there on small bronze stands.

Although they were opaque, they made him think of crystal balls and sinister fortunetellers in old movies, predicting dire fates.

'Anson,' Mitch whispered, and then a word uncommon to him, 'My God. Oh, God.'

# 37

The hard winds that came out of the eastern mountains were usually born with the rising or setting of the sun. Now, many hours after sunset, and hours before sunrise, a strong spring wind suddenly blew down upon the lowlands as if it had burst through a great door.

Along the alleyway where wind whistled, to the Chrysler, Mitch hurried but with the hesitant heart of a man making the short journey from his cell on death row to the execution chamber.

He didn't take time to roll down the windows. As he drove, he opened only the one in the driver's door.

A gruff wind huffed at him, pawed his hair, its breath warm and insistent.

Insane men lack self-control. They see conspiracies all around them and reveal their lunacy in irrational anger, in ludicrous fears. Genuinely insane men don't know they are deranged, and therefore they see no need to wear a mask.

Mitch wanted to believe that his brother was insane. If Anson was instead acting with cold-blooded calculation, he was a monster. If you had admired and loved a monster, your gullibility should shame you. Worse, it seemed that by your willingness to be deceived, you empowered the monster. You shared at least some small portion of the responsibility for his crimes.

Anson did not lack self-control. He never spoke of conspiracies. He feared nothing. As for masks, he had an aptitude for misdirection, a talent for disguise, a genius for deception. He was not insane.

Along the night streets, queen palms thrashed, like madwomen in frenzies tossing their hair, and bottle-brush trees shed millions of scarlet needles that were the petals of their exotic flowers.

The land rose, and low hills rolled into higher hills, and in the wind were scraps of paper, leaves, kiting pages from newspapers, a large transparent plastic bag billowing along like a jellyfish.

His parents' house was the only one on the block with lights in the windows.

Perhaps he should have been discreet, but he parked in the driveway. He put up the window, left the pistol in the car, brought the flashlight.

Filled with voices of chaos, rich with the smell of eucalyptus, the wind lashed the walkway with tree shadows.

He did not ring the doorbell. He had no false hope, only an awful need to know.

As he had thought it might be, the house was unlocked. He stepped into the foyer and closed the door behind him.

To his left, to his right, an uncountable number of Mitches receded from him in a mirror world, all of them with a ghastly expression, all of them lost.

The house was not silent, for the wind gibbered at windows, groaned in the eaves, and eucalyptus trailers scourged the walls.

In Daniel's study, a spectacle of shattered glass display shelves glittered on the floor, and scattered everywhere were the colorful polished spheres, as if a poltergeist had played billiards with them.

Room by room, Mitch searched the first floor, turning on lights where they were off. In truth, he expected to find nothing more on this level of the big house, and he did not. He told himself that he was just being thorough. But he knew that he was delaying his ascent to the second floor.

At the stairs, he gazed up, and heard himself say, 'Daniel,' but not loud, and 'Kathy,' no louder.

For what awaited Mitch, he should have had to descend. Climbing to it seemed all wrong. Sepulchers are not constructed at the tops of towers.

As he climbed, nature's long exhale grew more fierce. Windows thrummed. Roof beams creaked.

In the upstairs hall, a black object lay on the polished wood floor: the shape of an electric razor but a bit larger. The business end featured a four-inch-wide gap between two gleaming metal pegs.

He hesitated, then picked it up. On the side of the thing was a seesaw switch. When he pressed it, a jagged white arc of electricity *snapped* between the metal pegs, the poles.

This was a Taser, a self-defense weapon.

Chances were that Daniel and Kathy had not used it to defend themselves.

More likely, Anson had brought it with him and had assaulted them with it. A jolt from a Taser can disable a man for minutes, leave him helpless, muscles spasming as his nerves misfire.

Although Mitch knew where he must go, he delayed the terrible moment and went instead to the master bedroom.

The lights were on except for a nightstand lamp that had been knocked to the floor in a struggle, the bulb broken. The sheets were tangled. Pillows had slid off the bed.

The sleepers had been literally shocked awake.

Daniel owned a large collection of neckties, and perhaps a score were scattered across the carpet. Bright serpents of silk.

Glancing through other doors but not taking the time to inspect fully the spaces beyond, Mitch moved more purposefully to the room at the end of the shorter of the two upstairs halls.

Here the door was like all the others, but when he opened it, another door faced him. This one was heavily padded and covered with a black fabric.

Shaking badly, he hesitated. He had expected never to return here, never to cross this threshold again.

The inner door could be opened only from the hall, not from the chamber beyond. He turned the latch release. The well-fitted channels of an interlocking rubber seal parted with a sucking sound as he pushed the door inward.

Inside, there were no lamps, no ceiling fixture.

He switched on the flashlight.

After Daniel himself had layered floor, walls, and ceiling with eighteen inches of various soundproofing materials, the room had been reduced to a windowless nine-foot square. The ceiling was six feet.

The black material that upholstered every surface, densely woven and without sheen, soaked up the beam of the flashlight.

Modified sensory deprivation. They had said it was a tool for discipline, not a punishment, a method to focus the mind inward toward self-discovery — a technique, not a torture. Numerous studies had been published about the wonders of one degree or another of sensory deprivation.

Daniel and Kathy lay side by side: she in her pajamas, he in his underwear. Their hands and ankles had been bound with neckties. The knots were cruelly tight, biting the flesh.

The bindings between the wrists and those between the ankles had been connected with another necktie, drawn taut, to further limit each victim's movement.

They had not been gagged. Perhaps Anson had wanted to have a conversation with them.

And screams could not escape the learning room.

Although Mitch stooped just inside the door, the aggressive silence pulled at him, as quicksand pulls what it snares, as gravity the falling object. His rapid, ragged breathing was muffled to a whispery wheeze.

He could not hear the windstorm anymore,

but he was sure that the wind abided.

Looking at Kathy was harder than looking at Daniel, though not as difficult as Mitch had expected. If he could have prevented this, he would have stood between them and his brother. But now that it was done . . . it was done. And the heart sank rather than recoiled, and the mind fell into despondency but not into despair.

Daniel's face, eyes open, was wrenched by terror, but there was clearly puzzlement in it as well. At the penultimate moment, he must have wondered how this could be — how Anson, his one success, could be the death of him.

Systems of child-rearing and education were numberless, and no one ever died because of them, or at least not the men and women who dedicated themselves to conceiving and refining the theories.

Tasered, tied, and perhaps following a conversation, Daniel and Kathy had been stabbed. Mitch did not dwell upon the wounds.

The weapons were a pair of gardening shears and a hand trowel.

Mitch recognized them as having come from the rack of tools in his garage.

# 38

Mitch closed the bodies in the learning room, and he sat at the top of the stairs to think. Fear and shock and one Red Bull weren't sufficient to clear his thoughts as fully as four hours of sleep would have done.

Battalions of wind threw themselves against the house, and the walls shuddered but withstood the siege.

Mitch could have wept if he had dared to allow himself tears, but he would not have known for whom he was crying.

He had never seen Daniel or Kathy cry. They believed in applied reason and 'mutual supportive analysis' in place of easy emotion.

How could you cry for those who never cried for themselves, who talked and *talked* themselves through their disappointments, their misadventures, and even their bereavements?

No one who knew the truth of this family would fault him if he cried for himself, but he had not cried for himself since he was five because he had not wanted them to have the satisfaction of his tears.

He would not cry for his brother.

The wretched kind of pity that he had felt for Anson earlier was vapor now. It had not boiled away here in the learning room, but in the trunk of the vintage Chrysler.

During his drive north from Rancho Santa Fe,

with four windows open to ventilate the car, he let the draft blow from him all delusion and self-deception. The brother whom he had thought he knew, had thought he loved, in fact had never existed. Mitch had loved not a real person but instead a sociopath's performance, a phantom.

Now Anson had seized the moment to take vengeance on Daniel and Kathy, pinning the crimes on his brother, whom he thought would never be found.

If Holly was not ransomed, her kidnappers would kill her and perhaps dispose of her body at sea. Mitch would take the fall for her murder — and, somehow, for the shooting of Jason Osteen.

Such a killing spree would thrill the cable-channel true-crime shows. If he was missing — in fact dead in a desert grave — the search for him would be their leading story for weeks if not for months.

In time he might become a legend like D. B. Cooper, the airline hijacker who, decades earlier, had parachuted out of a plane with a fortune in cash, never to be heard from again.

Mitch considered returning to the learning room to collect the gardening shears and the hand trowel. The thought of wrenching the blades from the bodies repulsed him. He had done worse in recent hours; but he could not do this.

Besides, clever Anson had probably salted other evidence in addition to the gardening tools. Finding it would take time, and Mitch had no time to spare.

His wristwatch read six minutes past three in the morning. In less than nine hours, the kidnappers would call Anson with further instructions.

Forty-five of the original sixty hours remained until the midnight-Wednesday deadline.

This would be over long before then. New developments required new rules, and Mitch was going to set them.

With an imitation of wolves, the wind called him into the night.

After turning off the upstairs lights, he went down to the kitchen. In the past, Daniel had always kept a box of Hershey's bars in the refrigerator. Daniel liked his chocolate cold.

The box waited on the bottom shelf, only one bar missing. These had always been Daniel's treats, off limits to everyone else.

Mitch took the entire box. He was too exhausted and too tightly knotted with anxiety to be hungry, but he hoped that sugar might substitute for sleep.

He turned out the first-floor lights and left the house by the front door.

Brooms of fallen palm fronds swept the street, and in their wake came a rolling trash can spewing its contents. Impatiens withered and shredded themselves, shrubs shook as if trying to pull themselves up by their roots, a ripped window awning — actually green, but black in this light — flapped madly like the flag of some demonic nation, the eucalyptuses gave the wind a thousand hissing voices, and it seemed as if the moon would be blown down and the stars snuffed out like candles.

In the haunted Chrysler, Mitch set out in search of Anson.

# 39

Holly works at the nail even though she makes no progress with it, because if she doesn't work at the nail, she will have nothing to do, and with nothing to do, she will go mad.

For some reason, she remembers Glenn Close playing a mad-woman in *Fatal Attraction*. Even if she were to go crazy, Holly is not capable of boiling anyone's pet bunny in a soup pot, unless of course her family is starving and has nothing to eat or the bunny is possessed by a demon. Then all bets are off.

Suddenly the nail begins to wiggle, and that's exciting. She is so excited that she almost needs the bedpan that her kidnappers left with her.

Her excitement wanes as, during the next half-hour, she manages to extract only about a quarter of an inch of the nail from the floor plank. Then it binds and won't budge farther.

Nevertheless, a quarter of an inch is better than nothing. The spike might be — what? — three inches long. Cumulatively — discounting the breaks she took for the pizza they allowed her to have, and to rest her fingers — she has spent perhaps seven hours on the nail. If she can tease it out just a little faster, at the rate of an inch a day, by the Wednesday-midnight deadline, she will have only an inch to go.

In the event that Mitch has raised the ransom by that time, they will all just have to wait another day until she extracts the damn nail.

She has always been an optimist. People have called her sunny and cheerful and buoyant and ebullient; and annoyed by her unflagging positive outlook, a sourpuss once asked her if she was the love child of Mickey Mouse and Tinkerbell.

She could have been mean and told him the truth, that her father died in a traffic accident and her mother in childbirth, that she had been raised by a grandmother rich in love and mirth.

Instead she told him *Yes, but because Tink doesn't have the hips for childbirth, I was carried to term by Daisy Duck.*

At the moment, uncharacteristically, she finds it difficult to keep her spirits up. Being kidnapped fractures your funny bone.

She has two broken fingernails, and the pads of her fingers are sore. If she hadn't wrapped them in the tail of her blouse, to pad them, while she worked on the nail, they would probably be bleeding.

In the scheme of things, these injuries are insignificant. If her captors start cutting off her fingers like they promised Mitch, *that* would be something to bitch about.

She takes a break from her work with the nail. She lies back on the air mattress in the dark.

Although she is exhausted, she does not expect to sleep. Then she is dreaming about being in a lightless place different from the room in which the kidnappers have imprisoned her.

In the dream, she is not tethered to a ringbolt in the floor. She is walking in darkness, carrying a bundle in her arms.

240

She is not in a room but in a series of passageways. A maze of tunnels. A labyrinth.

The bundle grows heavy. Her arms ache. She doesn't know what she carries, but something terrible will happen if she puts it down.

A dim glow draws her. She arrives in a chamber brightened by a single candle.

Mitch is here. She's so happy to see him. Her father and mother, whom she has never known except from photographs, are here, too.

The bundle in her arms is a sleeping baby. Her sleeping baby.

Smiling, her mother comes forward to take the baby. Holly's arms ache, but she holds fast to the precious bundle.

Mitch says *Give us the baby, sweetheart. He should be with us. You don't belong here.*

Her parents are dead, and so is Mitch, and when she lets go of the infant, it will not just be sleeping anymore.

She refuses to give her son to them — and then somehow it is in her mother's arms. Her father blows out the candle.

Holly wakes to a howling beast that is only the wind, but beast enough, hammering the walls, shaking dust down from the roof beams.

A soft glow, not a candle but a small flashlight, brings minimal relief from the darkness in which she has been imprisoned. It reveals the knitted black ski mask, the chapped lips, and the beryl-blue eyes of one of her keepers kneeling before her — the one who worries her.

'I've brought you candy,' he says.

He holds out to her a Mr. Goodbar.

His fingers are long and white. His nails are bitten.

Holly dislikes touching anything that he has touched. Hiding her distaste, she accepts the candy bar.

'They're asleep. This is my shift.' He puts on the floor in front of her a can of cola beaded with icy sweat. 'You like Pepsi?'

'Yes. Thank you.'

'Do you know Chamisal, New Mexico?' he asks.

He has a soft, musical voice. It could almost be a woman's voice, but not quite.

'Chamisal?' she says. 'No. I've never been there.'

'I've had experiences there,' he says. 'My life was changed.'

Wind booms and something rattles on the roof, and she uses the noise as an excuse to look up, hoping to see a memorable detail of her prison for later testimony.

She was brought here in a blindfold. At the end, they came up narrow steps. She thinks she might be in an attic.

Half the lens of the small flashlight has been taped over. The ceiling remains unrevealed in gloom. The light reaches only to the nearest bare-board wall, and all else around her is lost in shadow.

They are careful.

'Have you been to Rio Lucio, New Mexico?' he asks.

'No. Not there, either.'

'In Rio Lucio, there is a small stucco house

242

painted blue with yellow trim. Why don't you eat your chocolate?'

'I'm saving it for later.'

'Who knows how much time any of us has?' he asks. 'Enjoy it now. I like to watch you eat.'

Reluctantly, she peels the wrapper off the candy bar.

'A saintly woman named Ermina Lavato lives in the blue-and-yellow stucco house in Rio Lucio. She is seventy-two.'

He believes that statements like this constitute conversation. His pauses suggest that obvious rejoinders are available to Holly.

After swallowing chocolate, she says, 'Is Ermina a relative?'

'No. She's of Hispanic origin. She makes exquisite chicken fajitas in a kitchen that looks like it came from the 1920s.'

'I'm not much of a cook,' Holly says inanely.

His gaze is riveted on her mouth, and she takes a bite from the Mr. Goodbar with the feeling that she's engaged in an obscene act.

'Ermina is very poor. The house is small but very beautiful. Each room is painted a different soothing color.'

As he stares at her mouth, she returns the scrutiny, to the extent his mask allows. His teeth are yellow. The incisors are sharp, the canines unusually pointed.

'Her bedroom walls hold forty-two images of the Holy Mother.'

His lips look as if they are perpetually chapped. Sometimes he chews at the loose shreds of skin when he isn't talking.

'In the living room are thirty-nine images of the Sacred Heart of Jesus, pierced by thorns.'

The cracks in his lips glisten as if they might start seeping.

'In Ermina Lavato's backyard, I buried a treasure.'

'As a gift for her?' Holly asks.

'No. She would not approve of what I buried. Drink your Pepsi.'

She does not want to drink from a can he handled. She opens it anyway, and takes a sip.

'Do you know Penasco, New Mexico?'

'I haven't traveled much in New Mexico.'

He is silent for a moment, and the wind howls into his silence, and his gaze drops to her throat as she swallows Pepsi. Then: 'My life changed in Penasco.'

'I thought that was Chamisal.'

'My life has changed often in New Mexico. It's a place of change and great mystery.'

Having thought of a use for the Pepsi can, Holly sets it aside with the hope he will allow her to keep it if she hasn't finished the cola by the time he leaves.

'You would enjoy Chamisal, Penasco, Rodarte, so many beautiful and mysterious places.'

She considers her words before she speaks. 'Let's hope I live to see them.'

He meets her stare directly. His eyes are the blue of a somber sky that suggests an impending storm even in the absence of clouds.

In a voice still softer than usual, not in a whisper but with a quiet tenderness, he says, 'May I speak to you in confidence?'

If he touches her, she will scream until she wakes the others.

Interpreting her expression as consent, he says, 'There were five of us, and now just three.'

This is not what she has expected. She holds his gaze though it disturbs her.

'To improve the split from five ways to four, we killed Jason.'

She cringes inwardly at the revelation of a name. She doesn't want to know names or see faces.

'Now Johnny Knox has disappeared,' he says. 'Johnny was running surveillance, hasn't called in. The three of us — we didn't agree to improve the split from four. The issue was never raised.'

*Mitch*, she thinks at once.

Outside, the tenor of the wind changes. Ceasing to shriek, it rushes with a great shush, counseling Holly in the wisdom of silence.

'The other two were out on errands yesterday,' he continues, 'separately, at different times. Either could have killed Johnny.'

To reward him for these revelations, she eats more chocolate.

Watching her mouth once more, he says, 'Maybe they decided on a two-way split. Or one of them may want to have it all.'

Not wishing to appear to sow discord, she says, 'They wouldn't do that.'

'They might,' he says. 'Do you know Vallecito, New Mexico?'

Licking chocolate from her lips, Holly says, 'No.'

'Austere,' he says. 'So many of these places are

austere but so beautiful. My life changed in Vallecito.'

'How did it change?'

Instead of answering, he says, 'You should see Las Trampas, New Mexico, in the snow. A scattering of humble buildings, white fields, low hills dark with chaparral, and the sky as white as the fields.'

'You're something of a poet,' she says, and half means it.

'They have no casinos in Las Vegas, New Mexico. They have *life* and they have mystery.'

His white hands come together, not in contemplation, certainly not in prayer, but as though each possesses its own awareness, as if they are pleased by the feel of each other.

'In Rio Lucio, Eloisa Sandoval has a shrine to Saint Anthony in her small adobe-walled kitchen. Twelve ceramic figures arranged in tiers, one for each child and grandchild. Candles every evening in the vespers hour.'

She hopes that he will make new revelations about his partners, but she knows that she must appear discreetly intrigued by everything he says.

'Ernest Sandoval drives a '64 Chevy Impala with giant steel chain links for a steering wheel, a custom-painted dashboard, and a ceiling upholstered in red velvet.'

The long fingers with spatulate pads smooth one another, smooth and smooth.

'Ernest is interested in saints with whom his pious wife is unfamiliar. And he knows . . . amazing places.'

The Mr. Goodbar has begun to cloy in Holly's

mouth, to stick in her throat, but she takes another bite of it.

'Ancient spirits dwell in New Mexico, since before the existence of humanity. Are you a seeker?'

If she encourages him too much, he will read her as insincere. 'I don't think so. Sometimes we all feel . . . something is missing. But that's everyone. That's human nature.'

'I see a seeker in you, Holly Rafferty. A tiny seed of spirit waiting to bloom.'

His eyes are as clear as a limpid stream, but cloaked by silt at the bottom are strange forms that she cannot identify.

Lowering her gaze, she says demurely, 'I'm afraid you see too much in me. I'm not a deep thinker.'

'The secret is not to think. We think in words. And what lies beneath the reality we see is a truth that words can't contain. The secret is to feel.'

'See, to you that's a simple concept, but even that's too deep for me.' She laughs softly at herself. 'My biggest dream is to be in real estate.'

'You underestimate yourself,' he assures her. 'Within you are . . . enormous possibilities.'

His large bony wrists and long pale hands are utterly hairless, either naturally or because he uses a depilatory cream.

# 40

With hobgoblins of wind threatening at the open window in the driver's door, Mitch cruised past Anson's house in Corona del Mar.

Large creamy-white flowers had been shaken from the big magnolia tree and had blown in a drift against the front door, revealed in a stoop lamp that remained on all night. Otherwise, the house was dark.

He did not believe that Anson had come home, washed up, and gone happily to sleep almost at once after killing their parents. He must be out somewhere — and up to something.

Mitch's Honda no longer stood at the curb where he had left it when he had first come here at the direction of the kidnappers.

In the next block, he parked, finished a Hershey's bar, rolled up the window, and locked the Chrysler Windsor. Unfortunately, it drew attention to itself among the surrounding contemporary vehicles, museum grandeur in a game arcade.

Mitch walked to the alleyway on which Anson's garage had access. Lights blazed throughout the lower floor of the rear condo above the pair of two-car garages.

Some people might have work that kept them busy just past three-thirty in the morning. Or insomnia.

Standing in the alleyway, Mitch planted his

feet wide to resist the rushing wind. He studied the high curtained windows.

Since Campbell's library, he had entered a new reality. He saw things more clearly now than he had seen them from his former perspective.

If Anson had eight million dollars and a fully paid-off yacht, he probably owned both condos, not just one, as he had claimed. He lived in the front unit and used the back condo for the office in which he applied linguistic theory to software design, or whatever the hell he did to get rich.

The toiler in the night, behind those curtained windows, was not a neighbor. Anson himself sat up there, bent to a computer.

Perhaps he was plotting a course, by yacht, to a haven beyond the authority of all law.

A service gate opened onto a narrow walkway beside the garage. Mitch followed it into the brick courtyard that separated the two condos. The courtyard lights were off.

Bordering the brick patio were planting beds lush with nandina and a variety of ferns, plus bromeliads and anthuriums to provide a punctuation of red blooms.

The houses to the front and back, the tall side fences, and the neighboring houses crowding close on their narrow lots all blocked the wind. Though still marked by blustering cross-currents, a more genteel version slipped down the roof slopes and danced with the courtyard greenery instead of whipping it.

Mitch slipped under the arching fronds of a Tasmanian tree fern, which swayed, trembled. He crouched there, peering out at the patio.

The skirt of broad, spreading, lacy fronds rose and dipped, rose and dipped, but the patio was not entirely screened from him at any time. If he remained alert, he couldn't miss a man passing from the back condo to the front.

In the shelter of the tree-fern canopy, he smelled rich planting soil, an inorganic fertilizer, and the vaguely musky scent of moss.

At first this comforted him, reminded him of life when it had been simpler, just sixteen hours ago. After a few minutes, however, the melange of odors brought to mind instead the smell of blood.

In the condo above the garages, the lights went out.

Perhaps assisted by the windstorm, a door slammed shut. The chorus of wind voices did not entirely cover the thud of heavy hurried footsteps that descended exterior stairs to the courtyard.

Between the fronds, Mitch glimpsed a bearish figure crossing the brick patio.

Anson was not aware of his brother behind him, closing, and let out a strangled cry only when the Taser short-circuited his nervous system.

When Anson staggered forward, trying to stay on his feet, Mitch remained close. The Taser delivered another fifty-thousand-volt kiss.

Anson embraced the bricks. He rolled onto his back. His burly body twitched. His arms flopped loosely. His head rolled side to side, and he made noises that suggested he might be in danger of swallowing his tongue.

Mitch didn't want Anson to swallow his tongue, but he wasn't going to take any action to prevent it from happening, either.

# 41

Apocalyptic flocks of wind beat wings against the walls and swoop the roof, and the darkness itself seems to vibrate.

The hairless hands, white as doves, groom each other in the dim glow of the half-taped flashlight.

The gentle voice regales her: 'In El Valle, New Mexico, there is a graveyard where the grass is seldom cut. Some graves have stones, and some do not.'

Holly has finished the chocolate. She feels half sick. Her mouth tastes like blood. She uses Pepsi as a mouthwash.

'A few graves without headstones are surrounded by small picket fences crafted from the slats of old fruit and vegetable crates.'

All this is leading somewhere, but his thoughts proceed along neural pathways that can be anticipated only by a mind as bent as his.

'Loved ones paint the pickets in pastels — robin's-egg blue, pale green, the yellow of faded sunflowers.'

In spite of the sharp enigmas underlying their soft color, his eyes repel her less, right now, than do his hands.

'Under a quarter moon, hours after a new grave was closed, we did some spade work and opened the wooden casket of a child.'

'The yellow of faded sunflowers,' Holly

251

repeats, trying to fill her mind with that color as defense against the image of a child in a coffin.

'She was eight, taken by cancer. They buried her with a Saint Christopher medal folded in her left hand, a porcelain figurine of Cinderella in her right because she loved that story.'

The sunflowers will not sustain, and in her mind's eye, Holly sees the small hands holding tight to the protection of the saint and to the promise of the poor girl who became a princess.

'By virtue of some hours in the grave of an innocent, those objects acquired great power. They were death-washed and spirit-polished.'

The longer she meets his eyes, the less familiar they become.

'We took from her hands the medal and the figurine, and replaced them with . . . other items.'

One white hand vanishes into a pocket of his black jacket. When it reappears, it holds the Saint Christopher medal by a silver chain.

He says, 'Here. Take it.'

That the object comes from a grave does not repulse her, but that it has been taken from the hand of a dead child offends.

More is happening here than he is putting into words. There is a subtext that Holly does not understand.

She senses that to reject the medal for any reason will have terrible consequences. She holds out her right hand, and he drops the medal into it. The chain ravels in random coils on her palm.

'Do you know Espanola, New Mexico?'

Folding her hand around the medal, she says,

'It's another place I've missed.'

'My life will be changed there,' he reveals as he picks up the flashlight and rises to his feet.

He leaves her in pitch black with the half-full can of Pepsi, which she expects him to take. Her intention is — or had been — to squash the can and to create from it a miniature pry bar with which to work on the stubborn nail.

The Saint Christopher medal will do a better job. Cast in brass and plated with silver or nickel, it is much harder than the soft aluminum of the can.

Her keeper's visit has changed the quality of this lightless space. It had been a lonely darkness. Now Holly imagines it inhabited by rats and waterbugs and legions of crawling things.

# 42

Anson fell hard in front of the back door, and the wind seemed to cheer his collapse.

Like a creature accustomed to filtering its oxygen from water and now helpless on a beach, he twitched, spasmed. His hands flopped, and his knuckles rapped on the bricks.

He gawped at Mitch, moving his mouth, as if trying to speak, or maybe he was trying to scream in pain. All that came out was a thin squeal, a mere thread of sound, as if his esophagus had constricted to the diameter of a pin.

Mitch tried the door. Unlocked. He pushed it open and stepped into the kitchen.

The lights were off. He didn't switch them on.

Not sure how long the effects of the shock would last, hoping for at least a minute or two, he put the Taser on a counter and returned to the open door.

Warily, he grabbed Anson by the ankles, but his brother was not capable of trying to kick him. Mitch dragged him into the house, and winced when the back of Anson's head stuttered against the raised threshold.

Closing the door, he turned on the lights. The blinds were shut, as they had been when he and Anson received the phone call from the kidnappers.

The pot of *zuppa massaia* remained on the

stove, cold but still fragrant.

Adjacent to the kitchen lay a laundry room. He checked it and found it to be as he remembered: small, no windows.

At the kitchen table, the four dinette chairs were retro-chic stainless steel and red vinyl. He moved one of them to the laundry room.

On the floor, hugging himself as if he were freezing, but most likely trying to stop the twitching, trying to get control of the less dramatic but still continuous muscle spasms, Anson made the pitiable sounds of a dog in pain.

The agony might be real. It might be a performance. Mitch kept a safe distance.

He retrieved the Taser. Reaching to the small of his back, he withdrew the pistol that he had tucked under his belt.

'Anson, I want you to roll over, facedown.'

His brother's head lolled from side to side, not in refusal but perhaps involuntarily.

Anticipation of revenge had been in its way a different kind of sugar rush. In reality, nothing about it tasted sweet.

'Listen to me. I want you to roll over and crawl as best you can to the laundry room.'

Drool escaped a corner of Anson's mouth. His chin glistened.

'I'm giving you a chance to do it the easy way.'

Anson continued to appear disoriented and not in easy control of his body.

Mitch wondered if two Taser shots in quick succession, and the second held perhaps too long, could have done permanent damage. Anson seemed to have been worse than stunned.

The big man's fall might have contained an element of tragedy if he had fallen from a height, but he had gone from low to lower.

Mitch hounded him, repeatedly making the same commands. Then: 'Damn it, Anson, if I have to, I can give you a third shock and drag your ass in there while you're helpless.'

The back door rattled, distracting Mitch. Only the hand of the wind tested the latch as a strong gust swept more boldly into the sheltered courtyard.

When he looked at Anson again, he saw an acute awareness in his brother's eyes, a sly calculation, which vanished in that glaze of disorientation. Anson's eyes rolled back in his head.

Mitch waited half a minute. Then he moved quickly toward his brother.

Anson sensed him coming, thought he was going to use the Taser, and sat up to block it, grab it.

Instead Mitch squeezed off a shot, intentionally missing his brother, but not by much. At the report of the pistol, Anson flinched back in surprise, and Mitch slammed the gun against the side of his head, hard enough to hurt bad — hard enough, as it turned out, to knock him unconscious.

The point had been to gain Anson's cooperation by convincing him that he was not dealing with the same Mitch. But this worked, too.

# 43

He *ain't heavy, he's my brother*. Bullshit. He was Mitch's brother, and he was *heavy*.

Dragging him across the polished wood floor of the kitchen and into the laundry room proved harder than Mitch expected. Hoisting him into the chair was one door away from impossible, but Mitch got it done.

The upholstered panel on the back of the chair fit between two steel verticals. Between each side of that padded panel and the frame was an open space.

He pulled Anson's hands through those gaps. With the handcuffs that he himself had worn earlier, he shackled his brother's wrists behind the chair.

Among the items in a utility drawer were three spare electrical extension cords. A thick orange cord was about forty feet long.

After weaving it through the chair's legs and stretcher bars, Mitch tied it around the washing machine. Far less flexible than rope, the rubber cord would allow only loose knots, so he tied three.

Although Anson might be able to rise into a half crouch, he would have to lift the chair with him. But anchored to the washer, he could not go anywhere.

The blow with the pistol had cut his ear. He was bleeding but not heavily.

His pulse was slow but steady. He might come around quickly.

Leaving the overhead light on, Mitch went upstairs to the master bedroom. He saw what he expected: two small nightlights plugged into wall outlets, neither switched on at the moment.

As a child, Anson had slept with a lamp on low. As a teenager, he had settled for a night-light similar to these. In every room of this house, as preparation for a power failure, he kept a flashlight that received fresh batteries four times a year.

Downstairs again, Mitch glanced in the laundry room. Anson remained unconscious in the chair.

Mitch searched the kitchen drawers until he found where Anson kept keys. He plucked out a spare house key. He also took the keys for three different cars, including his Honda, and left the house by the back door.

He doubted that the neighbors could have heard the shot — or, having heard it, could have recognized it for what it was — after it had been filtered through the boom and cry of the wind at war with itself. Nevertheless, he was relieved to see no lights in the houses to either side.

He climbed the stairs to the condo above the garages and tried the door, which was locked. As he expected, the key to Anson's house also opened this one.

Inside, he found Anson's home office occupying space that would normally be a living room and dining area. The nautical paintings were by some of the artists featured in the front condo.

Four computer workstations were served by a single wheeled office chair. The size of the logic units, far larger than anything ordinarily seen in a home, suggested his work required rapid multitiered computation and massive data storage.

Mitch wasn't a computer maven. He had no illusions that he could boot up these machines — if *boot up* was even a term in use anymore — and discover the nature of the work that had made his brother rich.

Besides, Anson would have layers of security, passwords and procedures, to keep out even serious hackers. He had always been delighted by the elaborate codes and arcane symbolism of the maps that pirates drew to their caches of treasure in those tales that enthralled him as a boy.

Mitch left, locked the door, and went down to the first of the garages. Here were the Expedition that he had driven to Campbell's estate in Rancho Santa Fe and the 1947 Buick Super Woody Wagon.

In the other two-car garage were an empty stall and Mitch's Honda, which he had left on the street.

Perhaps Anson had stored it here after driving it to Orange and taking two of Mitch's garden tools as well as some of his clothes, to Daniel and Kathy's place to murder them, and then to Mitch's again to plant the incriminating evidence.

Mitch opened the trunk. John Knox's body remained wrapped in the weathered canvas tarp.

The accident in the loft seemed to have happened in a long-ago time, in another life.

He returned to the first garage, started the Expedition, and moved it to the empty stall in the second garage.

After moving his Honda to park it beside the Buick wagon, he closed the big roll-up door on that garage.

Grimly, he wrestled the recalcitrant body from the trunk of the Honda. While it lay on the garage floor, he rolled the corpse out of the tarp.

Serious putrescence had not set in yet. The dead man had a sinister sweet-and-sour smell, however, that Mitch was eager to get away from.

The wind keened at the small high windows of the garage, as if it had a taste for the macabre and had blown itself a long way across the world to see Mitch at this gruesome work.

He thought that all this dragging around of bodies should have about it a quality of farce, especially considering that Knox was stiff with rigor mortis and hellaciously cumbersome. But at the moment he had a serious case of laugh-deficit disorder.

After he had loaded Knox into the Buick wagon and closed the tailgate, he folded the tarp and put it in the trunk of the Honda. Eventually he would dispose of it in a Dumpster or in a stranger's trash can.

He couldn't recall ever having been this exhausted: physically, mentally, emotionally. His eyes felt singed, his joints half-melted, his muscles fully cooked and tender enough to fall off the bone.

Maybe the sugar and caffeine in the Hershey's bars prevented his engine from stalling. Fear fueled him, too. But what most kept his wheels turning was the thought of Holly in the hands of monsters.

*Till death us do part* was the stated commitment in their vows. For Mitch, however, the loss of her would not release him. The commitment would endure. The rest of his life would pass in patient waiting.

He walked the alleyway to the street, returned to the Chrysler Windsor, and drove it back to the second garage. He parked it beside the Expedition and closed the roll-down door.

He consulted his wristwatch — 4:09.

In ninety minutes, maybe a little longer, maybe a little less, the furious wind would blow dawn in from the east. Because of dust flung high into the atmosphere, the first light would be pink, and it would rapidly squall across the heavens, fading to the color of a more mature sky as it was blown toward the sea.

Since he had met Holly, he had greeted every day with great expectations. This day was different.

He returned to the house and found Anson awake in the laundry room, and in a mood.

# 44

The cut on his left ear had crusted shut, and body heat was quickly drying the blood that had trickled down his cheek and neck.

His bearish good looks had settled into harder edges, as though a genetic contagion had introduced major wolf DNA into his face. Jaws clenched so tight that his facial muscles knotted, eyes molten with rage, Anson sat in seething silence.

The wind wasn't loud here. A vent pipe carried sighs and whispers from outside into the dryer, so it seemed as if a troubled spirit haunted that machine.

Mitch said, 'You're going to help me get Holly back alive.'

That statement elicited neither agreement nor refusal, only a glower.

'They'll be calling in a little more than seven and a half hours with wiring instructions.'

Paradoxically, confined in the chair, restrained, Anson looked bigger than he had before. Shackles emphasized his physical power, and it seemed that, like some figure out of myth, if he attained the pinnacle of his potential rage, he would be able to snap his bonds as if they were string.

In Mitch's absence, Anson had tried determinedly to wrench the chair free of the washing machine. The steel legs of the chair had scraped and chattered against the tile floor, leaving scars that revealed the intensity of his futile effort. Also, the washer had been pulled out of alignment with the clothes dryer.

'You said you could put it together by phone, by computer,' Mitch reminded him. 'You said three hours tops.'

Anson spat on the floor between them.

'If you've got eight million, you can spare two for Holly. When it's done, you and I never see each other again. You get to go back to the sewer of a life you've made for yourself.'

If Anson discovered that Mitch knew about Daniel and Kathy dead in the learning room, there would be no way to force his cooperation. He would think Mitch had already undone the planted evidence to focus the eye of the law on the true perpetrator.

As long as he believed those murders were not yet known, he could hope that cooperation would lead to a moment when Mitch made a mistake that reversed their fortunes.

'Campbell didn't just let you go,' Anson said.

'No.'

'So . . . how?'

'Killed those two.'

'*You?*'

'Now I've got to live with that.'

'You popped Vosky and Creed?'

'I don't know their names.'

'Those were their names, all right.'

'Because of you,' Mitch said.

'Vosky and Creed? It doesn't compute.'

'Then Campbell must have let me go.'

'Campbell would never let you go.'

'So believe what you want.'

From under a beetled brow, Anson studied him with sour eyes. 'Where did you get it — the Taser?'

'Vosky and Creed,' Mitch lied.

'You just took it away from them, huh?'

'Like I told you — I took everything away from them. Now I'm giving you a few hours to think about things.'

'You can have the money.'

'That's not what I want you to think about.'

'You can have it, but I've got some conditions.'

'You don't get to make the rules,' Mitch said.

'It's my two million.'

'No. It's mine now. I've earned it.'

'Cool down, all right?'

'If you were them, you'd screw her first.'

'Hey, you know, that's just a thing I said.'

'If you were them, you'd kill her but screw her first.'

'It was just something to say. Anyway, I'm not them.'

'No, you're not them. You're the cause of them.'

'Wrong. Things happen. They just happen.'

'Without you, they wouldn't be happening to me.'

'If you want to look at it that way, you will.'

'Here's what you need to think about — who I am now.'

'You want me to think about who you are?'

'No more *fratello piccolo*. Huh? You understand?'

'But you *are* my little brother.'

'If you think of me that way, you'll pull some dumb move I would have fallen for then, but I won't fall for it now.'

'If we can make a deal, I'm not pulling any moves.'

'We've already made the deal.'

'You've got to cut me some slack, man.'

'So you can hang me with it?'

'How can any deal work without at least a little trust?'

'You just sit here and think about how fast you could be dead.'

Mitch switched off the lights and stepped across the threshold.

In the dark, windowless laundry room, Anson said, 'What're you doing?'

'Providing the best learning environment,' Mitch said, and pulled the door shut.

'Mickey?' Anson called.

*Mickey*. After all this, *Mickey*.

'Mickey, don't do this.'

At the kitchen sink, Mitch scrubbed his hands, using a lot of soap and hot water, trying to wash away the tactile memory of John Knox's body, which felt as if it had been imprinted on his skin.

From the refrigerator, he got a package of cheddar-cheese slices and a squeeze bottle of mustard. He found a loaf of bread and made a cold cheese sandwich.

'I hear you out there,' Anson called from the laundry room. 'What are you doing, Mickey?'

Mitch put the sandwich on a plate. He added a dill pickle. From the refrigerator he got a bottle of beer.

'What's the point of this, Mickey? We've already got a deal. There's no point to this.'

Mitch tilted another kitchen chair under the knob of the laundry-room door, bracing it.

'What's that?' Anson asked. 'What's happening?'

Mitch switched off the kitchen lights. He went upstairs to Anson's bedroom.

After putting the pistol and the Taser on the nightstand, he sat on the bed, his back against the padded headboard.

He didn't turn down the quilted silk bedspread. He didn't take off his shoes.

After eating the sandwich and the pickle, and drinking the beer, he set the clock radio for 8:30 A.M.

He wanted Anson to have time to think, but he was taking this four-hour break primarily because his own thinking had been slowed by exhaustion. He needed a clear head for what was coming.

Raging across the roof, beating on the windows, speaking in the wild voice of a mob, the wind seemed to mock him, to promise that his every plan would end in chaos.

This was a Santa Ana, the dry wind that harried moisture from the vegetation in the canyons around which many southern California communities had been built, turning that dense growth into tinder. An arsonist would toss a burning rag, another would use a cigarette lighter, another would strike a match — and for days the news would be filled with fire.

The drapes were shut, and when he switched

266

off the lamp, a coverlet of darkness fell over him. He didn't use either of Anson's small night-lights.

Holly's lovely face rose into his mind, and he said aloud, 'God, please give me the strength and the wisdom to help her.'

This was the first time in his life that he had spoken to God.

He made no promises of piety and charity. He didn't think it worked that way. You could not make deals with God.

With the most important day of his life soon to dawn, he didn't think that he could sleep, but he slept.

# 45

The nail waits.

Holly sits in the dark, listening to the wind, fingering the Saint Christopher medal.

She sets aside the can of Pepsi without drinking the last half of it. She does not want to have to use the bedpan again, at least not when the sonofabitch on duty is the sonofabitch with the white hairless hands.

The thought of him emptying her bedpan creeps her out. Just asking him to do it would create an intolerable intimacy.

As she fingers the medal in her left hand, her right hand drops to her belly. Her waist is narrow, her stomach flat. The child grows in her, a secret, as private as a dream.

They say that if you listen to classical music while pregnant, your child will have a higher IQ. As an infant, he or she will cry less and be more content.

This may be true. Life is complex and mysterious. Cause and effect are not always clear. Quantum physicists say that sometimes effect comes before cause. She had watched a one-hour program about that on the Discovery Channel. She hadn't made much sense of it; and the scientists describing the various phenomena admitted they could not explain them, only observe them.

She moves her hand in slow circles over her

belly, thinking how fine it would be, how sweet, if the baby gave a twitch that she could feel. Of course, it is only a ball of cells at this stage, not yet capable of giving a *Hi, Mom* kick.

Even now, however, its full potential is there, a tiny person in the shell of her body, like a pearl steadily accreting in an oyster, and everything she does will affect her little passenger. No more wine with dinner. Cut way back on the coffee. Perform faithful but sensible exercise. Avoid another kidnapping.

Saint Christopher, being the protector of children, has brought her to a reconsideration of the nail as she blindly traces his image with her fingertips.

She's probably being irrational, taking this babies-learn-in-the-womb business too far. Yet it seems that if, while pregnant, she thrusts a nail into some guy's carotid artery or through his eye into his brain, the incident will surely have an effect on the baby.

Extremely strong emotion — again, according to the Discovery Channel — causes the brain to order the release into the blood of veritable floods of hormones or other chemicals. A homicidal frenzy would seem to qualify as a strong emotion.

If too much caffeine in the blood can put the unborn child at risk, torrents of killer-mommy enzyme can't be desirable. She intends to use the nail on a bad guy, of course, a really bad guy, but the baby has no way of knowing the victim isn't a good guy.

The baby won't be born with homicidal

269

tendencies because of a single incident of violent self-defense. Nevertheless, Holly broods about the nail.

Maybe this irrational worrying is a symptom of pregnancy, like morning sickness, which she hasn't experienced yet, or like a craving for chocolate ice cream with pickles.

Prudence also plays a role in her rethinking of the nail scheme. When you deal with people like those who had kidnapped her, you better not strike out against them unless you are certain that you can carry through with the assault successfully.

If you try to thrust a nail through someone's eye but instead stab him in the nose, you are going to have an angry nose-stabbed criminal psychopath on your case. Not good.

She is still fingering the Saint Christopher medal, pondering the pros and cons of fighting vicious gunmen with only a three-inch nail, when the representative of the New Mexico Tourist Board returns.

He comes behind a flashlight with a half-taped lens, as before, and still has the hands of a pianist from Hell. He kneels in front of her and puts the flashlight on the floor.

'You like the medallion,' he says, sounding pleased to see her smoothing it between her fingers as if it is a worry bead.

Instinct encourages her to play to his weirdness. 'It has an interesting . . . feel.'

'The girl in the coffin wore a simple white dress with cheap lace tacked to the collar and cuffs. She looked so peaceful.'

He has chewed all the shreds of loose skin from his chapped lips. They are mottled red and appear to be tender, swollen.

'She wore white gardenias in her hair. When we opened the lid, the pent-up perfume of the gardenias was *intense*.'

Holly closes her eyes to avoid his.

'We took the medallion and the figurine of Cinderella to a place near Angel Fire, New Mexico, where there's a vortex.'

Evidently he thought she knew what he meant by *vortex*.

His gentle voice becomes gentler, and almost sad, when he adds, 'I killed them both in their sleep.'

For a moment, she thinks this statement relates to the vortex in Angel Fire, New Mexico, and she tries to make sense of it in that context. When she realizes what he means, she opens her eyes.

'They pretended they didn't know what happened to John Knox, but at least one of them had to know, all right, and probably both.'

In a room nearby are two dead men. She didn't hear gunfire. Maybe he slit their throats.

She can picture his pale hairless hands wielding a straight razor with the grace of a magician rolling coins across his knuckles.

Holly has grown accustomed to the manacle on her ankle, to the chain that connects her to a ringbolt in the floor. Suddenly she is again acutely aware that she is not only imprisoned in a room with no windows but also is limited to the portion of the room that the chain permits her to reach.

He says, 'I would have been next, and they would have done a two-way split.'

Five people had planned her kidnapping. Only one remains.

If he touches her, there is no one to respond to her scream. They are alone together.

'What happens now?' she asks, and at once wishes that she hadn't.

'I'll speak to your husband at noon, as scheduled. Anson will have fronted him the money. Then it's up to you.'

She parses his third sentence, but it's a dry lemon from which she can't squeeze any juice. 'What do you mean?'

Instead of answering her question, he says, 'As part of a church festival, a small carnival comes to Penasco, New Mexico, in August.'

She has the crazy feeling that if she snatches off his knitted ski mask, there will be no features to his face other than the beryl-blue eyes and the mouth with yellow teeth and sore lips. No eyebrows, no nose, no ears, the skin as smooth and featureless as white vinyl.

'Just a Ferris wheel and a few other rides, a few games — and last year a fortuneteller.'

His hands swoop up to describe the shape of the Ferris wheel but then come to roost on his thighs.

'The fortuneteller calls herself Madame Tiresias, but of course that is not her real name.'

Holly is squeezing the medallion so tightly in one hand that her knuckles ache and the raised image of the saint is no doubt impressed in her palm.

'Madame Tiresias is a fraud, but the funny thing is, she has powers of which she's unaware.'

He pauses between each statement as if what he has said is so profound that he wants her to have time to absorb it.

'She would not *have* to be a fraud if she could recognize what she really is, and I intend to show her this year.'

Speaking without a tremor in her voice requires self-control, but Holly brings him back to the question he would not answer: 'What did you mean — then it will be up to me?'

When he smiles, part of his mouth disappears from the horizontal slit in the mask. This makes his smile seem sly and knowing, as if no one's secrets are safe from him.

'You know what I mean,' he says. 'You're not Madame Tiresias. You have full knowledge of yourself.'

She senses that if she denies his assertion, she will test his patience and perhaps make him angry. His soft voice and his gentle manner are sheep's clothing, and Holly does not want to poke the wolf beneath the fleece.

'You've given me so much to think about,' she says.

'I am aware of that. You've been living behind a curtain, and now you know there's not just a window under it, but a whole new world beyond.'

Afraid that one wrong word will shatter the spell that the killer has cast over himself, Holly says only, 'Yes.'

He rises to his feet. 'You have some hours yet to decide. Do you need anything?'

A *shotgun*, she thinks, but she says, 'No.'

'I know what your decision will be, but you need to reach it on your own. Have you ever been to Guadalupita, New Mexico?'

'No.'

His smile curves up behind the slit in the black mask. 'You will go there, and you will be amazed.'

He follows his flashlight, leaving her alone in darkness.

Gradually Holly realizes that the wind is still blowing hard. From the moment he'd told her that he killed the other kidnappers, the wind had vanished from her consciousness.

For a while she has heard only his voice. His sinuous, insidious voice.

She has not even heard her heart, but she hears it now and feels it, too, shaking the cage of ribs against which it pounds.

The baby, tiny ball of cells, is now bathed in the fight-or-flight chemicals that her brain has ordered released into her blood. Maybe that isn't so bad. Maybe it's even good. Maybe being marinated in that flood will make Baby Rafferty, him or her, tougher than would otherwise be the case.

This is a world that increasingly requires toughness of good people.

With the Saint Christopher medal, Holly sets diligently to work on the stubborn nail.

# Part Three

## Until Death
## Us Do Part.

# 46

The alarm woke Mitch at eight-thirty, and the wind that had worried his dreams still churned the real world.

He sat on the edge of the bed for a minute, yawning, looking at the backs of his hands, at the palms. After what those hands had done the previous night, they ought to have looked different from the way they had always looked before, but he could discern no change.

Passing the mirrored closet doors, he saw that his clothes were not unusually wrinkled. He had awakened in the same position in which he had fallen asleep; and he must not have moved in four hours.

In the bathroom, searching drawers, he found several unopened toothbrushes. He unwrapped one and used it, then shaved with Anson's electric razor.

Carrying the pistol and the Taser, he went downstairs to the kitchen.

The chair was still braced under the laundry-room doorknob. No sound came from in there.

He cracked three eggs, spiced them with Tabasco sauce, scrambled them, sprinkled Parmesan on them, and ate them with two slices of buttered toast and a glass of orange juice.

By habit, he began to gather the dishes to wash them, but then realized the absurdity of being a thoughtful guest under these circumstances. He left the dirty dishes on the table.

When he opened the laundry and switched on the lights, he found Anson cuffed as before, soaked in sweat. The room wasn't unusually warm.

'Have you thought about who I am?' Mitch asked.

Anson didn't appear angry anymore. He slumped in the chair and hung his burly head. He did not look physically smaller; but in some way he had been diminished.

When his brother didn't answer, Mitch repeated the question: 'Have you thought about who I am?'

Anson raised his head. His eyes were bloodshot, but his lips were pale. Jewels of sweat glittered in his beard stubble.

'I'm in a bad way here,' he complained in a voice that he had never used before, one with a whine and with the particular note of offense that suggested he felt victimized.

'One more time. Have you thought about who I am?'

'You're Mitch, but you're not the Mitch I know.'

'That's a start.'

'There's some part of you now . . . I don't know what you are.'

'I'm a husband. I cultivate. Preserve.'

'What's that supposed to mean?'

'I don't expect you to understand.'

'I've got to go to the bathroom.'

'Go ahead.'

'I'm bursting. I really have to piss.'

'You won't offend me.'

'You mean *here*?'

'It's messy but it's convenient.'

'Don't do this to me, bro.'

'Don't call me bro.'

Anson said, 'You're still my brother.'

'Biologically.'

'Man, this isn't right.'

'No, it isn't.'

The legs of the chair had scraped a lot more glaze off the floor tiles. Two tiles were cracked.

'Where do you keep the cash?' Mitch asked.

'I wouldn't take your dignity like this.'

'You handed me over to killers.'

'I didn't humiliate you first.'

'You said you'd rape my wife and kill her.'

'Are you stuck on that? I *explained* that.'

He had struggled so fiercely to free the chair from the washer that the thick orange extension cord had dimpled the metal of the machine at one corner.

'Where do you keep the cash, Anson?'

'I've got, I don't know, a few hundred in my wallet.'

'I'm not stupid. Don't handle me.'

Anson's voice cracked. 'This hurts like a sonofabitch.'

'What hurts?'

'My arms. My shoulders are on fire. Let me change position. Cuff my hands in front of me. This is torture.'

Almost pouting, Anson looked like a big little

boy. A boy with a coldly calculating reptilian brain.

'Let's talk about the cash first,' Mitch said.

'You think there's cash, like a lot of cash? There's not.'

'If I wire-transfer the money, I'll never see Holly again.'

'You might. They don't want you crying to the cops.'

'They won't risk her identifying them in court.'

'Campbell could persuade them to drop this.'

'By beating their mothers, raping their sisters?'

'You want Holly back or not?'

'I killed two of his men. He'd help me now?'

'Maybe. There'd be a respect thing now.'

'It wouldn't be a two-way respect thing.'

'Man, you've got to stay flexible about people.'

'I'm going to tell the kidnappers it has to be a cash trade in person.'

'Then it's not going to happen.'

'You've got cash somewhere,' Mitch insisted.

'Money earns interest, dividends. I don't put it in a mattress.'

'You read all those pirate stories.'

'So?'

'You *identified* with the pirates, thought they were way cool.'

Grimacing as if in pain, Anson said, 'Please, man, let me go to the bathroom. I'm in a real bad way.'

'Now you *are* a pirate. Even got your own boat, gonna run your business from sea. Pirates don't put their money in banks. They like to touch it, look at it. They bury it in lots of places so they can get to it easy when their fortunes change.'

'Mitch, please, man, I'm having bladder spasms.'

'The money you make consulting — yeah, it goes in the bank. But the money from jobs that are — how did you put it? — 'more directly criminal,' like whatever job you did with these guys and then cheated them on the split, *that* doesn't go in the bank. You don't pay taxes on it.'

Anson said nothing.

'I'm not going to march you over to your office and watch while you use the computer to move funds around, arrange a wire transfer. You're bigger than me. You're desperate. I'm not giving you a chance to turn the tables. You're in that chair till this is done.'

Accusatorily, Anson said, 'I was always there for you.'

'Not always.'

'As kids, I mean. I was always there for you when we were kids.'

'Actually,' Mitch said, 'we were there for each other.'

'We were. That's right. Real brothers. We can get back to that,' Anson assured him.

'Yeah? How do we get back to that?'

'I'm not saying it'll be easy. Maybe we start with some honesty. I screwed up, Mitch. It was horrible what I did to you. I was doing some drugs, man, and they messed with my head.'

'You weren't doing any drugs. Don't blame it on that. Where's the cash?'

'Bro, I swear to you, the dirty money gets laundered. It ends up in the bank, too.'

'I don't believe it.'

'You can grind me, but it doesn't change what's true.'

'Why don't you think about it some more?' Mitch advised.

'There's nothing to think about. What is is.'

Mitch switched off the light.

'Hey, no,' Anson said plaintively.

Stepping across the threshold, pulling the door shut behind him, Mitch closed his brother in the dark.

# 47

Mitch started in the attic. A trapdoor in the walk-in closet off the master bedroom gave access. A ladder folded down off the trap.

Two bare lightbulbs inadequately illuminated the high space, revealing cobwebs in the angles of the rafters.

Eager breathing, hissing, and hungry panting arose at every vent in the eaves, as though the attic were a canary cage and the wind a voracious cat.

Such was the disquieting nature of a Santa Ana wind that even the spiders were agitated by it. They moved restlessly on their webs.

Nothing was stored in the attic. He almost retreated, but was held by suspicion, by a hunch.

This empty space was floored with plywood. Anson would probably not conceal a hoard of cash under a sheet of plywood held down by sixteen nails. He wouldn't be able to get at it fast in an emergency.

Nevertheless, ducking to avoid the lower rafters, Mitch walked back and forth, listening to his hollow footsteps. An odd prophetic feeling seized him, a sense that he was on the brink of a discovery.

His attention was drawn to a nail. The other nails in the floor were pounded flat, but one was raised about a quarter of an inch.

He knelt in front of the nail to examine it. The

head was wide and flat. Judging by the size of the head and the thickness of the quarter-inch of shank revealed, it was at least three inches long.

When he pinched the nail between thumb and forefinger and tried to wiggle it, he found that it was firmly lodged.

An extraordinary feeling overcame him, akin to — but different from — what he had experienced when he had first seen the field of squirreltail grass transformed into a silvery whirlpool by the eddying breeze and the moonlight.

Suddenly he felt so close to Holly that he looked over his shoulder, half expecting her to be there. The feeling did not fade, but swelled, until a chill nubbed the flesh on the nape of his neck.

He left the attic and went down to the kitchen. In the drawer where he had found the car keys was a small collection of the most commonly used tools. He selected a screwdriver and a claw hammer.

From the laundry room, Anson said, 'What's going on?'

Mitch didn't reply.

In the attic once more, he applied the claw end of the hammer and pulled up the nail. Using the screwdriver as a wedge, tapping the handle with the hammer, he levered the next nail a quarter-inch out of the plywood, and then used the claw to extract it, too.

Agitated spiders plucked silent arpeggios from their silken harps, and the wind was never silent.

The chill on the back of his neck intensified nail by nail. When the last was extracted, he eagerly lifted aside the sheet of plywood.

He found only floor joists. Blankets of fiberglass insulation filled the spaces between the joists.

He lifted out the fiberglass. No strongbox or plastic-wrapped bundles of currency were concealed beneath the insulation.

The prophetic feeling had passed, as had the sense that somehow he had been close to Holly. He sat in mystification.

*What the hell was that all about?*

Surveying the attic, he felt no compulsion to take up other sheets of plywood.

His original assessment had been correct. In concern of a fire, if for no other reason, Anson wouldn't hide a lot of money where he couldn't get at it quickly.

Mitch left the spiders in darkness with the ever-seeking wind.

In the master closet, after putting up the folding ladder and the trapdoor, he continued his search. He looked behind the hanging clothes, checked drawers for false bottoms, felt under every shelf and along every molding for a hidden lever that might spring open a panel.

In the bedroom, he peered behind paintings in hope of finding a wall safe, although he doubted that Anson would be that obvious. He even rolled the king-size bed out of place, but he found no loose square of carpet concealing a floor vault.

Mitch worked through two bathrooms, a hall closet, and two spare bedrooms that had not been furnished. Nothing.

Downstairs, he began in the mahogany-paneled, book-lined study. There were so many potential hiding places that he had only half finished with the room when he glanced at his watch and saw it was 11:33.

The kidnappers would be calling in twenty-seven minutes.

In the kitchen, he picked up the pistol and went to the laundry room. When he opened the door, the stink of urine met him.

He switched on the light and found Anson in misery.

Most of the flood had been soaked up by his pants, his socks, his shoes, but a small yellow puddle had formed on the tiles at the feet of the chair.

Other than rage, the closest thing sociopaths have to human emotions is self-love and self-pity, the only love and only pity of which they are capable. Their extreme self-love is beyond mere rampant egomania.

Psychotic self-love includes nothing as worthy as self-respect, but it does encompass a kind of overweening pride. Anson could not feel shame, but his pride had fallen from a high place into a swamp of self-pity.

His tan could not conceal an ashen undertone. His face appeared spongy, fungoid. The blood-shot eyes were filmy pools of torment.

'Look what you've done to me,' he said.

'You did it to yourself.'

If self-pity left room in him for anger, he hid it well.

'This is sick, man.'

'It's way sick,' Mitch agreed.

'You're having a good laugh.'

'No. Nothing funny here.'

'You're laughing inside.'

'I hate this.'

'If you hate this, where's your shame now?'

Mitch said nothing.

'Where's your red face? Where's my blushing brother?'

'We're running out of time, Anson. They'll be calling soon. I want the cash.'

'What do I get? What's in it for me? Why am I supposed to just give and give?'

Arm extended full length, assuming the posture that Campbell had taken with Mitch himself, he pointed the gun at his brother's face.

'You give me the money, and I'll let you live.'

'What kind of life would I have?'

'You keep everything else you've got. I pay the ransom, take care of this without the police ever knowing there was a kidnapping, so nobody has to get a statement from you.'

No doubt Anson was thinking about Daniel and Kathy.

'You go on like before,' Mitch lied, 'make whatever kind of life you want.'

Anson would have been able to pin their parents' deaths on Mitch with ease if Mitch had been dead and buried in a desert grave beyond discovery. Not so easy now.

'I give you the money,' Anson said, 'you set me loose.'

'That's right.'

Dubious, he said, 'How?'

287

'Before I leave to make the trade, I Taser you again, and then I take off the cuffs. I leave while you're still twitching.'

Anson thought it over.

'Come on, pirate boy. Give up the treasure. If you don't tell me before the phone rings, it's over.'

Anson met his eyes.

Mitch didn't look away. 'I'll do it.'

'You're just like me,' Anson said.

'If that's what you want to think.'

Anson's gaze didn't waver. His eyes were bold. His eyes were direct and probing.

He was shackled to a chair. His shoulders ached and his arms ached. He had wet his pants. He was staring down the muzzle of a gun.

Yet his eyes were steady, and full of calculation. A graveyard rat, having tunneled to make nests in a series of skulls, seemed now to occupy this living head, peering out with rat-quick cunning.

'There's a floor safe in the kitchen,' Anson said.

# 48

The lower cabinet to the left of the sink featured two roll-out shelves. They contained pots and pans.

Mitch unloaded the shelves and detached them from the tracks in which they rolled, exposing the floor of the cabinet in perhaps one minute.

In the four corners were what appeared to be small wooden angle braces. They were in fact pins holding the otherwise unsecured floor panel in place.

He removed the pins, lifted the floor out of the cabinet, and exposed the concrete slab on which the house had been built. Sunk in the concrete was a floor safe.

The combination that Anson had given him worked on the first try. The heavy lid hinged away from him.

The fireproof box measured approximately two feet long, eighteen inches wide, and one foot deep. Inside were thick packets of hundred-dollar bills in kitchen plastic wrap sealed with clear tape.

The safe also contained a manila envelope. According to Anson, it held bearer bonds issued by a Swiss bank. They were almost as liquid as the hundred-dollar bills but more compact and easier to transport across borders.

Mitch transferred the treasure to the kitchen

table and checked the contents of the envelope. He counted six bonds denominated in U.S. dollars, one hundred thousand each, payable to the bearer regardless of whether or not he had been the purchaser.

Just a day previous, he would never have expected to be in possession of so much money; and he doubted that he would ever find himself with this much cash again in his life. Yet he experienced not even the briefest amazement or delight at the sight of such wealth.

This was Holly's ransom, and he was grateful to have it. This money was also why she had been kidnapped, and for that reason, he regarded it with such antipathy that he was loath to touch it.

The kitchen clock read 11:54.

Six minutes until the call.

He returned to the laundry, where he had left the door open and the light on.

As self-involved as he was self-saturated, Anson sat in the wet chair but was somewhere else. He didn't come back to the moment until Mitch spoke to him.

'Six hundred thousand in bonds. How much in cash?'

'The rest of it,' Anson said.

'The rest of the two million? So there's a million four hundred thousand in cash?'

'That's what I said. Isn't that what I said?'

'I'm going to count it.'

'Go ahead.'

'If it's not all there, the deal is off. I don't turn you loose when I leave.'

In frustration, Anson rattled his handcuffs against the chair. 'What're you trying to do to me?'

'I'm just saying how it is. For me to keep the deal, you have to keep the deal. I'll start counting now.'

Mitch turned away from the door, toward the kitchen table, and Anson said, 'There's eight hundred thousand in cash.'

'Not a million four?'

'The whole bundle, cash and bonds, is a million four. I got confused.'

'Yeah. Confused. I need six hundred thousand more.'

'That's all there is. I don't have any more.'

'You said you didn't have this, either.'

'I don't always lie,' Anson said.

'Pirates don't bury everything they've got in one place.'

'Will you stop with this pirate crap?'

'Why? Because it makes you feel like you've never grown up?'

The clock showed 11:55.

Inspiration struck Mitch, and he said, 'Stop with the pirate crap because maybe I'll think of the yacht. You bought yourself a sailing yacht. How much do you have stashed aboard it?'

'Nothing. I've got nothing on the boat. Haven't had time to fit it out with a safe.'

'If they kill Holly, I'll go through your records here,' Mitch said. 'I'll get the name of the boat, where it's moored. I'll go down to the harbor with an axe and a power drill.'

'Do what you have to do.'

'I'll rip it up bow to stern, and when I find the money and know you lied to me, I'll come back here and tape your mouth shut so you can't lie to me anymore.'

'I'm telling you the truth.'

'I'll close you here in the dark, no water, no food, close you in here to die of dehydration in your own filth. I'll sit right there in the kitchen, at your table, eating your food, listening to you die in the dark.'

Mitch didn't believe that he could kill anyone in such a cruel fashion, but to his own ear he sounded hard and cold and convincing.

If he lost Holly, maybe anything was possible. Because of her, he had come fully to life. Without her, a part of him would die, and he would be less of a man.

Anson seemed to follow that same chain of reasoning, for he said, 'All right. Okay. Four hundred thousand.'

'What?'

'In the boat. I'll tell you where to find it.'

'We're still two hundred thousand short.'

'There's no more. Not cash. I'd have to liquidate some stock.'

Mitch turned to look at the kitchen clock — 11:56.

'Four minutes. No time left for lies, Anson.'

'Would you for once believe me? Just for once? There's no more in easy cash.'

'I already have to change the conditions of the trade,' Mitch worried, 'no wire transfer. Now I also have to bargain them down two hundred thousand.'

'They'll take it,' Anson assured him. 'I know these pigs. Are they gonna turn down a million eight? No way. Not these pigs.'

'You better be right.'

'Listen, we're okay now, aren't we? Aren't we okay? So don't leave me in the dark.'

Mitch had already turned away from him. He didn't switch off the laundry-room light, and he didn't close the door.

At the table, he stared at the bearer bonds and the cash. He picked up the pen and the notepad and went to the phone.

He could not bear the sight of the telephone. Phones had not brought him good news lately.

He closed his eyes.

Three years ago, they were married with no family in attendance. Dorothy, the grandmother who had raised Holly, had passed suddenly five months previously. On her father's side were an aunt and two cousins. She didn't know them. They didn't care.

Mitch couldn't invite his brother and three sisters without extending an invitation to his parents. He didn't want Daniel and Kathy to be there.

He wasn't motivated by bitterness. He didn't exclude them in anger or as punishment. He'd been *afraid* for them to be present.

This marriage was his second chance at family, and if it failed, he wouldn't have the nerve to try a third time. Daniel and Kathy were a systemic disease of families, a disease that, allowed in at the roots, would surely deform the plant and wither its fruit.

Afterward, they told his family they had eloped, but actually they'd had a small ceremony and reception at the house for a limited number of friends. Iggy was right: The band had been woofy. Too many numbers with tambourines. And a guy singer who thought his best trick was extended passages in falsetto.

After everyone had gone and the band was a comic memory, he and Holly had danced alone, to a radio, on the portable dance floor that had been set up in the backyard for the event. She had been so lovely in the moonlight, almost otherworldly, that he unconsciously held her too tight, as if she might fade like a phantom, until she said, 'I'm breakable, you know,' and he relaxed, and she put her head on his shoulder. Although he was usually a clumsy dancer, he never once put a foot wrong, and around them turned the lush landscaping that was the consequence of his patient labor, and above them shone the stars that he had never offered her because he wasn't a man given to poetic declarations, but she owned the stars already, and the moon bowed to her, as well, and all the heavens, and the night.

The phone rang.

# 49

He answered on the second ring and said, 'This is Mitch.'

'Hello, Mitch. Are you feeling hopeful?'

This mellow voice was not the same as on the previous calls, and the change made Mitch uneasy.

'Yes. I'm hopeful,' he said.

'Good. Nothing can be achieved without hope. It was hope that brought me from Angel Fire to here, and it's hope that'll carry me back again.'

On consideration, the change didn't disturb Mitch so much as did the nature of the voice. The man spoke with a gentleness that was just one station up the dial from spooky.

'I want to talk to Holly.'

'Of course you do. She is the woman of the hour — and acquitting herself very well. This lady is a solid spirit.'

Mitch didn't know what to make of that. What the guy had said about Holly was true, but from him, it sounded creepy.

Holly came on the line. 'Are you okay, Mitch?'

'I'm all right. I'm going crazy, but I'm all right. I love you.'

'I'm okay, too. I haven't been hurt. Not really.'

'We're going to pull this off,' he assured her. 'I'm not going to let you down.'

'I never thought you would. Never.'

'I love you, Holly.'

'He wants the phone back,' she said, and returned it to her captor.

She had sounded constrained. Twice he'd told her that he loved her, but she had not responded in kind. Something was wrong.

The gentle voice returned: 'There's been one change in the plan, Mitch, one important change. Instead of a wire transfer, cash is king.'

Mitch had worried that he would not be able to talk them out of having the ransom sent by wire. He should have been relieved by this development. Instead it troubled him. It was another indication that something had happened to put the kidnappers off their game. A new voice on the phone, then Holly sounding guarded, and now a sudden preference for cash.

'Are you with me, Mitch?'

'Yeah. It's just, you've thrown me a curve here. You should know . . . Anson hasn't been as full of brotherly concern as maybe you thought he would be.'

The caller was amused. 'The others thought he would be. I was never sure. I don't expect genuine tears from a crocodile.'

'I'm handling the situation,' Mitch assured him.

'Have you been surprised by your brother?'

'Repeatedly. Listen, right now I can guarantee eight hundred thousand in cash and six hundred thousand in bearer bonds.'

Before Mitch could mention the additional four hundred thousand that was supposedly aboard Anson's boat, the kidnapper said, 'That's a disappointment, of course. That other six hundred thousand would buy a lot of time to seek.'

Mitch didn't catch the last word. 'To what?'

'Do you seek, Mitch?'

'Seek what?'

'If we knew the answer, there'd be no need to seek. A million four will be all right. I'll think of it as a discount for paying cash.'

Surprised by the ease with which the lower figure had been accepted, Mitch said, 'You can speak for everyone, your partners?'

'Yes. If I don't speak for them, who will?'

'Then . . . what's next?'

'You come alone.'

'All right.'

'Unarmed.'

'All right.'

'Pack the money and bonds in a plastic trash bag. Don't tie the top shut. Are you familiar with the Turnbridge house?'

'Everyone in the county knows the Turnbridge house.'

'Come there at three o'clock. Don't get cute and think you can come early and lie in wait. All you'll get for that is a dead wife.'

'I'll be there at three. Not a minute earlier. How do I get in?'

'The gate will appear to be chained, but the chain will be loose. After you drive onto the site, replace the chain as it was. What will you be driving?'

'My Honda.'

'Stop directly in front of the house. You'll see an SUV. Park well away from it. Park with the back of the Honda toward the house and open the trunk. I want to see no one's in the trunk.'

'All right.'

'At that point, I'll phone you on your cell with instructions.'

'Wait. My cell. It's dead.' Actually it was somewhere in Rancho Santa Fe. 'Can I use Anson's?'

'What's that number?'

Anson's cell phone lay on the kitchen table, beside the money and the bonds. Mitch snared it. 'I don't know the number. I have to switch it on and look. Give me a minute.'

As Mitch waited for the phone company logo to leave the screen, the man with the gentle voice said, 'Tell me, is Anson alive?'

Surprised by the question, Mitch said only, 'Yes.'

Amused, the caller said, 'The simple answer tells me so much.'

'What does it tell you?'

'He underestimated you.'

'You're reading too much into one word. Here's the cell number.'

After Mitch read the number and then repeated it, the man on the phone said, 'We want a smooth simple trade, Mitch. The best piece of business is one from which everyone walks away a winner.'

Mitch considered that this was the first time the man with the gentle voice had said *we* instead of *I*.

'Three o'clock,' the caller reminded him, and hung up.

# 50

Everything in the laundry room was white, everything except the red chair and Anson in it and the small yellow puddle.

Reeking, restless, rocking side to side on the chair, Anson was resigned to cooperation. 'Yeah, there's one of them talks like that. Name's Jimmy Null. He's a pro, but he's not a front guy. If he's on the phone with you, the others are dead.'

'Dead how?'

'Something went wrong, a disagreement about something, and he decided to bag the whole payoff.'

'So you think there's just one of them now?'

'That makes it harder for you, not easier.'

'Why harder?'

'Once he's wasted the others, his tendency will be to clean up totally behind himself.'

'Holly and me.'

'Only when he's got the money.' In his misery, Anson found a ghastly smile. 'You want to know about the money, bro? You want to know what I do for a living?'

Anson would be offering this information only if he believed that the knowledge would do his brother harm.

Mitch knew that the glint of vicious glee in Anson's eyes was an argument for continued ignorance, but his curiosity outweighed his caution.

Before either of them could speak, the telephone rang.

Mitch returned to the kitchen, briefly considered not answering, but worried that it might be Jimmy Null calling with additional instructions.

'Hello?'

'Anson?'

'He's not here.'

'Who's this?'

The voice didn't belong to Jimmy Null.

'I'm a friend of Anson's,' Mitch said.

Now that he'd taken the call, the best thing was to carry through with it as if all were normal here.

'When will he be back?' the caller asked.

'Tomorrow.'

'Should I try his cell?'

The voice teased Mitch's memory.

Picking up Anson's cell phone from the counter, Mitch said, 'He forgot to take it with him.'

'Can you give him a message?'

'Sure. Go ahead.'

'Tell him that Julian Campbell called.'

The glimmer of the gray eyes, the glitter of the gold Rolex.

'Anything else?' Mitch asked.

'That's everything. Although I do have one concern, friend of Anson.'

Mitch said nothing.

'Friend of Anson, are you there?'

'Yes.'

'I hope you're taking good care of my Chrysler Windsor. I love that car. See you later.'

# 51

Mitch located the kitchen drawer in which Anson kept two boxes of plastic trash-can liners. He chose the smaller of the sizes, a white thirteen-gallon bag.

He put the blocks of cash and the envelope of bearer bonds in the bag. He twisted the top but didn't tie a knot.

At this hour, in the usual traffic, Rancho Santa Fe was as much as two hours from Corona del Mar. Even if Campbell had associates at work here in Orange County, they wouldn't arrive immediately.

When Mitch returned to the laundry room, Anson said, 'Who called?'

'He was selling something.'

Sea-green and bloodshot, Anson's eyes were oceans murky with shark's work. 'It didn't sound like sales.'

'You were going to tell me what you do for a living.'

Malicious glee swam into Anson's eyes again. He wanted to share his triumph less out of pride than because somehow it was knowledge that would wound Mitch.

'Imagine you send data to a customer over the Internet, and on receipt it appears to be innocent material — say photos and a text history of Ireland.'

'Appears to be.'

'It's not like encrypted data, which is meaningless if you don't have the code. Instead it appears clear, unremarkable. But when you process it with a special software, the photos and text combine and re-form into completely different material, into *the hidden truth*.'

'What is the truth?'

'Wait. First . . . your customer downloads the software and never has a hard copy. If police search his computer and try to copy or analyze the operative software, the program self-destructs beyond reconstitution. Likewise documents stored on the computer in either original or converted form.'

Having striven to keep his computer knowledge to the minimum that the modern world would allow, Mitch wasn't sure that he saw the most useful applications of this, but one occurred to him.

'So terrorists could communicate over the Internet, and anyone sampling their transmissions would find them sharing only a history of Ireland.'

'Or France or Tahiti, or long analyses of John Wayne's films. No sinister material, no obvious encryption to raise suspicion. But terrorists aren't a stable, profitable market.'

'Who is?'

'There are many. But I want you to know especially about the work I did for Julian Campbell.'

'The entertainment entrepreneur,' Mitch said.

'It's true he owns casinos in several countries.

Partly he uses them to launder money from other activities.'

Mitch thought he knew the real Anson, a man far different from the one who had ridden south with him to Rancho Santa Fe. No more illusions. No more self-imposed blindness.

Yet in this essential moment, a chilling third iteration of the man revealed itself, almost as much a stranger to Mitch as had been the second Anson who first appeared in Campbell's library.

His face seemed to acquire a new tenant that slouched through the chambers of his skull and brought a darker light to those two familiar green windows.

Something about his body changed, as well. A more primitive hulk seemed to occupy the chair than he who'd sat there a minute previous, still a man but a man in whom the animal was more clearly visible.

This awareness came to Mitch before his brother had begun to reveal the business done with Campbell. He could not pretend that the effect was psychological, that Anson's revelation had transformed him in Mitch's eyes, for the change preceded the disclosure.

'One-half of one percent of men are pedophiles,' Anson said. 'In the U.S. — one and a half million. And millions of others worldwide.'

In this bright white room, Mitch felt on the threshold of a darkness, a terrible gate opening before him, and no turning back.

'Pedophiles are eager consumers of child pornography,' Anson continued. 'Though they might be buying it through a police sting operation that will destroy them, they risk everything to get it.'

Who did Hitler's work, Stalin's, Mao Tse-tung's? Neighbors did the work, friends, mothers and fathers did the work, and brothers.

'If the stuff comes in the form of dull text about the history of British theater and converts into exciting pictures and even video, if they can get their need filled safely, their appetite becomes insatiable.'

Mitch had left the pistol on the kitchen table. Perhaps he had unconsciously suspected some outrage like this and had not trusted himself with the weapon.

'Campbell has two hundred thousand customers. In two years, he expects a million worldwide, and revenues of five billion dollars.'

Mitch remembered the scrambled eggs and toast he had made in this creature's kitchen, and his stomach curdled at the thought of having eaten off plates, with utensils, that those hands had touched.

'Profit on gross sales is sixty percent. The adult performers do it for the fun. The young stars aren't paid. What do they need with money at their age? And I've got a little piece of Julian's business. I told you I have eight million, but it's three times that much.'

The laundry room was intolerably crowded. Mitch sensed that in addition to him and his brother, unseen legions were attendant.

'Bro, I just wanted you to understand how filthy the money is that's going to buy Holly. The rest of your life, when you kiss her, touch her, you're going to think about the source of all that dirty, dirty money.'

Chained helpless to the chair, sitting in urine, soaked in the fear sweat that earlier the darkness had wrung from him, Anson raised his head defiantly and thrust out his chest, and his eyes shone with triumph, as though having done what he had done, having facilitated Campbell's vile enterprise, was payment enough, that having had the opportunity to serve the appetite of the depraved at the expense of the innocent was all the reward he would need to sustain him through his current humiliation and through the personal ruination to come.

Some might call this madness, but Mitch knew its real name.

'I'm leaving,' he announced, for there was nothing else to be said that would matter.

'Taser me,' Anson demanded, as if to assert that Mitch did not have the power to hurt him in any lasting way.

'The deal we made?' Mitch said. 'Screw it.'

He switched out the lights and pulled shut the door. Because there are forces against which it is wise to take extra — and even irrational — precautions, he wedged the door shut with a chair. He might have nailed it shut, as well, if he'd had time.

He wondered if he would ever feel clean again.

A fit of the shakes took him. He felt as if he would be sick.

At the sink, he splashed cold water in his face.

The doorbell rang.

# 52

The chimes played a few bars of 'Ode to Joy.'

Only minutes had passed since Julian Campbell terminated their phone call. Five billion a year in revenues was a treasure that he would do anything to protect, but he couldn't have gotten a fresh pair of gunmen to Anson's place this quickly.

Mitch cranked off the water at the sink and, face dripping, tried to think if there was any reason he should risk checking on the identity of the visitor through a living-room window. His imagination failed him.

Time to get out of here.

He grabbed the trash bag that held the ransom and plucked the pistol off the table. He headed for the back door.

The Taser. He had left it on a counter by the ovens. He returned for it.

Again the unknown visitor rang the bell.

'Who's that?' Anson asked from the laundry room.

'The postman. Now shut up.'

Nearing the back door once more, Mitch remembered his brother's cell phone. It had been on the table beside the ransom, yet he had grabbed the bag and left the phone.

Julian Campbell's call, Anson's hideous revelations, and the doorbell, coming one on the heels of the other, had rocked him off balance.

After retrieving the cell phone, Mitch turned in a circle, surveying the kitchen. As far as he could tell, he had forgotten nothing else.

He turned off the lights, stepped out of the house, and locked the door behind him.

The inexhaustible wind played chase-and-hide with itself among the ferns and bamboo. Leathery, wind-seared banyan leaves, blown in from another property, scrabbled this way and that across the patio, scratching at the bricks.

Mitch went to the first of the two garages, entering by the courtyard door. Here his Honda waited, and John Knox ripened in the back of the Buick Super Woody Wagon.

He'd had a vague plan for hanging Knox's death around Anson's neck at the same time that he extricated himself from the setup for Daniel's and Kathy's murders. But Campbell's looming reentry into the situation left him feeling that he was roller-skating on ice, and the vague plan was now no plan at all.

None of that mattered at the moment anyway. When Holly was safe, John Knox and the bodies in the learning room and Anson handcuffed to the chair would matter again, and matter big-time, but now they were incidental to the main problem.

More than two and a half hours remained before he could swap the money for Holly. He opened the trunk of the Honda and tucked the bag into the wheel well.

In the front seat of the Woody, he found a garage-door remote. He clipped it to the Honda's sun visor, so he could close the roll-up door from the alleyway.

He put the pistol and the Taser in the storage pocket in the driver's door. Sitting behind the steering wheel, he could look down and see the weapons, and they were easier to reach than they would have been under the seat.

Triggering the remote control, he watched in the rearview mirror as the big door rolled up.

Backing out of the garage, he glanced to his right, saw the alleyway was clear — and stamped on the brakes in surprise as someone rapped on the driver's-door window. Snapping his head to the left, he discovered that he was face-to-face with Detective Taggart.

# 53

Muffled by glass: 'Hello there, Mr. Rafferty.'

Mitch stared at the detective too long before putting down the car window. His surprise would have been expected; however, he must have looked shocked, fearful.

Warm wind tossed Taggart's sports coat and flapped the collar of his yellow-and-tan Hawaiian shirt as he leaned close to the window. 'Do you have time for me?'

'Well, I do have a doctor's appointment,' Mitch said.

'Good. I won't keep you too long. Should we talk in the garage, out of this wind?'

John Knox's body lay exposed in the back of the station wagon. The homicide detective might be drawn to it by a keen nose for the earliest odors of decomposition, or by admiration for the beautiful old Buick.

'Sit with me in the car,' Mitch said, and he put up the window as he finished backing out of the garage.

He remoted the big door and parked parallel to it, out of the center of the alley, as it rolled down.

Getting into the passenger's seat, Taggart said, 'Have you called an exterminator about those termites?'

'Not yet.'

'Don't put it off too long.'

'I won't.'

Mitch sat facing forward, staring at the alley, determined to glance at Taggart only from time to time, because he remembered the penetrating power of the cop's stare.

'If it's pesticides you're worried about, they don't have to use them anymore.'

'I know. They can freeze the creepers in the walls.'

'Better yet, they've got this highly condensed orange extract that kills them on contact. All natural, and the house smells great.'

'Oranges. I'll have to look into that.'

'I guess you've been too busy to think about termites.'

An innocent man might wonder what this was about and might be impatient to get on with his day, so Mitch risked asking, 'Why are you here, Lieutenant?'

'I came to see your brother, but he didn't answer the door.'

'He's away until tomorrow.'

'Where's he gone?'

'Vegas.'

'Do you know his hotel?'

'He didn't say.'

'Didn't you hear the doorbell?' Taggart asked.

'I must have left before it rang. I had a few things to do in the garage.'

'Looking after the place for your brother while he's away?'

'That's right. Why do you want to talk to him?'

The detective drew up one leg and turned sideways in his seat, facing Mitch directly, as though to compel more eye contact. 'Your brother's phone numbers were in Jason Osteen's address book.'

Glad to have something truthful to say, Mitch reported: 'They met when Jason and I were roommates.'

'You didn't stay in touch with Jason, but your brother did?'

'I don't know. Maybe. They got along well.'

During the night and the morning, all the loose leaves and the litter and the dust had been blown to the sea. Now the wind carried no debris to suggest its form. As invisible as shock waves, massive slabs of crystalline air slammed along the alleyway, rocking the Honda.

Taggart said, 'Jason was hooked up with this girl named Leelee Morheim. You know her?'

'No.'

'Leelee says Jason hated your brother. Says your brother cheated Jason in some deal.'

'What deal?'

'Leelee doesn't know. But one thing's pretty clear about Jason — he didn't do honest work.'

That statement required Mitch to meet the detective's eyes and to frown with convincing puzzlement. 'Are you saying Anson was involved in something illegal?'

'Do you think that's possible?'

'He's got a Ph.D. in linguistics, and he's a computer geek.'

'I knew a professor of physics who murdered his wife, and a minister who murdered a child.'

Considering recent events, Mitch no longer

believed that the detective might be one of the kidnappers.

*If you had spilled your guts to him, Mitch, Holly would be dead now.*

Neither did he any longer worry that the kidnappers were keeping him under surveillance or were monitoring his conversations. The Honda might be fitted out with a transponder that allowed it to be tracked easily, but that was of no concern anymore, either.

If Anson was right, Jimmy Null — he of the gentle voice, with concern that Mitch should remain *hopeful* — had killed his partners. He was the whole show now. Here in the final hours of the operation, Null would be focused not on Mitch but on preparations to trade his hostage for the ransom.

This did not mean that Mitch could turn to Taggart for help. John Knox, laid out in the Woody Wagon as if it were a hearse, thrice dead of a broken neck and a crushed esophagus and a gunshot wound, would require some explaining. No homicide detective would be quickly convinced that Knox had perished in an accidental fall.

Daniel and Kathy would be no more easily explained than Knox.

When Anson was discovered in such miserable condition in the laundry room, he would appear to be a victim, not a victimizer. Given his talent for deception, he would play innocent with conviction, to the confusion of the authorities.

Only two and a half hours remained before the hostage swap. Mitch had little confidence that the police, as bureaucratic as any arm of the government, would be able to process what had happened thus far and do the right thing for Holly.

Besides, John Knox had died in one local jurisdiction, Daniel and Kathy in another, and Jason Osteen in a third. Those were three separate sets of bureaucracies.

Because this was a kidnapping, the FBI would most likely also have to be involved.

The moment Mitch revealed what had happened and asked for help, his freedom of movement would be curtailed. The responsibility for Holly's survival would devolve from him to strangers.

Dread filled him at the thought of having to sit helplessly as the minutes ticked away and the authorities, even if well meaning, tried to get their minds around the current situation and the events that had led to it.

Taggart said, 'How is Mrs. Rafferty?'

Mitch felt known to the bone, as if the detective had already untied many of the knots in the case and used that rope to snare him.

Reacting to Mitch's nonplussed expression, Taggart said, 'Did she get some relief from her migraine?'

'Oh. Yeah.' Mitch almost could not conceal his relief that the source of Taggart's interest in Holly was the mythical migraine. 'She's feeling better.'

'Not entirely well, though? Aspirin really isn't the ideal treatment for a migraine.'

Mitch sensed that a trap had been laid before

him, but he could not tell its nature — bear, snare, or deadfall — and he didn't know how to avoid it. 'Well, aspirin is what she's comfortable with.'

'But now she's missed a second day of work,' Taggart said.

The detective could have learned Holly's place of employment from Iggy Barnes. His knowledge didn't surprise Mitch, but that he had followed up on the migraine-headache story was alarming.

'Nancy Farasand says it's unusual for Mrs. Rafferty to take a sick day.'

Nancy Farasand was another secretary at the Realtor's office where Holly was employed. Mitch himself had spoken to her the previous afternoon.

'Do you know Ms. Farasand, Mitch?'

'Yes.'

'She strikes me as a very efficient person. She likes your wife very much, thinks very highly of her.'

'Holly likes Nancy, too.'

'And Ms. Farasand says it's not at all like your wife to fail to report in when she's going to miss work.'

This morning Mitch should have called in sick for Holly. He had forgotten.

He'd also forgotten to phone Iggy to cancel the day's schedule.

Having triumphed over two professional killers, he had been tripped up by inattention to a mundane task or two.

'Yesterday,' Detective Taggart said, 'you told

314

me that when you saw Jason Osteen shot, you were on the phone with your wife.'

The car had gotten stuffy. Mitch wanted to open the window to the wind.

Lieutenant Taggart was approximately Mitch's size, but now he seemed to be larger than Anson. Mitch felt crowded, in a corner.

'Is that still what you remember, Mitch, that you were on the phone with your wife?'

In fact, he had been on the phone with the kidnapper. What had seemed a safe and easy lie at the time might now be a noose into which he was being invited to place his neck, but he could see no way to abandon this falsehood without having a better one to use in its place.

'Yeah. I was on the phone with Holly.'

'You said she called to tell you that she was leaving work early because of a migraine.'

'That's right.'

'So you were on the phone with her when Osteen was shot.'

'Yes.'

'That was at eleven forty-three A.M. You said it was eleven forty-three.'

'I checked my watch right after the shot.'

'But Nancy Farasand tells me that Mrs. Rafferty called in sick *early* yesterday, that she wasn't in the office at all.'

Mitch did not reply. He could feel the hammer coming down.

'And Ms. Farasand says that you called her between twelve-fifteen and twelve-thirty yesterday afternoon.'

The interior of the Honda felt like a tighter

space than the trunk of the Chrysler Windsor.

Taggart said, 'You were still at the crime scene at that time, waiting for me to ask a series of follow-up questions. Your helper, Mr. Barnes, continued planting flowers. Do you remember?'

When the detective waited, Mitch said, 'Do I remember what?'

'Being at the crime scene,' Taggart said drily.

'Sure. Of course.'

'Ms. Farasand says that when you called her between twelve-fifteen and twelve-thirty, you asked to speak to your wife.'

'She's very efficient.'

'What I can't understand,' Taggart said, 'is why you would call the Realtor's office and ask to speak to your wife as much as forty-five minutes after, according to your own testimony, your wife had already called *you* to say that she was leaving there with a terrible migraine.'

Great clear turbulent tides of air drowned the alleyway.

As Mitch lowered his gaze to the dashboard clock, a helpless sinking of the heart overcame him.

'Mitch?'

'Yeah.'

'Look at me.'

Reluctantly, he met the detective's gaze.

Those hawkshaw eyes didn't pierce Mitch now, didn't drill at him as they had before. Instead, worse, they were sympathetic and invited confidence, encouraged trust.

Taggart said, 'Mitch . . . where is your wife?'

316

# 54

Mitch remembered the alley as it had been the previous evening, flooded with the crimson light of sunset, and the ginger cat stalking shadow to shadow behind radium-green eyes, and how the cat had seemed to morph into a bird.

He had allowed himself hope then. The hope had been Anson, and the hope had been a lie.

Now the sky was hard and wind-polished and a frigid blue, as if it were a dome of ice that borrowed its color by reflection from the ocean not far to the west of here.

The ginger cat was gone, and the bird, and nothing living moved. The sharp light was a flensing knife that stripped the shadows to the lean.

'Where is your wife?' Taggart asked again.

The money was in the car trunk. The time and place of the swap were set. The clock was ticking down to the moment. He had come so far, endured so much, gotten so close.

He had discovered Evil with an uppercase *E*, but he had also come to see something better in the world than he had seen before, something pure and true. He perceived mysterious meaning where he had previously seen only the green machine.

If things happened for a purpose, then perhaps there was a purpose he must not ignore in this encounter with the persistent detective.

*For richer or poorer. In sickness and in health. To love, honor, and cherish. Until death us do part.*

The vows were his. He had made them. Nobody else had made them to Holly. Only he had made them to her. He was the husband.

No one else would be so quick to kill for her, to die for her. To cherish means to *hold* dear and to *treat* as dear. To cherish means to do all you can for the welfare and the happiness of the one you cherish, to support and to comfort and to *protect her.*

Perhaps the purpose of bringing him together here with Taggart was to warn him that he had reached the limits of his ability to protect Holly without backup, to encourage him to realize that he could not go any further alone.

'Mitch, where is your wife?'

'What do you think of me?'

'In what sense?' Taggart asked.

'In every sense. What's your take on me?'

'People seem to think you're a stand-up guy.'

'I asked what *you* think.'

'I haven't known you until this. But inside you're all steel springs and ticking clocks.'

'I wasn't always.'

'No one could be. You'd blow up in a week. And you've changed.'

'You've only known me one day.'

'And you've changed.'

'I'm not a bad man. I guess all bad men say that.'

'Not so directly.'

In the sky, perhaps high enough to be above

318

the wind, miles too high to cast a shadow on the alley, a sun-silvered jet caught his eye as it sailed north. The world seemed shrunken now to this car, to this moment of peril, but the world was not shrunken, and the possible routes between any place and any other place were nearly infinite.

'Before I tell you where Holly is, I want a promise.'

'I'm just a cop. I can't make plea bargains.'

'So you think I've hurt her.'

'No. I'm just being level with you.'

'The thing is . . . we don't have much time. The promise I want is, when you hear the essence of it, you'll act fast, and not waste time picking at details.'

'The devil's in the details, Mitch.'

'When you hear this, you'll know where the devil is. But with so little time, I don't want to screw with police bureaucracies.'

'I'm one cop. All I can promise is — I'll do my best for you.'

Mitch took a deep breath. He blew it out. He said, 'Holly has been kidnapped. She's being held for ransom.'

Taggart stared at him. 'Am I missing something?'

'They want two million dollars or they'll kill her.'

'You're a gardener.'

'Don't I know.'

'Where would you get two million bucks?'

'They said I'd find a way. Then they shot Jason Osteen to impress on me how serious they are. I thought he was just a guy walking a dog, thought they shot some passerby to make a point.'

The detective's eyes were too sharp to read. His gaze filleted.

'Jason thought they were going to shoot the dog. So they scared obedience into me and at the same time cut the eventual split from five ways to four.'

'Go on,' Taggart said.

'Once I got home and saw the scene they staged for me there, once they had me in knots, they sent me to my brother for the money.'

'For real? He's got that much?'

'Anson once pulled some criminal operation with Jason Osteen, John Knox, Jimmy Null, and two others whose names I've never heard.'

'What was the operation?'

'I don't know. I wasn't part of it. I didn't know Anson was into this crap. And even if I did know what the operation was, it's one of the details you don't need now.'

'All right.'

'The essence is . . . Anson cheated them on the split, and they only found out what the real take was a lot later.'

'Why snatch your wife?' Taggart asked. 'Why not go after *him*?'

'He's untouchable. He's too valuable to some very important and very hard people. So they went after him through his little brother. Me. They figured he wouldn't want to see me lose my wife.'

Mitch thought he had made a flat statement, but Taggart saw the hidden hills in it. 'He

320

wouldn't give you the money.'

'Worse. He turned me over to some people.'

'Some people?'

'To be killed.'

'Your brother did?'

'My brother.'

'Why didn't they kill you?'

Mitch maintained eye contact. Everything was on the line now, and he could not hold back too much and expect cooperation. He said, 'Some things went wrong for them.'

'Sweet Jesus, Mitch.'

'So I came back to see my brother.'

'Must've been some reunion.'

'No champagne, but he had second thoughts about helping me.'

'He gave you the money?'

'He did.'

'Where is your brother now?'

'Alive but restrained. The swap is at three o'clock, and I've got reason to believe one of the kidnappers popped the others. Jimmy Null. Now it's just him holding Holly.'

'How much have you left out?'

'Most of it,' Mitch said truthfully.

The detective stared through the windshield at the alley.

From a coat pocket, he withdrew a roll of hard-caramel candies. He peeled the end of the roll, extracted a candy. He held the sweet circlet between his teeth while he folded shut the roll. As he returned the roll to his pocket, his tongue took the caramel from between his teeth. This procedure had the quality of a ritual.

'So?' Mitch said. 'You believe me?'

'I've got a bullshit detector even bigger than my prostate,' said Taggart. 'And it isn't ringing.'

Mitch didn't know whether to be relieved or not.

If he went alone to ransom Holly, and if they were both killed, at least he would not have to live with the knowledge that he had failed her.

If the authorities took it out of his hands, however, and if then Holly was killed but he lived, the responsibility would be a burden of intolerable weight.

He had to acknowledge that no possible scenario would put him in control, that inevitably fate was his partner in this. He must do what seemed right for Holly, and hope that what *seemed* right turned out to *be* right.

'Now what?' he asked.

'Mitch, kidnapping is a federal offense. We have to notify the FBI.'

'I'm afraid of the complication.'

'They're good. Nobody's more experienced with this kind of crime. Anyway, because we have only two hours, they won't be able to get a specialty team in place. They'll probably want us to take the lead.'

'How should I feel about that?'

'We're good. Our SWAT's first-rate. We have an experienced hostage negotiator.'

'So many people,' Mitch worried.

'I'll be running this. You think I'm trigger-happy?'

'No.'

'You don't think I'm a dog for details?' Taggart asked.

'I think maybe you're best of show.'

The detective grinned. 'Okay. So we'll get your wife back.'

Then he reached across the console and plucked the car key from the ignition.

Startled, Mitch said, 'Why'd you do that?'

'I don't want you having second thoughts, bolting off on your own, after all. That isn't what's best for her, Mitch.'

'I've made the decision. I need your help. You can trust me with the keys.'

'In a little while. I'm only looking out for you here, for you and Holly. I've got a wife I love, too, and two daughters — I told you about the daughters — so I know where you are right now, in your head. I know where you are. Trust me.'

The keys disappeared into a jacket pocket. From another pocket, the detective withdrew a cell phone.

As he switched on the phone, Taggart crunched what remained of the circlet of candy. A caramel aroma sweetened the air.

Mitch watched the detective speed-dial a number. A part of him felt that with the contact of that finger to that button, not only a call had been placed but also Holly's fate had been sealed.

As Taggart spoke police code to a dispatcher and gave Anson's address, Mitch looked for another sun-silvered jet high above. The sky was empty.

Terminating the call, pocketing the phone,

Taggart said, 'So your brother's back there in the house?'

Mitch could no longer pretend Anson was in Vegas. 'Yeah.'

'Where?'

'In the laundry room.'

'Let's go talk to him.'

'Why?'

'He pulled some sort of job with this Jimmy Null, right?'

'Yeah.'

'So he must know him well. If we're going to get Holly out of Null's hands smooth and easy, nice and safe, we need to know every damn thing about him we can learn.'

When Taggart opened the passenger's door to get out, a clear wind blasted into the Honda, bringing neither dust nor litter, but the promise of chaos.

For better or worse, the situation was spinning out of Mitch's control. He didn't think it would be for the better.

Taggart slammed the passenger's door, but Mitch sat behind the wheel for a moment, his thoughts spinning, tumbling, his mind busy, and not just his mind, and then he got out into the whipping wind.

# 55

The polished sky and the sharp light and the flaying wind, and from the overhead power lines, a keening like an animal in mourning.

Mitch led the detective to the painted wooden service gate. The wind tore it from his hand as he slipped the latch, and banged it against the garage wall.

Undoubtedly, Julian Campbell was sending men here, but they were no threat now, because they would not arrive before the police. The police were only minutes away.

Following the narrow brick walkway, which was sheltered from the worst of the wind, Mitch came upon a collection of dead beetles. Two were as big as quarters, one the diameter of a dime. On the underside they were yellow with stiff black legs. They were on their backs, balanced on curved shells, and a gentle eddy of wind spun them in slow circles.

Cuffed to a chair, sitting in urine, Anson would make a pathetic figure, and he would play the victim convincingly, with the skill of a cunning sociopath.

Even though Taggart had implied that he heard truth in Mitch's story, he might wonder at the hard treatment Anson had received. With no experience of Anson, having heard only the *condensed* version of events, the detective might think the treatment had been

325

worse than hard, had been cruel.

Crossing the courtyard, where the wind badgered again, Mitch was aware of the detective close behind him. Although they were in the open, he felt crowded, pinched by claustrophobia.

He could hear Anson's voice in his mind: *He told me that he killed our mom and dad. He stabbed them with garden tools. He said he'd come back to kill me, too.*

At the back door, Mitch's hands were shaking so much that he had trouble fitting the key in the lock.

*He killed Holly, Detective Taggart. He made up a story about her being kidnapped, and he came to me for money, but then he admitted killing her.*

Taggart knew that Jason Osteen hadn't earned an honest living. He knew from Leelee Morheim that Jason had done a job with Anson and had been cheated. So he knew Anson was bent.

Nevertheless, when Anson told a story conflicting with Mitch's, Taggart would consider it. Cops were always presented with competing stories. Surely the truth most often lay somewhere between them.

Finding the truth will take time, and time is a rat gnawing at Mitch's nerves. Time is a trapdoor under Holly, and time is a noose tightening around her neck.

The key found the keyway. The deadbolt clacked open.

Standing on the threshold, Mitch switched on the lights. At once he saw on the floor a long blood smear that hadn't concerned him before, but which alarmed him now.

When Anson had been clubbed alongside the head, his ear had torn. As he'd been dragged to the laundry room, he'd left a trail.

The wound had been minor. The smears on the floor suggested something worse than a bleeding ear.

By such misleading evidence were doubts raised and suspicions sharpened.

Trapdoor, noose, and gnawing rat, time sprung a coiled spring in Mitch, and as he entered the kitchen, he slipped open a button on his shirt, reached inside, and withdrew the Taser that was tucked under his belt, against his abdomen. As he'd delayed getting out of the Honda, he had retrieved the weapon from the storage pocket in the driver's door.

'The laundry room is this way,' Mitch said, leading Taggart a few steps forward before turning suddenly with the Taser.

The detective wasn't following as close as Mitch had thought. He was a prudent two steps back.

Some Tasers fire darts trailing wires, which deliver a disabling shock from a moderate distance. Others require that the business end be thrust against the target, resulting in an intimacy equal to that of an assault with a knife.

This was the second Taser model, and Mitch had to get in close, get in fast.

As Mitch thrust with his right arm, Taggart blocked with his left. The Taser was almost knocked out of Mitch's hand.

Retreating, the detective reached cross-body, under his sports jacket, with his right hand, surely going for a weapon in a shoulder holster.

Taggart backed into a counter, Mitch feinted left, thrust right, and here came the gun hand from under the jacket. Mitch wanted bare skin, didn't want to risk fabric providing partial insulation against the shock, and he got the detective in the throat.

Eyes rolling back in his head, jaw sagging, Taggart fired one round, his knees folded, and he dropped.

The shot seemed unusually loud. The shot shook the room.

# 56

Mitch was not wounded, but he thought about John Knox self-shot in the fall from the garage loft, and he knelt worriedly beside the detective.

On the floor at Taggart's side lay his pistol. Mitch shoved it out of reach.

Taggart shuddered as if chilled to the marrow, his hands clawed at the floor tiles, and bubbles of spit sputtered on his lips.

Faint, thin, pungent, a ribbon of smoke unraveled from Taggart's sports jacket. The bullet had burned a hole through it.

Mitch pulled back the jacket, looking for a wound. He didn't find one.

The relief he felt did not much buoy him. He was still guilty of assaulting a police officer.

This was the first time he had hurt an innocent person. Remorse, he found, actually had a taste: a bitterness rising at the back of the throat.

Pawing at Mitch's arm, the detective could not close his hand into a grip. He tried to say something, but his throat must be tight, his tongue thick, his lips numb.

Mitch wanted to avoid having to Taser him a second time. He said, 'I'm sorry,' and set to work.

The car key had vanished into Taggart's jacket. Mitch found it in the second pocket he searched.

In the laundry room, having digested the

gunshot and having come to a conclusion about what it might mean, Anson began shouting. Mitch ignored him.

Taking Taggart by the feet, Mitch dragged him out of the house, onto the brick patio. He left the detective's pistol in the kitchen.

As he pulled the back door shut, he heard the doorbell ring inside. The police were at the front of the house.

As Mitch took time to lock the door to delay their exposure to Anson and his lies, he said to Taggart, 'I love her too much to trust anyone else with this. I'm sorry.'

He sprinted across the courtyard, along the side of the garage, and through the open back gate into the windswept alleyway.

When no one answered the doorbell, the cops would come around the side of the house, into the courtyard, and find Taggart on the bricks. They would be in the alley seconds later.

He threw the Taser on the passenger's seat as he got behind the wheel. Key, switch, the roar of the engine.

In the storage pocket of the door was the pistol that belonged to one of Campbell's hired killers. Seven rounds remained in the magazine.

He wasn't going to pull a gun on the police. His only option was to get the hell out of there.

He drove east, fully expecting that a squad car would suddenly hove across the end of the alleyway, thwarting him.

Panic is fear expressed by numbers of people simultaneously, by an audience or a mob. But

Mitch had enough fear for a crowd, and *panic* seized him.

At the end of the alleyway, he turned right into the street. At the next intersection, he turned left, heading east again.

This area of Corona del Mar, itself a part of Newport Beach, was called the Village. A grid of streets, it could be sealed off with perhaps as few as three roadblocks.

He needed to get beyond those choke points. Fast.

In Julian Campbell's library, in the trunk of the Chrysler, and in that trunk a second time, he'd known fear, but nothing as intense as this. Then he had been afraid for himself; now he was afraid for Holly.

The worst that could happen to him was that he would be captured or shot by the police. He had weighed the costs of his options and had chosen the best game. Now he didn't care what happened to him except to the extent that if anything happened to him, Holly would stand alone.

In the Village, some of the streets were narrow. Mitch was on one of them. Vehicles were parked on both sides. With too much speed, he risked sheering a door off if somebody opened one.

Taggart could describe the Honda. In minutes, they would have the license-plate number from the Department of Motor Vehicles. He could not afford to rack up body damage that would make the car even more identifiable.

He arrived at a traffic signal at Pacific Coast Highway. Red.

Heavy traffic surged north and south on the divided highway. He couldn't jump the light and weave into the flow without precipitating a chain reaction of collisions, with himself at the center of the ultimate snarl.

He glanced at the rearview mirror. Some kind of paneled truck or muscle van approached, still a block away. The roof appeared to be outfitted with an array of emergency beacons, like those on a police vehicle.

This was a street lined with mature trees. The dappling shadows and piercework of light rippled in veils across the moving vehicle, making it difficult to identify.

Out on northbound lanes of the Pacific Coast Highway, a police car passed, parting the traffic before it with emergency beacons but not with a siren.

Behind the Honda, the worrisome vehicle cruised within half a block, at which point Mitch could read the word AMBULANCE on the brow above the windshield. They were in no hurry. They must be off duty or carrying the dead.

He exhaled a pent-up breath. The ambulance braked to a stop behind him, and his relief was short-lived when he wondered whether paramedics usually listened to a police scanner.

The traffic light changed to green. He crossed the southbound lanes and turned left, north on Coast Highway.

One bead of sweat chased another down the nape of his neck, under his collar, along the spillway of his spine.

He had traveled only a block on Coast

Highway when a siren shrilled behind him: this time, in the rearview mirror, a police car.

Only fools led cops on a chase. They had air resources as well as a lot of iron on the ground.

Defeated, Mitch steered toward the curb. As he vacated the lane, the squad car shot past him and away.

From the curb, Mitch watched until the cruiser left the highway two blocks ahead. It turned left into the north end of the Village.

Evidently Taggart hadn't yet sufficiently recovered his wits to give them a description of the Honda.

Mitch took a very deep breath. He took another. He wiped the back of his neck with one hand. He blotted his hands on his jeans.

He had assaulted a police officer.

Easing the Honda back into the northbound traffic, he wondered if he had lost his mind. He felt resolved, and perhaps reckless in a venturous sense, but not shortsighted. Of course, a lunatic could not recognize madness from the inside of his bubble.

# 57

After Holly extracts the nail from the plank, she turns it over and over in her stiff sore fingers, assessing whether or not it is as lethal as she imagined when it was sheathed in wood.

Straight, more than three but less than four inches long, with a thick shank, it qualifies as a spike, all right. The point is not as sharp as, say, the wicked point of a poultry skewer, but plenty sharp enough.

While the wind sings of violence, she spends time imagining the ways the spike might be employed against the creep. Her imagination is fertile enough to disturb her.

After quickly grossing herself out, she changes the subject from the uses of the spike to the places where it might be hidden. What value it has is the value of surprise.

Although the spike probably won't show if tucked in a pocket of her jeans, she worries that she'll not be able to extract it quickly in a crisis. When they had transported her from her house to this place, they had bound her wrists tightly with a scarf. If he does the same when he takes her away from here, she will not be able to pull her hands apart and, therefore, might not be able to get her fingers easily into a particular pocket.

Her belt offers no possibilities, but in the dark, by touch, she considers her sneakers. She can't carry the nail inside the shoe; it will rub and blister her foot, at the least. Maybe she can conceal it on the outside of the shoe.

She loosens the laces on her left sneaker, carefully tucks the nail between the tongue and one of the flaps, and reties the shoe.

When she gets to her feet and walks a circle around the ringbolt to which she is tethered, she quickly discovers that the rigid nail is an impediment to a smoothly flexed step. She can't avoid limping.

Finally she pulls up her sweater and secrets the nail in her bra. She isn't as extravagantly endowed as the average female mud wrestler, but Nature has been more than fair. To prevent the nail from slipping out between the cups, she presses the point through the elastic facing, thus pinning it in place.

She has armed herself.

With the task complete, her preparations seem pathetic.

Restless, she turns to the ringbolt, wondering if she can set herself free or at least augment her meager weaponry.

With her questing hands, she had earlier determined that the ringbolt is welded to a half-inch-thick steel plate that measures about eight inches on a side. The plate is held to the floor by what must be four countersunk screws.

She is unable to say with certainty that they are screws, for some liquid has been poured into the sink around each one and has formed a hard puddle. This denies her access to the slot in the head of each screw, if indeed they are screws.

Discouraged, she lies on her back on the air

335

mattress, her head raised on the pillow portion.

Earlier, she had slept fitfully. Her emotional exhaustion breeds physical fatigue, and she knows that she could sleep again. But she does not want to doze off.

She is afraid that she will wake only as he falls upon her.

She lies with her eyes open, though this darkness is deeper than the one behind her eyelids, and she listens to the wind, though there is no comfort in it.

A timeless time later, when she wakes, she is still in darkness absolute, but she knows she isn't alone. Some subtle scent alerts her or perhaps an intuitive sense of being encroached upon.

She sits up with a start, the air mattress squeaking under her, the chain rattling against the floor between manacle and ringbolt.

'It's only me,' he assures her.

Holly's eyes strain at the blackness because it seems that the gravity of his madness ought to condense the darkness around him into something yet darker, but he remains invisible.

'I was watching you sleep,' he says, 'then after a while, I was concerned that my flashlight would wake you.'

Judging his position by his voice is not as easy as she might have expected.

'This is nice,' he says, 'being with you in the numinous dark.'

To her right. No more than three feet away. Perhaps on his knees, perhaps standing.

'Are you afraid?' he asks.

'No,' she lies without hesitation.

'You would disappoint me if you were afraid. I believe you are arising into your full spirit, and one who is arising must be beyond fear.'

As he speaks, he seems to move behind her. She turns her head, listening intently.

'In El Valle, New Mexico, one night the snow came down as thick as ever it has anywhere.'

If she is correct, he has moved to her right side and stands over her, having made no sound that the wind failed to mask.

'The valley floor received six inches in four hours, and the land was eerie in the snowlight . . .'

Hairs quiver, flesh prickles on the back of her neck at the thought of him moving confidently in pitch-black conditions. He does not reveal himself even by eyeshine, as might a cat.

' . . . eerie in a way it is nowhere else in the world, the flats receding and the low hills rising as if they are just fields of mist and walls of fog, illusions of shapes and dimensions, reflections of reflections, and those reflections only reflections of a dream.'

The gentle voice is in front of her now, and Holly chooses to believe that it has not moved, that it has always been in front of her.

Startled from sleep, she should expect her senses to be at first unreliable. Such perfect darkness displaces sound, disorients.

He says, 'The storm was windless at ground level, but hard wind blew at higher elevations, because when the snow abated, most of the clouds were quickly torn into rags and were flung away. Between the remaining clouds, the sky was black, festooned with ornate necklaces of stars.'

She can feel the nail between her breasts, warmed by her body heat, and tries to take comfort from it.

'The glassmaker had fireworks left over from the past July, and the woman who dreamed of dead horses offered to help him set them up and set them off.'

His stories always lead somewhere, although Holly has learned to dread their destinations.

'There were star shells, Catherine wheels, fizgigs, girandoles, twice-changing chrysanthemums, and golden palm trees . . . '

His voice grows softer, and he is close now. He may be leaning toward her, his face but a foot from her face.

'Red and green and sapphire-blue and gold bursts brightened the black sky, but they were also colorful and diffusely reflected on the fields of snow, soft swaths of pulsing color on the fields of snow.'

As the killer talks, Holly has the feeling that he will kiss her here in the darkness. What will his reaction be when inevitably she recoils in revulsion?

'Some last snow was falling, a few late flakes as big as silver dollars, descending in wide lazy gyres. They caught the color, too.'

She leans back and turns her head aside in fearful anticipation of the kiss. Then she thinks it might come not on her lips but on the nape of her neck.

'Shimmering with red and blue and gold fire, the flakes slowly glimmered to the ground, as if something magical were aflame high in the night, some glorious palace burning on the other side of Heaven, shedding jewel-bright embers.'

He pauses, clearly expecting a response.

As long as he is kept talking, he will not kiss.

Holly says, 'It sounds so magnificent, so beautiful. I wish I'd been there.'

'*I* wish you'd been there,' he agrees.

Realizing that what she's said might be taken as an invitation, she hurries to entreat him: 'There must be more. What else happened in El Valle that night? Tell me more.'

'The woman who dreamed of dead horses had a friend who claimed to be a countess from some eastern European country. Have you ever known a countess?'

'No.'

'The countess had a problem with depression. She balanced it by taking ecstasy. She took too much ecstasy and walked into that field of snow transfigured by fireworks. Happier than she had ever been in her life, she killed herself.'

Another pause requires a response, and Holly can think of nothing she dares to say except, 'How sad.'

'I *knew* you would see. Yes, sad. Sad and stupid. El Valle is a portal that makes possible a journey to great change. On that night, and in *that special moment*, transcendence was offered to everyone present. Yet there are always some who cannot see.'

'The countess.'

'Yes. The countess.'

The pressurized darkness seems to brew itself into an ever blacker reduction.

She feels his warm breath upon her brow, upon her eyes. It has no scent. And then it is gone.

Maybe she didn't feel his breath, after all, only a draft.

She wishes to believe it was a draft, and she thinks of clean things like her husband and the baby, and the bright sun.

He says, 'Do you believe in signs, Holly Rafferty?'

'Yes.'

'Omens. Portents. Harbingers, oracle owls, storm petrels, black cats and broken mirrors, mysterious lights in the sky. Have you ever seen a sign, Holly Rafferty?'

'I don't think so.'

'Do you hope to see a sign?'

She knows what he wants her to say, and she is quick to say it. 'Yes. I hope to see one.'

Upon her left cheek, she feels warm breath, and then upon her lips.

If this is him — and in her heart she knows there is no *if* — he remains undifferentiated from the gloom although only inches separate them.

The darkness of the room calls forth a darkness in her mind. She imagines him kneeling naked before her, his pale body decorated by arcane symbols painted with the blood of those he killed.

Struggling to keep her quickening fear from her voice, she says, 'You've seen many signs, haven't you?'

The breath, the breath, the breath upon her lips, but not the kiss, and then not the breath, either, as he withdraws and says, 'I've seen scores. I have the eye for them.'

'Please tell me about one.'

He is silent. His silence is a sharp and looming weight, a sword above her head.

Perhaps he has begun to wonder if she is talking to forestall the kiss.

If at all possible, she must avoid offending him. As important as it is to leave this place without being violated, it is likewise important to leave this place without disabusing him of the strange dark romantic fantasy that appears to have him in its grip.

He seems to believe that she will eventually decide that she must go to Guadalupita, New Mexico, with him and that in Guadalupita she will 'be amazed.' As long as he continues in this belief, which she has so subtly tried to reinforce without raising suspicion, she might be able to find some advantage over him when it matters most, in the moment of her greatest crisis.

When his silence begins to seem ominously long, he says, 'This was just as summer became autumn that year, and everyone said the birds had left early for the south, and wolves were seen where they had not been in a decade.'

Wary in the dark, Holly sits very erect, with her arms crossed over her breasts.

'The sky had a hollow look. You felt like you could shatter it with a stone. Have you ever been to Eagle Nest, New Mexico?'

'No.'

'I was driving south from Eagle Nest, on a two-lane blacktop, at least twenty miles east of

341

Taos. These two girls were across the highway, hitchhiking north.'

Along the roof, the wind finds a new niche or protrusion from which to strike another voice for itself, and now it imitates the ululant cry of hunting coyotes.

'They were college age but not college girls. They were serious seekers, you could see, and confident in their good hiking boots and backpacks, with their walking sticks, and all their experience.'

He pauses, perhaps for drama, perhaps savoring the memory.

'I saw the sign and knew at once that it was a sign. Hovering above their heads, a blackbird, its wings spread wide, not flapping, the bird riding so effortlessly on a thermal, but moving precisely no faster or slower than the girls were walking.'

She regrets having elicited this story. She closes her eyes against the images that she fears he might describe.

'Only six feet above their heads and a foot or two behind them, the bird hovered, but the girls were unaware of it. They were unaware of it, and I knew what that meant.'

Holly fears the darkness around her too much to close her eyes to it. She opens them even though she can see nothing.

'Do you know what the sign of the bird meant, Holly Rafferty?'

'Death,' she says.

'Yes, exactly right. You *are* arising into full spirit. I saw the bird and believed that death was settling on the girls, that they were not long for this world.'

'And . . . were they?'

'Winter came early that year. Many snows followed one another, and the cold was very hard. The spring thaw extended into summer, and when the snow melted, their bodies were found in late June, dumped in a field near Arroyo Hondo, all the way around Wheeler Peak from where I'd seen them on the road. I recognized their pictures in the paper.'

Holly says a silent prayer for the families of the unknown girls.

'Who knows what happened to them?' he continues. 'They were found naked, so we can imagine some of what they endured. But though it seems to us a horrible death, and tragic because of their youth, there is always a possibility of enlightenment even in the worst of situations. If we're seekers, we learn from everything, and grow. Perhaps any death involves moments of illuminating beauty and the potential for transcendence.'

He switches on his flashlight and is sitting immediately before her, cross-legged on the floor.

Had the light surprised her earlier in their conversation, she might have flinched. Now she is not as easily surprised, nor is she likely to flinch from any light, so welcome is it.

He wears the ski mask in which are visible only his chewed-sore lips and his beryl-blue eyes. He is neither naked nor painted with the blood of those he killed.

'It's time to go,' he says. 'You will be ransomed for a million four hundred thousand, and when I

343

have the money, then the time will have come for decision.'

The dollar figure stuns her. It might be a lie.

Holly has lost all track of time, but she is confused and amazed by what his words imply. 'Is it already . . . midnight Wednesday?'

Within his knitted mask, he smiles. 'Only a few minutes before one o'clock Tuesday afternoon,' he says. 'Your persuasive husband has encouraged his brother to come through with the money quicker than ever seemed possible. This whole thing has moved so smoothly that it's obviously coasting on the wheels of destiny.'

Rising to his feet, he gestures for her to rise, as well, and she obeys.

Behind her back, he binds her wrists together with a blue silk scarf, as before.

Stepping in front of her again, he tenderly smoothes her hair back from her forehead, for some of it has fallen over her face. As he performs this grooming, with hands as cold as they are pale, he stares continuously into her eyes in a spirit of romantic challenge.

She dares not look away from him, and she closes her eyes only when he presses to them thick gauze pads that have been moistened to make them stick. He binds the pads in place with a longer length of silk, which he loops three times around her head and ties firmly at the back of her skull.

His hands brush her right ankle, and he unlocks the manacle, freeing her from the chain and the ringbolt.

He plays the flashlight over her blindfold, and

she sees dim light penetrate the gauze and silk. Evidently satisfied by the job he's done, he lowers the light.

'When we've reached the ransom drop,' he promises, 'the scarves will come off. They're only to incapacitate you during transport.'

Because he is not the one who hit her and pulled her hair to make her scream, she can sound credible when she says, 'You've never been cruel to me.'

He studies her in silence. She *assumes* that he studies her, for she feels naked, undressed by his stare.

The wind, the dark again, the hideous expectation all make her heart jump like a rabbit battering itself against the wire walls of a trap cage.

Holly feels his breath brush lightly across her lips, and she endures it.

After he exhales four times upon her, he whispers, 'At night in Guadalupita, the sky is so vast that the moon seems shrunken, small, and the stars you can see, horizon to horizon, number more than all the human deaths in history. Now we must go.'

He takes Holly by one arm, and she does not shrink from his repulsive touch, but moves with him across the room and through an open doorway.

Here are the steps again, up which they led her the previous day. He patiently guides her descent, but she cannot hold a railing and therefore places each foot tentatively.

From attic to second floor, to first floor, and

then into the garage, he encourages her: 'A landing now. Very good. Duck your head. And now to the left. Be careful here. And now a threshold.'

In the garage, she hears him open the door of a vehicle.

'This is the van that brought you here,' he says, and helps her through the rear entrance, into the cargo space. The carpeted floor smells as foul as she remembered it. 'Lie on your side.'

He exits, closes the door behind him. The signature metallic sound of a key in a lock eliminates any consideration that she might be able to let herself out somewhere en route.

The driver's door opens, and he gets in behind the wheel. 'This is a two-seat van. The seats are open to the cargo area, which is why you hear me so clearly. You do hear me clearly?'

'Yes.'

He closes his door. 'I can turn in my seat and see you. On our trip here, there were men to sit with you, to make sure that you behaved. I'm alone now. So . . . somewhere along the way, if we stop at a red light and you think a scream will be heard, I'll have to deal with you more harshly than I would like.'

'I won't scream.'

'Good. But please let me explain. On the passenger's seat beside me is a pistol fitted with a silencer. The instant that you begin to scream, I'll pick up the pistol, turn around in my seat, and shoot you dead. Whether you're dead or alive, I'll collect the ransom. You see the way it is?'

'Yes.'

'That sounded cold, didn't it?' he asks.

'I understand . . . your position.'

'Be honest now. It did sound cold.'

'Yes.'

'Consider this. I could have gagged you, but I didn't. I could have shoved a rubber ball in your pretty mouth and sealed your lips with duct tape. Couldn't I have done that easily?'

'Yes.'

'Why didn't I?'

'Because you know you can trust me,' she says.

'I *hope* that I can trust you. And because I'm a man of hope, who lives his life with hope in every hour, I did not gag you, Holly. A gag of the type I described is effective but extremely unpleasant. I didn't want an unpleasantness like that between us in case . . . in *hope* of Gaudalupita.'

Her mind works to deceive more smoothly than she would have thought possible one day ago.

In a voice not at all seductive but solemn with respect, she recites for him details that suggest he has indeed cast a spell over her: 'Guadalupita, Rodarte, Rio Lucio, Penasco, where your life was changed, and Chamisal, where it was also changed, Vallecito, Las Trampas, and Espanola, where your life will be changed again.'

He is silent for a moment. Then: 'I'm sorry for the discomfort, Holly. It will be over soon, and then transcendence . . . if you want it.'

# 58

The architecture of the gun shop had been inspired by dry-goods stores in countless Western movies. A flat railed roof, vertical-clapboard walls, a covered boardwalk the length of the long building, and a hitching post raised the expectation that at any moment John Wayne would walk out of the front door, dressed as he had been in *The Searchers*.

Feeling less like John Wayne than like any supporting character who gets shot in the second act, Mitch sat in the Honda, in the gun-shop parking lot, examining the pistol that he had brought back from Rancho Santa Fe.

Several things were engraved in the steel, if it was steel. Some were numbers and letters that meant nothing to him. Others provided useful information for a guy who knew squat about handguns.

Near the muzzle, in script, were the words *Super Tuned*. Farther back on the slide the word CHAMPION looked as if it had been laser-incised in block letters, and CAL .45 was directly under it.

Mitch preferred not to deliver the ransom with only seven rounds in the magazine. Now he knew that he needed to purchase .45-caliber ammunition.

Seven rounds were probably more than enough. Gunfights most likely dragged on only in movies. In real life, somebody fired the first shot, somebody responded, and within a total of four rounds, one of the somebodies was wounded or dead.

Buying more ammunition was not about fulfilling a genuine need, but a psychological one. He didn't care. Additional ammo would make him feel better prepared.

On the other side of the slide, he found the word SPRINGFIELD. He took this to be the maker.

The word CHAMPION most likely referred to the model of the gun. He had a Springfield Champion .45 pistol. That sounded more likely than a Champion Springfield .45 pistol.

He wanted to avoid drawing attention to himself when he went into the shop. He hoped to sound like he knew what he was talking about.

After ejecting the magazine from the pistol, he extracted a cartridge from the magazine. The casing identified it as .45 ACP, but he didn't know what the letters meant.

He returned the cartridge to the magazine and put the magazine in a pocket of his jeans. He slid the pistol under the driver's seat.

From the glove box, he retrieved John Knox's wallet. Using the dead man's money pricked his conscience, but he had no choice. His own wallet had been taken from him in Julian Campbell's library. He took the entire $585 and returned the wallet to the glove box.

He got out into the wind, locked the car, and went into the gun shop. The word *shop* seemed inadequate for such a large store. There were aisles and aisles of gun-related paraphernalia.

At the long cashier's counter, he got help from a large man with a walrus mustache. His name tag identified him as ROLAND.

'A Springfield Champion,' Roland said. 'That's a stainless-steel version of a Colt Commander, isn't it?'

Mitch had no clue if it was or not, but he suspected that Roland knew his stuff. 'That's right.'

'Beveled magazine well, throated barrel, a lowered and flared ejection port all come standard.'

'It's a sweet gun,' Mitch said, hoping people actually talked that way. 'I want three extra magazines. For target shooting.'

He added the last three words because it seemed that most people wouldn't have a use for spare magazines unless they were planning to knock over a bank or take potshots at people from a clock tower.

Roland appeared not in the least suspicious. 'Did you go for Springfield's whole Super Tuned package?'

Remembering the words engraved near the muzzle, Mitch said, 'Yes. The whole package.'

'Any further customization?'

'No,' Mitch guessed.

'You didn't bring the gun? I'd feel better if I could see it.'

Incorrectly, Mitch had thought if he carried a pistol into the store, he'd look like a shoplifter or a stickup artist or something.

'I've got this.' He put the magazine on the counter.

'I'd rather have the gun, but let's see if we can work with this.'

Five minutes later, Mitch had paid for three magazines and a box of one hundred .45 ACP cartridges.

Throughout the transaction, he had expected alarm bells to go off. He felt suspected, watched, and known for what he was. Clearly, his nerves didn't have the tensile strength required of a fugitive from the law.

As he was about to leave the shop, he looked through the glass door and saw a police cruiser in the parking lot, blocking his car. A cop stood at the driver's door, peering into the locked Honda.

# 59

On second look, Mitch realized that the driver's door of the cruiser wasn't emblazoned with the seal of a city but with the name — First Enforcement — and ornate logo of a private-security firm. The uniformed man at the Honda must be a security guard, not a police officer.

Nevertheless, the Honda would be of interest to him only if he knew an all-points bulletin had been put out for it. Evidently this guy *did* listen to a police scanner.

The guard left his car athwart the Honda and approached the gun shop. He appeared purposeful.

He had most likely stopped to do some personal business and had lucked onto the Honda. Now he was psyched up for a citizen's arrest and a taste of glory.

A real cop would have called for backup before coming into the store. Mitch supposed he should be grateful for getting even that much of a break.

The parking lot wrapped two sides of the freestanding building, and there were two entrances. Mitch backed away from this door and headed quickly for the other.

He left by the side exit and hurried to the front of the store. The security guard had gone inside.

Mitch was alone in the wind. Not for long. He

sprinted to the Honda.

The First Enforcement car trapped him. The back of the parking space featured a steel-pipe safety barrier atop a six-inch concrete curb because, from the lot, the land sloped steeply down six feet to a sidewalk.

No good. No way out. He would have to abandon the Honda.

He unlocked the driver's door and retrieved the Springfield Champion .45 from under the seat.

As he closed the car door, somebody coming out of the gun shop drew his attention. Not the security guard.

He popped the trunk and snatched the white plastic trash bag from the wheel well. He put the pistol and the gun-shop purchases with the money, twisted the neck of the bag, closed the trunk, and walked away.

After passing behind five parked vehicles, he stepped between two SUVs. He peered in each, hoping one of the drivers had left the keys in the ignition, but he wasn't lucky.

He walked briskly — did not run — diagonally across the blacktop, toward the side of the building from which he had recently exited.

As he reached the corner, his peripheral vision caught movement at the front door of the gun shop. When he glanced along the covered boardwalk, he glimpsed the security guard coming out of the store.

He did not think that the guard had seen him, and then he was out of sight, past the corner.

The side parking lot ended at a low concrete-block wall. He vaulted it, onto a property belonging to a fast-food franchise.

Cautioning himself not to run like a fugitive, he crossed the parking lot, passed a queue of vehicles waiting in line for takeout, the air redolent of exhaust fumes and greasy French fries, rounded the back of the restaurant, came to another low wall, vaulted it.

Ahead lay a small strip center with six or eight stores. He slowed down, looking in the windows as he passed, just a guy out on an errand, with one point four million to spend.

As he came to the end of the block, a squad car went by on the main boulevard, emergency beacons flashing red-blue, red-blue, red-blue, heading in the direction of the gun shop. And immediately behind it sped another one.

Mitch turned left on the small cross street, away from the boulevard. He picked up his pace again.

The commercial zone was only one lot wide, facing the boulevard. Behind lay a residential neighborhood.

In the first block were condos and apartment houses. After that he found single-family homes, most of them two stories, occasionally a bungalow.

The street trees were huge old podocarpuses that cast a lot of shade. Most lawns were green, trimmed, shrubs well kept. But every community has landscape slobs eager to exert their rights to be bad neighbors.

When the police didn't find him at the gun shop, they would search surrounding neighborhoods. In a few minutes, they could have half a dozen or more units cruising the area.

He had assaulted a police officer. They tended to put his kind at the top of their priority list.

Most of the vehicles parked on this residential street were SUVs. He slowed down, squinting through the passenger-door windows at the ignitions, hoping to spot a key.

When he glanced at his watch, he saw the time was 1:14. The exchange was set for 3:00, and now he didn't have wheels.

# 60

The ride lasts about fifteen minutes, and Holly, bound and blindfolded, is too busy scheming to consider a scream.

This time when her lunatic chauffeur stops, she hears him put the van in park and apply the hand brake. He gets out, leaving his door open.

In Rio Lucio, New Mexico, a saintly woman named Ermina Something lives in a blue-and-green or maybe blue-and-yellow stucco house. She is seventy-two.

The killer returns to the van and drives it forward about twenty feet, and then gets out again.

In Ermina Something's living room are maybe forty-two or thirty-nine images of the Sacred Heart of Jesus, pierced by thorns.

This has given Holly an idea. The idea is daring. And scary. But it feels right.

When the killer returns to the van, Holly guesses that he has opened a gate to admit them to someplace, and then has closed it behind them.

In Ermina Something's backyard, the killer buried a 'treasure' of which the old woman would not approve. Holly wonders what that treasure might be, but hopes she will never know.

The van coasts forward maybe sixty feet, on an unpaved surface. Small stones crunch together and rattle under the tires.

He stops again and this time switches off the engine. 'We're here.'

'Good,' she says, for she is trying to play this not as if she is a frightened hostage but as if she is a woman whose spirit is arising to its fullness.

He unlocks the back door and helps her out of the van.

The warm wind smells vaguely of wood smoke. Maybe canyons are afire far to the east.

For the first time in more than twenty-four hours, she feels sun on her face. The sun feels so good she could cry.

Supporting her right arm, escorting her in an almost courtly fashion, he leads her across bare earth, through weeds. Then they follow a hard surface with a vague limy smell.

When they stop, a strange muffled sound is repeated three times — *thup, thup, thup* — accompanied by splintering-wood and shrieking-metal noises.

'What's that?' she asks.

'I shot open the door.'

Now she knows what a pistol fitted with a silencer sounds like. *Thup, thup, thup*. Three shots.

He conducts her across the threshold of the place into which he has shot his way. 'Not much farther.'

The echoes of their slow footsteps give her a sense of cavernous spaces. 'It feels like a church.'

'In a way it is,' he says. 'We are in the cathedral of excessive exuberance.'

She smells plaster and sawdust. She can still hear the wind, but the walls must be well insulated and the windows triple-pane, for the blustery voice is muted.

Eventually they come into a space that sounds smaller than those before it, with a lower ceiling.

After halting her, the killer says, 'Wait here.' He lets go of her arm.

She hears a familiar sound that makes her heart sink: the rattle of a chain.

Here the scent of sawdust is not as strong as in previous spaces, but when she remembers their threat to cut off her fingers, she wonders if the room contains a table saw.

'One point four million dollars,' she says calculatedly. 'That buys a lot of seeking.'

'It buys a lot of everything,' he replies.

He touches her arm again, and she does not recoil. Around her left wrist, he wraps a chain and makes some kind of connection.

'When there's always a need to work,' she says, 'there's never really time to seek,' and though she knows this is ignorance, she hopes it is the kind of ignorance to which he relates.

'Work is a toad squatting on our lives,' he says, and she knows she has struck a chord with him.

He unties the scarf that binds her hands, and she thanks him.

When he removes her blindfold, she squints and blinks, adjusting to the light, and discovers that she's in a house under construction.

After entering this place, he has put on his ski mask again. He is at least pretending that she can choose her husband over him and that he will let them live.

'This would have been the kitchen,' he says.

The space is enormous for a kitchen, maybe fifty feet by thirty feet, the ultimate for catering large parties. The limestone floor is adrift in dust. Finished drywall is in place, although no cabinets or appliances have been installed.

A metal pipe about two inches in diameter, perhaps a gas line, protrudes from low in a wall. The other end of her chain has been padlocked to this pipe, as it was padlocked to her wrist. The metal cap on the end of the pipe, almost a full inch wider than the pipe itself, prevents the chain from being slipped loose.

He has given her eight feet of links. She can sit, stand, and even move around a little.

'Where are we?' she wonders.

'The Turnbridge house.'

'Ah. But why? Do you have some connection with it?'

'I've been here a few times,' he says, 'though I've always made a more discreet entrance than shooting out the lock. He draws me. He's still here.'

'Who?'

'Turnbridge. He hasn't moved on. His spirit's here, curled up tight on itself like one of the ten thousand dead pill bugs that litter the place.'

Holly says, 'I've been thinking about Ermina in Rio Lucio.'

'Ermina Lavato.'

'Yes,' she says, as if she had not forgotten the surname. 'I can almost see the rooms of her house, each a different soothing color. I don't know why I keep thinking of her.'

Within his knitted mask, his blue eyes regard

her with feverish intensity.

Closing her eyes, standing with her arms limp at her sides and with her face tilted toward the ceiling, she speaks in a murmur. 'I can see her bedroom walls covered with images of the Holy Mother.'

'Forty-two,' he says.

'And there are candles, aren't there?' she guesses.

'Yes. Votive candles.'

'It's a lovely room. She's happy there.'

'She's very poor,' he says, 'but happier than any rich man.'

'And her quaint kitchen from the 1920s, the aroma of chicken fajitas.' She takes a deep breath, savoring, and lets it out.

He says nothing.

Opening her eyes, Holly says, 'I've never been there, I've never met her. Why can't I get her and her house out of my mind?'

His continued silence begins to worry her. She is afraid that she has overacted, struck a false note.

Finally he says, 'Sometimes people who've never met can resonate with each other.'

She considers the word: 'Resonate.'

'In one sense, you live far from her, but in another sense you might be neighbors.'

If Holly reads him right, she has sparked more interest than suspicion. Of course, it may be a fatal mistake to think that she can ever read him right.

'Strange,' she says, and drops the subject.

He wets his peeled lips with his tongue, licks

them again, and yet again. Then: 'I've got some preparations to make. I'm sorry for the chain. It won't be necessary much longer.'

After he has left the kitchen, she listens to his footsteps fading through vast hollow rooms.

The cold shakes seize her. She isn't able to get them under control, and the links of her chain sing against one another.

# 61

Mitch in the shuddering shade of the wind-tossed podocarpuses, squinting through windows, finally began to test the doors of the vehicles parked at the curb. When they weren't locked, he opened them and leaned inside.

If keys weren't in the ignition, they might be in a cup holder or tucked behind a sun visor. Each time that he didn't find keys in those places, either, he closed the door and moved on.

Born of desperation, his boldness nevertheless surprised him. Because a police car might turn one corner or another momentarily, however, caution rather than assurance would be his downfall.

He hoped that these residents were not people with a sense of community, that they had not joined the Neighborhood Watch program. Their police mentor would have coached them to notice and report suspicious specimens exactly like him.

For laid-back southern California, for low-crime Newport Beach, a depressing percentage of these people locked their parked cars. Their paranoia gradually began to piss him off.

When he had gone over two blocks, he saw ahead a Lexus parked in a driveway, the engine idling, the driver's door open. No one sat behind the wheel.

The garage door also stood open. He

362

cautiously approached the car, but no one was in the garage, either. The driver had dashed back into the house for a forgotten item.

The Lexus would be reported stolen within minutes, but the cops wouldn't be looking for it immediately. There would be a process for reporting a stolen car; a process was part of a system, a system the work of a bureaucracy, the business of bureaucracy delay.

He might have a couple of hours before the plates were on a hot sheet. He needed no more time than two hours.

Because the car faced the street, he slipped behind the wheel, dropped the trash bag on the passenger's seat, pulled the door shut, and rolled at once out of the driveway, turning right, away from the boulevard and the gun shop.

At the corner, ignoring the stop sign, he turned right once more and went a third of a block before he heard a thin shaky voice in the backseat say, 'What is your name, honey?'

An elderly man slumped in a corner. He wore Coke-bottle glasses, a hearing aid, and his pants just under his breasts. He appeared to be a hundred years old. Time had shrunken him, though not every part in proportion to every other.

'Oh, you're Debbie,' the old man said. 'Where are we going, Debbie?'

Crime led to more crime, and here were the wages of crime: certain destruction. Mitch himself had now become a kidnapper.

'Are we going to the pie store?' the old man inquired, a note of hope in his quavery voice.

Maybe some Alzheimer's was happening here.

'Yes,' Mitch said, 'we're going to the pie store,' and he turned right again at the next corner.

'I like pie.'

'Everybody likes pie,' Mitch agreed.

If his heart had not been knocking hard enough to hurt, if his wife's life had not depended on his remaining free, if he had not expected to encounter roving police at any moment, and if he had not expected them to shoot first and discuss the fine points of his civil rights later, he might have found this amusing. But it wasn't amusing; it was surreal.

'You aren't Debbie,' the old man said. 'I'm Norman, but you're not Debbie.'

'No. You're right. I'm not.'

'Who are you?'

'I'm just a guy who made a mistake.'

Norman thought about that until Mitch turned right at the third corner, and then he said, 'You're gonna hurt me. That's what you're gonna do.'

The fear in the old man's voice inspired pity. 'No, no. Nobody is gonna hurt you.'

'You're gonna hurt me, you're a bad man.'

'No, I just made a mistake. I'm taking you right back home,' Mitch assured him.

'Where are we? This isn't home. We're nowhere near home.' The voice, to this point wispy, suddenly gained volume and shrillness. *'You're a bad sonofabitch!'*

'Don't get yourself worked up. Please don't.' Mitch felt sorry for the old man, responsible for him. 'We're almost there. You'll be home in a minute.'

'*You're a bad sonofabitch! You're a bad sonofabitch!*'

At the fourth corner, Mitch turned right, onto the street where he'd stolen the car.

'*YOU'RE A BAD SONOFABITCH!*'

In the desiccated depths of that time-ravaged body, Norman found the voice of a bellowing youth.

'*YOU'RE A BAD SONOFABITCH!*'

'Please, Norman. You're gonna give yourself a heart attack.'

He had hoped to be able to pull the car into the driveway and leave it where he'd found it, with nobody the wiser. But a woman had come out of the house into the street. She spotted him turning the corner.

She looked terrified. She must have thought that Norman had gotten behind the wheel.

'*YOU'RE A BAD SONOFABITCH, A BAD, BAD SONOFABITCH!*'

Mitch stopped in the street near the woman, put the car in park, tramped on the emergency brake, grabbed the trash bag, and got out, leaving the door open behind him.

Fortysomething, slightly stout, she was an attractive woman with Rod Stewart hair that a beautician had painstakingly streaked with blond highlights. She wore a business suit and heels too high to be sensible for a trip to the pie store.

'Are you Debbie?' Mitch asked.

Bewildered, she said, 'Am I Debbie?'

Maybe there was no Debbie.

Norman still shrieked in the car, and Mitch said, 'I'm so sorry. Big mistake.'

He walked away from her, toward the first of the four corners around which he had driven Norman, and heard her say 'Grandpapa? Are you all right, Grandpapa?'

When he reached the stop sign, he turned and saw the woman leaning in the car, comforting the old man.

Mitch rounded the corner and hurried out of her line of sight. Not running. Walking briskly.

A block later, as he reached the next corner, a horn blared behind him. The woman was pursuing him in the Lexus.

He could see her through the windshield: one hand on the wheel, the other holding a cell phone. She was not calling her sister in Omaha. She was not calling for a time check. She was calling 911.

# 62

Leaning into the resisting wind, Mitch hurried along the sidewalk, and miraculously escaped being stung when a violent gust shook a cloud of bees out of a tree nest.

The determined woman in the Lexus stayed far enough back that she could hang a U-turn and elude him if he changed directions and sprinted toward her, but she maintained sight of him. He started to run, and she accelerated to match his pace.

Evidently she intended to keep him located until the police arrived. Mitch admired her guts even though he wanted to shoot out her tires.

The cops would be here soon. Having found his Honda, they knew that he was in the area. The attempted theft of a Lexus just a few blocks from the gun shop would ring all their bells.

The car horn blared, blared again, and then relentlessly. She hoped to alert her neighbors to the presence of a criminal in their midst. The over-the-top urgency of the horn blasts suggested Osama bin Laden was loose on the street.

Mitch left the sidewalk, crossed a yard, opened a gate, and hurried around the side of a house, hoping he wouldn't find a pit bull in the backyard. No doubt most pit bulls were as nice as nuns, but considering the way his luck was cutting, he wouldn't run into Sister Pit but instead would stumble over a demon dog.

The backyard proved to be shallow, encircled by a seven-foot cedar fence with pointed staves. He didn't see a gate. After tying the twisted neck of the trash bag to his belt, he climbed into a coral tree, crossed the fence on a limb, and dropped into an alley.

Police would expect him to prefer these service alleys to streets, so he couldn't use them.

He passed through a vacant lot, sheltered by the weeping boughs of long-untrimmed California pepper trees, which whirled and flounced like the many-layered skirts of eighteenth-century dancers in a waltz.

As he was crossing the next street in midblock, a police car swept through the intersection to the east. The shriek of its brakes told him that he had been seen.

Across a yard, over a fence, across an alley, through a gate, across a yard, across another street, very fast now, the plastic bag slapping against his leg. He worried that it would split, spilling bricks of hundred-dollar bills.

The last line of houses backed up to a small canyon, about two hundred feet deep and three hundred wide. He scaled a wrought-iron fence and was at once on a steep slope of loose eroded soil. Gravity and sliding earth carried him down.

Like a surfer chasing bliss along the treacherous face of a fully macking monolith, he tried to stay upright, but the sandy earth proved to be not as accommodating as the sea. His feet went out from under him, and on his back he slid the last ten yards, raising a wake of white dust, then thrashed feetfirst through a sudden wall of tall grass and taller weeds.

He came to a stop under a canopy of branches. From high above, the floor of the canyon had appeared to be choked with greenery, but Mitch hadn't expected large trees. Yet in addition to some of the scrub trees and brush that he had envisioned, he found an eclectic forest.

California buckeyes were garlanded with fragrant white flowers. Bristling windmill palms thrived with California laurels and black myrobalan plums. Many of the trees were gnarled and twisted and rough, junk specimens, as though the urban-canyon soil fed mutagens to their roots, but there were acer japonicums and Tasmanian snow gums that he would have been pleased to use in any high-end landscaping job.

A few rats scattered on his arrival, and a snake slithered away through the shadows. Maybe a rattlesnake. He couldn't be sure.

While he remained in the cover of the trees, no one could see him from the canyon rim. He no longer was at risk of immediate apprehension.

So many branches of different trees interlaced that even the raging wind could not peel back the canopy and let the sun shine in directly. The light was green and watery. Shadows trembled, swayed like sea anemones.

A shallow stream slipped through the canyon, no surprise this recently after the rainy season. The water table might be so close to the surface here that a small artesian well maintained the flow all year.

He untied the plastic trash-can liner from his

belt and examined it. The bag had been punctured in three places and had sustained a one-inch tear, but nothing seemed to have fallen out of it.

Mitch fashioned a loose temporary knot in the neck of the bag and carried it against his body, in the crook of his left arm.

As he remembered the lay of the land, the canyon narrowed and the floor rose dramatically toward the west. The purling water eased lazily from that direction, and he paralleled it at a faster pace.

A damp carpet of dead leaves cushioned his step. The pleasant melange of moist earth, wet leaves, and sporing toadstools gave weight to the air.

Although the population of Orange County exceeded three million, the bottom of the canyon felt so remote that he might have been miles from civilization. Until he heard the helicopter.

He was surprised they were up in this wind.

Judging by sound alone, the chopper crossed the canyon directly over Mitch's head. It went north and circled the neighborhood through which he'd made his run, swelling louder, fading, then louder again.

They were searching for him from the air, but in the wrong place. They didn't know he'd descended into the canyon.

He kept moving — but then halted and cried out softly in surprise when Anson's phone rang. He pulled it from his pocket, relieved that he hadn't lost or damaged it.

'This is Mitch.'

Jimmy Null said, 'Are you feeling hopeful?'

'Yes. Let me talk to Holly.'

'Not this time. You'll see her soon. I'm moving the meet from three to two o'clock.'

'You can't do that.'

'I just did it.'

'What time is it now?'

'One-thirty,' Jimmy Null said.

'Hey, no, I can't make two o'clock.'

'Why not? Anson's place is only minutes from the Turnbridge house.'

'I'm not at Anson's place.'

'Where are you, what are you doing?' Null asked.

Feet planted wide in wet leaves, Mitch said, 'Driving around, passing time.'

'That's stupid. You should've stayed at his place, been ready.'

'Make it two-thirty. I've got the money right here. A million four. I've got it with me.'

'Let me tell you something.'

Mitch waited, and when Null didn't go on, he said, 'What? Tell me what?'

'About the money. Let me tell you something about the money.'

'All right.'

'I don't live for money. I've got some money. There are things that mean more to me than money.'

Something was wrong. Mitch had felt it before, when talking to Holly, when she had sounded constrained and had not told him that she loved him.

'Listen, I've come so far, *we've* come so far,

371

it's only right we finish this.'

'Two o'clock,' Null said. 'That's the new time. You aren't where you need to be at two sharp, it's over. No second chance.'

'All right.'

'Two o'clock.'

'All right.'

Jimmy Null terminated the call.

Mitch ran.

# 63

Chained to the gas pipe, Holly knows what she must do, what she *will* do, and therefore she can pass her time only by worrying about all the ways things could go wrong or by marveling at what she can see of the uncompleted mansion.

Thomas Turnbridge would have had one fantastic kitchen if he had lived. When all the equipment had been installed, a high-end caterer with platoons of staff could have cooked and served from here a sit-down dinner for six hundred on the terraces.

Turnbridge had been a dot-com billionaire. The company that he founded — and that made him rich — produced no product, but it had been on the cutting edge of advertising applications for the Internet.

By the time *Forbes* estimated Turnbridge's net worth at three billion, he was buying homes on a dramatic Pacific-view bluff in an established neighborhood. He bought nine, side by side, by paying more than twice the going price. He spent over sixty million dollars on the houses and tore them down to make a single three-acre estate, a parcel with few if any equals on the southern California coast.

A major architectural firm committed a team of thirty to the design of a three-level house encompassing eighty-five thousand square feet, a figure that excluded the massive subterranean garages and mechanical plant. It was to be in the style of an Alberto Pinto-designed residence in Brazil.

Such elements as interior-exterior waterfalls, an underground shooting range, and an indoor ice-skating rink required heroic work of the structural, systems, and soil engineers. Two years were required for plans. During the first two years of construction, the builder worked solely on the foundation and subterranean spaces.

No budget. Turnbridge spent whatever was required.

Exquisite marbles and granites were purchased in matched lots. The exterior of the house would be clad in French limestone; sixty seamless limestone columns, from plinth to abacus, were fabricated at a cost of seventy thousand dollars each.

Turnbridge had been as passionately committed to the company he had created as to the house he was building. He believed it would become one of the ten largest corporations in the world.

He believed this even after a rapidly evolving Internet exposed flaws in his business model. From the start, he sold his shares only to finance lifestyle, not to broaden investments. When his company's stock price fell, he borrowed to buy more shares at market. The price fell further, and he leveraged more purchases.

When the share price never recovered and the company imploded, Turnbridge was ruined. Construction of the house came to a halt.

Pursued by creditors, investors, and an angry

ex-wife, Thomas Turnbridge came home to his unfinished house, sat in a folding chair on the master-bedroom balcony, and with a 240-degree ocean-and-city-lights view to enchant him, washed down an overdose of barbiturates with an icy bottle of Dom Perignon.

Carrion birds found him a day before his ex-wife did.

Although the three-acre coastal property is a plum, it has not sold after Turnbridge's death. A snarl of lawsuits entangle it. The actual value of the land now appraises at the sixty million dollars that Turnbridge overpaid for it, which allows only a small pool of potential buyers.

To complete this project as specified in the plans, a buyer will need to spend fifty million on the finish work, so he better like the style. If he demos existing construction and starts again, he needs to be prepared to spend five million on top of the sixty million for the land, because he will be dealing with steel-and-concrete construction meant to ride out an 8.2 quake with no damage.

As a hope-to-be real-estate agent, Holly doesn't dream of getting the commission for the Turnbridge house. She will be content selling properties in middle-class neighborhoods to people who are thrilled to have their own homes.

In fact, if she could trade her modest real-estate dream for a guarantee that she and Mitch would survive the ransom exchange, she would be content to remain a secretary. She is a good secretary and a good wife; she will try hard to be a good mom, too, and she will be happy with that, with life, with love.

But no such deal can be made; her fate remains in her own hands, literally and figuratively. She will have to act when the time comes for action. She has a plan. She is ready for the risk, the pain, the blood.

The creep returns. He has put on a gray windbreaker and a pair of thin, supple gloves.

She is sitting on the floor when he enters, but she gets to her feet as he approaches her.

Violating the concept of personal space, he stands as close to Holly as a man would stand just before taking her in his arms to dance.

'In Duvijio and Eloisa Pacheco's house in Rio Lucio, there are two red wooden chairs in the living room, railback chairs with carved cape tops.'

He places his right hand on her left shoulder, and she is glad that it is gloved.

'On one red chair,' he continues, 'stands a cheap ceramic figurine of Saint Anthony. On the companion chair stands a ceramic of a boy dressed for church.'

'Who is the boy?'

'The figurine represents their son, also named Anthony, who was run down and killed by a drunk driver when he was six. That was fifty years ago, when Duvijio and Eloisa were in their twenties.'

Not yet a mother but hopeful of being one, she cannot imagine the pain of such a loss, the horror of its suddenness. She says, 'A shrine.'

'Yes, a shrine of red chairs. No one has sat in those chairs in fifty years. The chairs are for the two figurines.'

'The two Anthonys,' she corrects.

He may not recognize it as a correction.

'Imagine,' he says, 'the grief and the hope and the love and the despair that have been focused on those figurines. Half a century of intense yearning has imbued those objects with tremendous power.'

She remembers the girl in the lace-trimmed dress, buried with the Saint Christopher medal and the Cinderella figurine.

'I will visit Duvijio and Eloisa one day when they are not home, and take the ceramic of the boy.'

This man is many things, including a cruel strip-miner of other people's faith and hope and treasured memories.

'I have no interest in the other Anthony, the saint, but the boy is a totem of magical potential. I will take the boy to Espanola — '

'Where your life will change again.'

'Profoundly,' he says. 'And perhaps not only my life.'

She closes her eyes and whispers, 'Red chairs,' as if she is picturing the scene.

This seems to be encouragement enough for him right now, because after a silence, he says, 'Mitch will be here in a little more than twenty minutes.'

Her heart races at this news, but her hope is tempered by her fear, and she does not open her eyes.

'I'll go now to watch for him. He'll bring the money into this room — and then it will be time to decide.'

'In Espanola, is there a woman with two white dogs?'

'Is that what you see?'

'Dogs that seem to vanish in the snow.'

'I don't know. But if you see them, then I'm sure they must be in Espanola.'

'I see myself laughing with her, and the dogs so white.' She opens her eyes and meets his. 'You better go watch for him.'

'Twenty minutes,' he promises, and leaves the kitchen.

Holly stands quite still for a moment, amazed by herself.

White dogs, indeed. Where had that come from? White dogs and a laughing woman.

She almost laughs now at his gullibility, but there is no humor in the fact that she has gotten inside his head deep enough to know what imagery will work with him. That she could travel in his mad world at all does not seem entirely admirable.

The shakes seize her, and she sits down. Her hands are cold, and a chill traces every turn of her bowels.

She reaches under her sweater, between her breasts, and extracts the nail from her bra.

Although the nail is sharp, she wishes it were sharper. She has no means to file it to a keener point.

Using the head of the nail, she scratches industriously at the drywall until she has produced a small pile of powdered plaster.

The time has come.

When Holly was a little girl, for a while she

feared an array of night monsters born of a good imagination: in closet, under bed, at the windows.

Her grandmother, good Dorothy, had taught her a poem that, she claimed, would repel every monster: vaporize those in the closet, turn to dust those under the bed, and send those at the windows away to swamps and caves where they belonged.

Years later, Holly learned that this poem, which cured her fear of monsters, was titled 'A Soldier — His Prayer.' It had been written by an unknown British soldier and had been found on a slip of paper in a trench in Tunisia during the battle of El Agheila.

Quietly but aloud, she recites it now:

'Stay with me, God. The night is dark,
The night is cold: My little spark
Of courage dies. The night is long;
Be with me, God, and make me strong.'

She hesitates then, but only for a moment. The time has come.

# 64

Shoes caked with mud and wet leaves, clothes rumpled and dirty, a white trash bag cradled in his arms and pressed against his chest as if it were a precious baby, eyes so bright with desperation that they might have been lamps to light his way if this had been night, Mitch hurried along the shoulder of the highway.

No officer of the law, happening to drive past, would fail to give him special scrutiny. He had the look of a fugitive or a madman, or both.

Fifty yards ahead stood a combination service station and minimart. Advertising a tire sale, scores of bright pennants snapped in the wind.

He wondered if ten thousand dollars cash would buy him a ride to the Turnbridge house. Probably not. The way he looked, most people would expect him to kill them en route.

A guy looking like a hobo, waving around ten thousand bucks, wanting to buy a ride, would make the station manager nervous. He might call the cops.

Yet buying a ride seemed to be his only option other than carjacking someone at gunpoint, which he would not do. The owner of the car might foolishly grab for the gun and be accidentally shot.

As he drew near the service station, a Cadillac Escalade angled off the highway and stopped at the outermost pumps. A tall blonde got out, clutching her purse, and strode into the minimart, leaving the driver's door open.

The two rows of pumps were both self-service. No attendants were in sight.

Another customer was fueling a Ford Explorer. He focused on his windows, working with a squeegee.

Mitch shambled up to the Escalade and peered through the open door. The keys were in the ignition.

Leaning inside, he checked the backseat. No grandpapa, no child in a safety seat, no pit bull.

He climbed in behind the wheel, pulled the door shut, started the engine, and drove onto the highway.

Although he half expected people to run after him, waving their arms and shouting, the rearview mirror revealed no one.

The highway was divided. He considered driving over the median planter strip. The Escalade could handle it. Fate being what fate is, a patrol car would happen by at just that moment.

He sped north a few hundred yards to a turning lane, and then headed south.

When he passed the service station, no tall angry blonde had yet put in an appearance. He raced past, but with respect for the posted speed limit.

Ordinarily, he was not an impatient driver who ranted at slow or clueless motorists. During this trip, he wished upon them all kinds of plagues and hideous misfortunes.

By 1:56, he arrived in the neighborhood where

Turnbridge's folly stood incomplete. Out of sight of the mansion, he pulled to the curb.

Cursing the stubborn buttons, he stripped out of his shirt. Jimmy Null would most likely make him take it off anyway, to prove that he was not concealing a weapon.

He had been told to come unarmed. He wanted to appear to be in compliance with that demand.

From the trash bag, he retrieved the box of .45 ammunition, and from a pocket of his jeans, he withdrew the original magazine for the Springfield Champion. He added three cartridges to the seven already in the magazine.

A movie memory served him well. He pulled back the slide and inserted an eleventh round in the chamber.

The cartridges slipped in his sweaty trembling fingers, so he had time to load only two of the three spare magazines. He stashed the box of ammo and the extra magazine under the driver's seat.

One minute till two o'clock.

He shoved the two loaded magazines in the pockets of his jeans, put the loaded pistol in the bag with the money, twisted the top of the bag but didn't knot it, and drove to the Turnbridge place.

A long chain-link construction fence fitted with privacy panels of green plastic fabric separated the street from the big Turnbridge property. The nearby residents who had put up with this ugliness for years must wish the entrepreneur hadn't killed himself if only so they could now torment him with lawyers and neighborly invective.

The gate was closed, draped with chain. As Jimmy Null promised, it wasn't locked.

Mitch drove onto the property and parked with the back of the SUV facing the house. He got out and opened all five doors, hoping by this gesture to express his desire to fulfill the terms of the agreement to the best of his ability.

He closed the construction gate and draped the chain in place once more.

Carrying the trash bag, he walked to a spot between the Escalade and the house, stopped, and waited.

The day was warm, not hot, but the sun was hard. The light cut at his eyes, and the wind.

Anson's cell phone rang.

He took the call. 'This is Mitch.'

Jimmy Null said, 'It's a minute past two. Oh, now it's two past. You're late.'

# 65

The unfinished house appeared as large as a hotel. Jimmy Null could have been watching Mitch from any of scores of windows.

'You were supposed to come in your Honda,' he said.

'It broke down.'

'Where'd you get the Escalade?'

'Stole it.'

'No shit.'

'None.'

'Park it parallel to the house, so I can see straight through the front and back seats.'

Mitch did as told, leaving the doors open as he repositioned the vehicle. He stepped away from the SUV and waited with the trash bag, the phone to his ear.

He wondered if Null would shoot him dead from a distance and come take the money. He wondered why he *wouldn't* do that.

'I'm disturbed you didn't come in the Honda.'

'I told you, it broke down.'

'What happened?'

'Flat tire. You brought the swap forward an hour, so I didn't have time to change it.'

'A stolen car — the cops could have chased your ass here.'

'No one saw me take it.'

'Where'd you learn to hot-wire a car?'

'The keys were in the ignition.'

Null considered in silence. Then: 'Enter the house by the front door. Stay on the phone.'

Mitch saw that the door had been shot open. He went inside.

The entry hall was immense. Although no finish work had been done, even Julian Campbell would have been impressed.

After leaving Mitch to stew for a minute, Jimmy Null said, 'Pass through the colonnade into the living room directly ahead of you.'

Mitch went into the living room, where the west windows extended floor to ceiling. Even through dusty glass, the view was so stunning that he could understand why Turnbridge had wanted to die with it.

'All right. I'm here.'

'Turn left and cross the room,' Null directed. 'A wide doorway leads into a secondary drawing room.'

None of the doors were hung. Those separating these two rooms would have to be nine feet tall to fill the opening.

When Mitch reached the drawing room, which offered an equally spectacular view, Null said, 'You'll see another wide doorway across from the one you're standing in, and a single door to your left.'

'Yes.'

'The single leads to a hallway. The hall passes other rooms and leads to the kitchen. She's in the kitchen. But don't go near her.'

Moving across the drawing room toward the specified doorway, Mitch said, 'Why not?'

'Because I'm still making the rules. She's

385

chained to a pipe. I have the key. You stop just inside the kitchen.'

The hallway seemed to recede from him the farther he followed it, but he knew the telescoping effect had to be psychological. He was frantic to see Holly.

He didn't look in any of the rooms he passed. Null might have been in one of them. It didn't matter.

When Mitch entered the kitchen, he saw her at once, and his heart swelled, and his mouth went dry. Everything that he had been through, every pain that he had suffered, every terrible thing that he had done was in that instant all worthwhile.

# 66

Because the creep arrives in the kitchen to stand beside her during the last of his phone conversation, Holly hears him give the final directions.

She holds her breath, listening for footsteps. When she hears Mitch approaching, hot tears threaten, but she blinks them back.

A moment later Mitch enters the room. He says her name so tenderly. Her husband.

She has stood with her arms crossed over her breasts, her hands fisted in her armpits. Now she lowers her arms and stands with her hands fisted at her sides.

The creep, who has drawn a wicked-looking pistol, is intently focused on Mitch. 'Arms straight out like a bird.'

Mitch obeys, a white trash bag dangling from his right hand.

His clothes are filthy. His hair is windblown. His face has lost all color. He is beautiful.

The killer says, 'Come slowly forward.'

As instructed, Mitch approaches, and the creep tells him to stop fifteen feet away.

As Mitch halts, the killer says, 'Put the bag on the floor.'

Mitch lowers the bag to the dusty limestone. It settles but does not flop open.

Covering Mitch with the pistol, the killer says, 'I want to see the money. Kneel in front of the bag.'

Holly doesn't like to see Mitch kneeling. This is the position that executioners instruct their victims to take before the coup de grâce.

She must act, but the time feels not quite right. If she makes her move too soon, the scheme might fail. Instinct tells her to wait, though waiting with Mitch on his knees is so hard.

'Show me the money,' the killer says, and he has a two-hand grip on the pistol, finger tightened on the trigger.

Mitch opens the neck of the bag and withdraws a plastic-wrapped brick of cash. He tears off one end of the plastic, and riffles the hundred-dollar bills with his thumb.

'The bearer bonds?' the killer asks.

Mitch drops the cash into the sack.

The creep tenses, thrusting the pistol forward as Mitch reaches into the bag again, and he does not relax even when Mitch produces only a large envelope.

From the envelope, Mitch extracts half a dozen official-looking certificates. He holds one forward for the killer to read.

'All right. Put them back in the envelope.'

Mitch obeys, still on his knees.

The creep says, 'Mitch, if your wife had a chance for previously undreamed-of personal fulfillment, the opportunity for enlightenment, for *transcendence*, surely you would want her to follow that better destiny.'

Bewildered by this turn, Mitch does not know what to say, but Holly does. The time has come.

She says, 'I've been sent a sign, my future is New Mexico.'

Raising her hands from her sides, opening her fists, she reveals her bloody wounds.

An involuntary cry escapes Mitch, the killer glances at Holly, and her stigmata drip for his astonishment.

The nail holes are not superficial, though they don't go all the way through her hands. She stabbed herself and worked the wounds with brutal determination.

The worst had been having to bite back every cry of pain. If he had heard her agony expressed, the killer would have come to see what she was doing.

At once, the wounds had bled too much. She had packed them with powdered plaster to stop the bleeding. Before the plaster worked, blood had dripped on the floor, but she had covered it with a quick redistribution of the thick dust.

With her hands fisted in her armpits, as Mitch entered the room, Holly had clawed the plugs of plaster from the wounds, tearing them open once more.

Blood flows now for the killer's fascination, and Holly says, 'In Espanola, where your life will change, lives a woman named Rosa Gonzales with two white dogs.'

With her left hand, she pulls down the neck of her sweater, revealing cleavage.

His gaze rises from her breasts to her eyes.

She slips her right hand between her breasts, palms the nail, and fears not being able to hold it in her slippery fingers.

The killer glances at Mitch.

She grips the nail well enough, reveals it, and

rams it into the killer's face, going for his eye, but instead pinning his mask to him, piercing the hollow of his cheek and ripping.

Screaming, tongue flailing on the nail, he reels back from her, and his pistol fires wildly, bullets thudding into walls.

She sees Mitch rising and moving fast, with a gun of his own.

# 67

Mitch shouted, 'Holly, move,' and she was moving on the first syllable of Holly, separating herself from Jimmy Null as much as her chain allowed.

Point-blank, aiming abdomen, hitting chest, pulling down from the recoil, firing again, pulling down, firing, firing, he thought a couple of shots went wide, but saw three or four rounds tearing into the windbreaker, each roar so big booming through the big house.

Null reeled backward, off balance. His pistol had an extended magazine. It seemed to be fully automatic. Bullets stitched a wall, part of the ceiling.

Because he now had only a one-hand grip on the weapon, maybe the recoil tore it from him, maybe he lost all strength, but for whatever reason, it flew. The gun hit the wall, clattered to the limestone.

Driven backward by the impact of the .45s, rocked on his heels, Null staggered, dropped on his side, rolled onto his face.

When the echoes of the echoes of the gunfire faded, Mitch could hear Jimmy Null's ragged wheezing. Maybe that was how you breathed when you had a fatal chest wound.

Mitch wasn't proud of what he did next, didn't even take any savage delight in it. In fact he almost didn't do it, but he knew that *almost* would buy no dispensation when the time came to reckon for the way he lived his life.

He stepped over the wheezing man and shot him twice in the back. He would have shot him a third time, but he had expended all eleven rounds in the pistol.

Crouching defensively during the gunfire, Holly rose to meet Mitch as he turned to her.

'Anyone else?' he asked.

'Just him, just him.'

She exploded into him, threw her arms around him. He had never before been held so tight, with such sweet ferocity.

'Your hands.'

'They're okay.'

'Your hands,' he insisted.

'They're okay, you're alive, they're okay.'

He kissed every part of her face. Her mouth, her eyes, her brow, her eyes again, salty now with tears, her mouth.

The room stank of gunfire, a dead man lay on the floor, Holly was bleeding, and Mitch's legs felt weak. He wanted fresh air, the brisk wind, sunshine to kiss her in.

'Let's get out of here,' he said.

'The chain.'

A small stainless-steel padlock coupled the links around her wrist.

'He has the key,' she said.

Staring at the body, Mitch withdrew a spare magazine from a pocket of his jeans. He ejected the spent clip, replaced it with the fresh.

Pressing the muzzle against the back of the kidnapper's head, he said, 'One move, I'll blow your brains out,' but of course he got no answer.

Nevertheless, he pressed hard on the gun and, with his free hand, was able to search the side pockets of the windbreaker. He found the key in the second one.

The chain fell away from her wrist as the dropped padlock rapped the limestone floor.

'Your hands,' he said, 'your beautiful hands.'

The sight of her blood pierced him, and he thought of the staged scene in their kitchen, the bloody hand prints, but this was worse, so much worse to see her bleeding.

'What happened to your hands?'

'New Mexico. It's not as bad as it looks. I'll explain. Let's go. Let's get out of here.'

He snatched the bag of ransom off the floor. She started toward a doorway, but he led her to the entrance from the hall, which was the only route he knew.

They walked with her right arm around his shoulders and his left arm around her waist, past empty rooms haunted or not, and his heart knocked no softer and no slower than when he had been in the quick of the gunfire. Maybe it would race like this for the rest of his life.

The hall was long, and in the drawing room, they could not help looking toward the vast, dust-filmed view.

As they stepped into the living room, an engine roared to life elsewhere in the house. The racket rattled room to hall to room, and chattered off the high ceilings, making it impossible to determine where it originated.

'Motorcycle,' she said.

'Bulletproof,' Mitch said. 'A vest under the windbreaker.'

The impact of the slugs, especially the two in the back, jarring the spine, must have knocked Jimmy Null briefly unconscious.

He had not intended to leave in the van that he'd driven here. Having stashed a motorcycle near the kitchen, perhaps in the breakfast room, he'd been prepared to leave — if things went wrong — through any wing of the house, any door. Once outside the house, he could flee not only by the construction gate that led into the street but also by switchbacking down the bluff, or by some third route.

As the clatter of the engine swelled, Mitch knew that Jimmy was not intent on fleeing. It wasn't the ransom that drew him, either.

Whatever had happened between him and Holly — New Mexico and Rosa Gonzales and two white dogs and bloody stigmata — all *that* drew him, and he was drawn, too, by the humiliation of the nail in the face. For the nail, he wanted Holly more than money, wanted her dead.

Logic suggested that he was at their backs and would come from the drawing room.

Mitch hurried Holly across the enormous living room, toward the equally huge receiving hall and the front door beyond.

Logic flopped. They had crossed less than half the living room when Jimmy Null on a Kawasaki shot out of somewhere, bulleting along the colonnade that separated them from the receiving room.

Mitch drew her back as Null steered between columns into the receiving room. He made a wide turn out there and came straight at them, across that room, across the width of the colonnade, gaining speed.

Null didn't have his pistol. Out of ammunition. Or wild with rage, the gun forgotten.

Shoving Holly behind him, Mitch raised the Champion in both hands, remembering the front sight, a white dot, and opened fire as Null was passing across the colonnade.

Aiming chest this time, hoping for head. Fifty feet and closing, thunder crashing off walls. First shot high, pull it down, second, *pull it down*, thirty feet and closing, third shot. *PULL IT DOWN!* The fourth turned off Jimmy Null's brain so abruptly, his hands *sprang* away from the handlebars.

The dead man stopped, the cycle did not, rearing on its back wheel, tire barking, smoking, screaming forward until it toppled, tumbled toward them, past them, hit one of the big windows, and shattered through, gone.

Be sure. Evil has cockroach endurance. Be sure, be sure. The Champion in both hands, approach him cool, no hurry now, circle him. Step around the spatters on the floor. Gray-pink spatters, bits of bone and twists of hair. He can't be alive. Take nothing for granted.

Mitch peeled up the mask to see the face, but it wasn't a face anymore, and they were done now. They were done.

# 68

In the summer that Anthony is three years old, they celebrate Mitch's thirty-second birthday with a backyard party.

Big Green owns three trucks now, and there are five employees besides Iggy Barnes. They all come with their wives and kids, and Iggy brings a wahine named Madelaine.

Holly has made good friends — as she always makes good friends — at the real-estate agency where she is second in sales so far this year.

Although Dorothy followed Anthony by just twelve months, they have not moved to a bigger house. Holly had been raised here; this house is her history. Besides, already they have made quite a history here together.

They will add a second story before there is a third child. And there will be a third.

Evil has been across this threshold, but the memory of it will not drive them from the place. Love scrubs the worst stains clean. Anyway, there can be no retreat in the face of evil, only resistance. And commitment.

Sandy Taggart comes, as well, with his wife, Jennifer, and their two daughters. He brings the day's newspaper, wondering if Mitch has seen the story, which he has not: Julian Campbell, between conviction and appeal, throat slit in prison — a contract hit suspected, but no inmate yet identified as the killer.

Although Anson is in a different prison from the one to which Campbell was sent, he will eventually hear about the hit. It will give him something to ponder as his attorneys work to stave off his own lethal injection.

Mitch's youngest sister, Portia, comes to the party all the way from Birmingham, Alabama, with her restaurateur husband Frank and their five children. Megan and Connie remain distant in more than one sense, but Mitch and Portia have grown close, and he entertains hope of finding a way to gather his other two sisters to him, in time.

Daniel and Kathy had produced five children because he said continuation of the species could not be left to the irrationalists. Materialists must breed as vigorously as believers or the world would go to Hell by way of God.

Portia had balanced her father's five with five of her own, and raised them by traditional standards that did not involve a learning room.

On this birthday evening, they eat a feast at tables on the patio and lawn, and Anthony sits proudly on his special chair. Mitch built it for him to a design sketched by Holly, and she painted it a cheerful red.

'This chair,' she had told Anthony, 'is in memory of a boy who was six years old for fifty years and much loved for fifty-six years. If you ever think that you aren't loved, you will sit in this chair and know you are loved as much as that other Anthony was loved, as much as any boy ever has been loved.'

Anthony, being three, had said, 'Can I have ice cream?'

After dinner, there is a portable dance floor on the lawn, and the band is not as woofy as the one at their wedding. No tambourines and no accordion.

Later, much later, when the band has departed and all the guests are gone, when Anthony and Dorothy are sound asleep on the back-porch glider, Mitch asks Holly to dance to the music of a radio, now that they have the entire floor to themselves. He holds her close but not too tight, for she is breakable. As they dance, husband and wife, she puts a hand to his face, as though after all this time she is still amazed that he brought her home to him. He kisses the scar in the palm of her hand, and then the scar in the other. Under a great casting of stars, in the moonlight, she is so lovely that words fail him, as they have so often failed him before. Although he knows her as well as he knows himself, she is as mysterious as she is lovely, an eternal depth in her eyes, but she is no more mysterious than are the stars and the moon and all things on the earth.